continued on next page . . .

following the wake

gemma o'connor

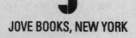

JOVE BOOKS, NEW YORK

This is a work of fiction. Names, characters, places, and incidents either are the product of the author's imagination or are used fictitiously, and any resemblance to actual persons living or dead, business establishments, events, or locales is entirely coincidental.

FOLLOWING THE WAKE

A Jove Book / published by arrangement with the author

PRINTING HISTORY
Jove edition / July 2004

ISBN: 0-515-13772-3

A JOVE BOOK®
Jove Books are published by The Berkley Publishing Group, a division of Penguin Group (USA) Inc., 375 Hudson Street, New York, New York 10014. JOVE and the "J" design are trademarks belonging to Penguin Group (USA) Inc.

PRINTED IN THE UNITED STATES OF AMERICA

10 9 8 7 6 5 4 3 2 1

See him! Whom? . . .
See him! How? . . .
See it! What? His innocence.
Look! Look where? On our offence.
See him filled with love . . .

Break in grief, thou loving heart;
For a child whom thou didst nourish,
Yea, a friend whom thou didst cherish,
Gathers wicked foes around three
And doth like a serpent wound thee.

Chorus 1; Aria 12; from J. S. Bach: St. Matthew Passion
Edited in English by Neil Jenkins

For Pauline

The *Dublin Daily News*, Thursday, September 12

The tragic and untimely death is announced of award-winning journalist Fiona Moore, who was fatally injured in a hit-and-run incident in Dublin city centre. Ms. Moore worked for this newspaper for the past five years and won the coveted Columnist of the Year award last year. Forty-eight and recently divorced, she leaves a nineteen-year-old son and ten-year-old daughter.

Comment page 4; Obituary page 6

regression 1

one

THE WATERS OF the Glár Estuary are black and peaty. Opaque, yet where the river runs over the rounded pebbles of the estuary it appears quite clear. When I plunged my hand in, I could see tiny particles suspended in the pale water, and if I let my feet sink into the slimy brown silt, the colour oozed out and swirled around, hiding them. The river was my refuge. Once, I fell into the space between my fa-

ther's boat and the dock when the tide was in and the water
was deep. I remember thinking as I floated down, down,
how calm it was, how cool, mysterious, and silent. I touched
the bottom before I made any attempt to surface, kicking my
waterlogged shoes away as I rose. I wasn't in a hurry. The
water enfolded me, kept me safe, and I knew that whenever
things got too bad, I could always slip off the dock and tread
water under the slatted planks until my father went off up to
the house. I don't think it ever occurred to me that he might
pull me out of danger. Or that he would notice if I drowned.
I must have reckoned he'd be glad to see the back of me.

By contrast, my mother never allowed me out of her
sight. Her comforting presence is what I remember. She was
as terrified of my father as I was, but when she was with me,
I had no fear. She fended off the bad stuff. Most of it, anyway. Papa was always irritated and angry; with her, with me,
with the whole goddamn world. He had a nasty habit of
grinding his teeth just before he exploded. His temper was
vicious, and he didn't seem to care which of us he had a go
at. It was all the same to him if she put herself between us.
I don't think she ever knew how much I was taking in, how
I willed her to clock him one, make him disappear. I used to
drum the floor with my heels, wishing it was him I was
pounding. Now that I've grown up, everyone thinks I'm a
pushover, but I think maybe I've inherited his foul moods,
and it scares me. Sometimes I have to sit on my hands to
stop me lashing out. I'm not sure anyone realises. Certainly
not my mother, who often misses the point, being a bit
vague. Though it could be an act. Maybe, like me, she has
things to hide?

Cressie worried about me all the time. That's what I call
her now, though when I was little I called her Mama. It was
the first word she taught me, and for a long time the only
word I could say. My earliest memory is of the two of us sitting on the floor of an empty room, with her clutching me in
her arms. She is holding a warm, damp washcloth to the side
of my face, and it is slowly dripping blood, which disappears into old, rough, quarry tiles. Mama is weeping. The
tears roll slowly down her face. Silently. I want her to stop.

I can see our dog, Finnegan, keeping guard at the door. His tail is down, but his mouth opens and shuts. There is no sound.

I tagged along beside my mother everywhere she went. People smiled when they talked to her and patted my head and tried to make me smile as well. Others—I suppose they must have been our neighbours—waved when we passed in the car, but I don't remember anyone clearly except old John Spain, who was our friend. I called him Tar—not because he was a sailor, which he was, but simply because anything beginning with *T* was easiest for me when I first began to talk. Frank Recaldo, who eventually became my stepfather, was Tank for the same reason.

Every day, rain or shine, Tar went out fishing in his boat. Usually, he rowed; he hardly ever used the outboard motor. He always wore bright yellow oilskin overalls and jacket with the hood up, or sometimes a navy cloth cap. He was famous for his lobsters and often brought us one, or a crab. I loved watching the lobster turn from dark blue to pink when it was dropped into boiling water. He was also famous because he'd once been a priest. I don't remember if someone told me that or if I just picked it up along the way. Tar didn't have many friends. At least, I don't remember him ever talking to anyone except us and an American woman who lived near him on the far side of the river. I remember her because she always laughed whenever she saw me with John Spain. The way her red, red lips stretched over her long white teeth fascinated me. She was horrible; I hated her. My father must have liked her though, because I sometimes saw her on his yacht *Azzurra*.

John Spain. The man and the place became so entangled, I sometimes thought of the river as Spain. I used to dream I was back. Always the same age, about six or seven, wearing a blue jersey and shorts with yellow wellies, plodding along the waterline. Sometimes I am sitting in the prow of Tar's boat, trailing my hand in the water until a fish surfaces and snaps it off. I watch the blood boiling on the surface, pouring from my upheld arm.

Tar taught me to swim. It amused him that I had no fear

of the cold water. I suppose I was too young to understand or explain that underwater, hearing didn't matter; I felt normal. Looking was the thing and learning when to hold your breath and when to expand your lungs. I remember him standing patiently, in his waders, by the edge of the water, while I dived in and out of the rising tide, pretending I was a dolphin. Sometimes he tied a long strip torn from an old sheet under my armpits and let me slip off the side of the boat. We didn't let on to my mother, or she'd have stopped it, and I would never have learned Tar's great lesson: how to listen. Really listen. One day he asked me what it felt like to have water in my ears. To make me understand, he cupped his hand in the water and let it flow into his own ear. I laughed and drummed the surface with my hand. I wanted to say it gurgled—which was odd, because I hadn't the word. If I couldn't hear, then how could I know something so complicated? Tar looked at me a long time as if he was trying to figure something out. Then, without warning, he tipped me over the side again, and when I surfaced, he had his mouth on the surface, saying my name: "Gil, Gil." I felt it rippling and vibrating through the water. "Gil, Gi, Gi, Gi." I held on to the edge of the boat and tried to copy him. "Gi, Gi, Gi, *Gil.*"

Tar gave me his quiet smile and hauled me aboard and sat me on the thwart beside him. "You Gil, me Tar," he said, and I could feel the rumble of his strong, deep voice vibrate through the wooden seat back. When we got back to his cottage, he wrote "Gil" and then "Tar" in big letters on a sheet of yellow paper and stuck it on the wall. That was how he began to teach me how to speak and read. As far as I know, he didn't mention the incident to my mother, and never again to me. We just fell into a way of communicating which somehow allowed that in certain circumstances I was not totally deaf.

I loved being on the boat with Tar. There was something written—too difficult for me to read—written in tiny gold letters on the inside of the prow. Tar told me it was his dead wife's name and that when he was alone, he talked to her. I liked that. I liked the thought that even when you were dead, someone still loved you. He was brilliant, the only person besides Cressie I felt truly safe with. And *no*, he did *not* touch me up, though someone told my father he did. How do I know that? I've no idea, I just do. It happened just before we left the estuary. I sometimes wonder if that is why John Spain died.

My parents were always fighting. My father didn't seem to be able to walk past me without taking a sneaky side-swipe. When Cressie tried to protect me, he'd turn on her. Sometimes she was black and blue all over. I watched her all the time. I could tell she was hurting by the way she walked. Knew when she wore her hair loose that she was hiding a black eye. Once, towards the end, I saw him burn the back of her hand with a cigarette. He just stubbed it out, casually. Three times. He didn't stop talking even when she opened her mouth in a scream. They were at the kitchen table. I was standing beside her, as usual. I believe now he was trying to drive us away, though of course I didn't understand any of that at the time. It made sense once I discovered the house belonged to my mother's family. My parents only went to Ireland when my mother inherited Coribeen.

My father is dead, and my memory of what he looked like is vague. I cannot see his face. A blurred image of long legs and blond hair—like mine. I still find it unbelievable that I knew so little about him until I was about fourteen, when Grandfather Hollingsworth dragged my mother over to Oxford to look after him. "You look just like your father" was pretty well the first thing he ever said to me. "Strange chap, Sweeney. Good-looking, athletic. Successful. Never figured out what he saw in your poor mother." I ignored that little crack and asked if his name had been Gil. Grandfather gave me a very strange look. "No," he said. "It was Valentine Jason Sweeney." All I could think of was that such a poncy name didn't tally with the ogre in my head. So my real name was Sweeney, was it? After that, I used to secretly write "Gil Sweeney, Spain/Ireland/The World/The Universe" on my schoolbooks, and it was the beginning of trying to piece together my father's history and the reasons why we left the estuary.

Frank adopted me about the same time my little sister Katie May was born. But even before that, I thought of myself as Gil Recaldo. I find it odd now that I didn't seem to have any idea what my real name was. I was just Gil. It might have been because of my hearing difficulty. Who knows? It was a very long time before I realised that losing my birth name might have repercussions. Even so, I knew deep down that one day I'd be driven to seek an explanation.

It took ages to establish exactly where the estuary was because I'd only ever had two place names in my head: Coribeen and Trianach. I didn't remember them as sounds but as written words. I read much earlier than I talked, so I might have seen them on signposts. I thought Coribeen was a village when, in fact, it was the name of our house as well as the hinterland on that side of the river. But it wasn't until I finally got to Passage South after I left school and saw the admiralty chart on the wall of Hussey's pub that it all fell into place.

Trianach was the real key. I first found it on an ordnance survey map of West Cork in my last year at school when I was doing a project on grain shipments from Ireland to England during the nineteenth-century famines. The name jumped out at me and I was completely enthralled. It appeared to be a small island on the River Glár, but linked to the land by a causeway—a kind of near-island. Neither my mother nor Frank Recaldo had ever spoken to me of either place. Maybe they thought I didn't remember, or that if I did and it wasn't mentioned it would fade from my mind. They were wrong; the river was always in my head. The river and Tar. The more I learned about Trianach, the more I wanted to go home. Not that I knew where my original home was exactly, and when, in a roundabout way, I tried to question Frank, he clammed up. I knew better than to tackle my mother, who'd just get upset.

A strange girl called Halcyon appeared on the scene soon after we left the estuary. She was some sort of relation of Murray Magraw, an Oxford friend of my parents. She used to come and stay sometimes when I was a kid. I could never understand why my mother bothered with her, because she was totally weird. A big gallumping girl who used to follow me around pawing me. I didn't mind at first, but she seemed to become more peculiar with every visit, especially after my sister Katie May was born. She was completely fixated on my mother and dead jealous of the baby; she was always trying to attack her until Frank said she couldn't come to the house anymore. Sound man, Frank.

Halcyon's another bone of contention between Frank and Cressie, who insists on visiting her at the convent in Tipperary whenever she's back home in Ireland—which isn't often these days. "You spend more time with her than with me," Frank used to moan, and I can see his point. I haven't seen Halcyon for years, but for some reason she always reminded me of my father. She had the same kind of swirling fury. Totally unpredictable. Thinking of either of them brings back that sinking feeling in my gut.

My mother never got over leaving Coribeen. Not really. She was deeply upset over the deaths of my father and Tar. Tar especially. Frank left with us. No, that's wrong, we left with him. He was always hanging around, even before my father died, so I assume he and my mother must have been having it off, and being Cressie, she would have been terrified of people knowing about it and turning against them. I suppose if it came out, things might have been awkward, him being the local copper and all.

Even before we left Coribeen, the whole world turned upside down: Cressie bawling her head off, Frank looking fierce, people talking in whispers, and no sign of John Spain or my father. I was staying with a family I didn't know, my arm was broken, and we seemed to be forever tearing along country roads in Frank's clapped-out jeep, which we had until four or five years ago.

I carried one completely clear memory away with me: the night they set fire to John Spain's boat. There were hundreds of people standing on the pier looking out to sea. I remember the red flames licking through the thick smoke and my mother telling me that all true sailors are buried at sea. Funny. My father was a sailor, too, an Olympic yachtsman, but there was no funeral for him. I only remembered that a few weeks ago, when I stood on that same pier at Passage South looking across the bay to the rocks where Tar used to take me to watch the seals.

After we left the estuary, we went to Kerry to stay with Frank's brother. We have a summer cottage there now. I was completely bewildered and kept asking for Tar. I'd ask, and Cressie would burst out crying. Frank would tell me not to upset her. So of course I stopped asking. I suppose that's how the embargo on information thing started.

two

E-mail from Fiona Moore
To: Sean Brophy, Arts Editor, *Dublin Daily News*

Hi. This comes with a proposal for a series of
articles entitled "Irish Artists in Profile" I
thought might interest you. I've already started
work and hope to have the first couple ready in
the next few weeks. If you want more info, contact Jez Murphy at *Jeu d'esprit* (the San Francisco art and literary review). I've been
freelancing for him for the past few years. CV
enclosed.
Fiona Moore

OF ALL THE things Cressida Recaldo resented in her first husband Valentine Sweeney—and there were many—being
deprived of her beloved Coribeen was the worst. For that,
she never forgave him. Viewed dispassionately, it might
have seemed the least heinous of his crimes, because he was
a violent, murderous brute. Yet somehow, in the aftermath of

Val's death, when Cressida and her lover Recaldo fled the estuary to avoid the scandal breaking around their heads, being cut adrift from her small and carefully constructed world affected her most. That and the death at sea—while in pursuit of her fleeing husband—of John Spain, the old man who had helped her lead Gil out of his silent world.

Born and brought up in a small village in Oxfordshire, she had lived in Ireland for eighteen years, and it suited her, which was strange, because she was dogged by one disaster after another right from the start when, as a young bride, she went to view the Georgian farmhouse she inherited from her Anglo-Irish forebears. Coribeen was a ruin, but it was situated on the glorious Glár River, and she was bewitched with the countryside, the house, and the estuary. She hardly registered that the property had no surrounding land and only the most meagre access to the road.

It was fortunate that Val Sweeney—an Englishman despite his name—was wealthy. A keen yachtsman as well as an astute businessman, he saw the possibilities of the land around Coribeen with its long river frontage and private mooring. Even before embarking on the house restoration, Sweeney quietly bought the surrounding twenty-five acres. It was some years before Cressida discovered that, due to some fast footwork by persons unknown or at least unnamed, her title to the house included no land, not even the original narrow track from the main road. Together, land and house were extremely valuable; divided, less so. The land could be sold without the house, but the converse did not hold. With neither land nor access, the house was worthless. In effect, Cressida could not sell her inheritance without her husband's agreement.

Ignorance was bliss for Cressida that first year. A few weeks after completing the purchase of the land, Sweeney's beloved yacht *Azzurra* was moored at the bottom of the garden. The couple originally intended Coribeen as a holiday home, but Cressida was eager to get settled. She moved in, ostensibly to oversee the work, while it was still a building site. Her trips to London gradually dwindled, and once baby Gil was born, she took up permanent residence while V. J.—

as he was universally known—returned at weekends. For him, Coribeen was an investment; he never intended to settle in Ireland. He didn't really like it. Soon weekly visits became monthly. The arrangement suited them both.

When Gil was two years old, he developed severe hearing difficulties. His parents reacted differently to this setback; V. J. took it as a personal insult, while Cressida became totally focussed on helping her little son. She learned sign language and how to lip-read and taught Gil herself until a neighbour offered to help. There were those who thought it inadvisable to allow an elderly, solitary ex-priest near the child, even if he was once a distinguished academic. But Cressida knew better; John Spain was more than a good friend, he was also her confidant and advisor. She regarded him as a kind of surrogate father and would have trusted him with her life.

With the discovery of Gil's deafness, the Sweeneys' relationship began to go seriously wrong. Overnight, V. J. seemed to lose all sense of propriety. Always something of a womaniser, now he openly flaunted his relationship with Evangeline Walter, an American who lived across the river. He also began to drink heavily, and with drink, he became violent and abusive towards his wife and child. His neglected business failed and within a couple of years he was practically bankrupt. As money dried up, he determined to sell Coribeen, house and land together, and started a campaign to force Cressida to agree to surrender her title to the house. For such a gentle girl, she proved surprisingly resistant to even the most ferocious beatings. As she saw it, her marriage was in shreds, and she had a handicapped child to look after; Coribeen was her only safeguard against the future. She refused to budge.

It was around this point that Francis Xavier Recaldo, a former detective inspector at garda headquarters in Dublin, amateur musician, and aspiring travel writer, entered the picture. After a premature heart attack, he had retired to quiet and sleepy Passage South as resident policeman. Tall, handsome, and vulnerable, he was precisely the kind of man to appeal to a shy and neglected young woman. So of course they fell in love, though they managed to conduct their affair with the utmost secrecy. Or so they thought.

Then disaster struck the estuary. Early one autumn morning, John Spain found Evangeline Walter dead in her garden. V. J. Sweeney went missing, suspected of killing her. As the lover of Sweeney's wife, Garda Recaldo was in an extremely invidious position. The investigating detectives shipped in from the city certainly thought so. By the time incontrovertible evidence against Sweeney was found, both he and Spain had drowned. Life on the estuary was over; Cressie and Gil fled, under Frank Recaldo's protection.

V. J. Sweeney's name was never released to the press. He remained forever "suspect drowned at sea." The police believed they had their man, and the case was closed.

Against all expectation, there wasn't a whisper in the press of Recaldo and Cressie's personal involvement, although they were aware of the usual village gossip. And that, of course, was the real reason they packed their bags and took off. There was also another reason: since V. J.'s liaison with Evangeline Walter was well known, his guilt would have been speculated upon. Someone, sometime, would blurt it out and the thought of her son being branded as the child of a murderer appalled Cressida.

Some months later, Coribeen was sold at a knockdown price, there being few enough willing to live in a house associated with a recent murder. Deep in her heart Cressida knew that her old friend John Spain would have advised against the panic selling of her beloved home. But Frank had urged it, and once she realised that he had no future in the garda, especially in West Cork, she felt she had no choice but to leave. "One day," John Spain once told her, "you will have to learn to make your own decisions—for yourself and your son. Remember that. No one else, no one, no matter how loving, will ever put Gil's interest first. You have to take responsibility, Cressida, for your life and his."

Wisely or not, they packed their bags and took off. Just before the birth of their daughter, Katherine Mary—Katie May—they married quietly. Shortly afterwards, Frank legally adopted Gil and made his name change official.

Oddly, Gil never mentioned the estuary except at the very beginning, when he kept asking for John Spain. Nor did he ever speak of his father. And after an anxious year or so, Cressida and Frank concluded he had forgotten his previous life. He was a happy, charming child who threw off his shyness as his hearing gradually improved.

They settled in Dublin, in a small semi-detached house in an outer city suburb within walking distance of the mountains. The Dublin house and a tiny holiday cottage in Kerry, near Frank's family, cost more than Cressida made from the sale of Coribeen. The balance ate up most of Frank's capital. He invested what remained to provide, however inadequately, for Gil's school fees. But at least they were clear of a mortgage. Frank's travel series—*Walking to Music around Ireland*—sold reasonably well, and with his pension, occasional journalism, and the rental income from the cottage, they kept the wolf from the door.

Over time, the Recaldos melted into their surroundings and convinced themselves that they were what they appeared: an unremarkable, ordinary family. Secretly, Cressida never stopped fearing that one day her—and Gil's—past history would be discovered, but as the years went by, she became a little more relaxed. It seemed that nothing could ever intrude into their private, safe cocoon. And perhaps that would have been so, had not Frank, weary of earning so little from his travel series, turned his hand to crime under the pen name Frank Ventry. His first detective novel achieved a modest success, but his second hit the jackpot. Fame beckoned, and the Recaldos were unprepared for it.

regression 2

three

Duncreagh Listening Post

(archive discovered by Gil Recaldo)
Body of woman found in the river by fisherman.
Name withheld until relatives informed. Foul play
suspected.

JUST AFTER MY fourteenth birthday, my grandfather fell ill,
and my mother was called upon to play Florence Nightingale.
She thought it would only be for a few weeks, but it took
four years for the old bugger to pop his clogs. Frank and I
stayed in Dublin because I didn't want to change schools,
and Frank was tramping the length and breadth of Ireland
for his "Walking" series. There were other reasons: not
much spare cash flying around, the Oxford house was too
small, and neither of us got on with Grandfather. But the
real clincher was that during the second year, Frank went
back to working, part time, for the Irish police. His friend
Chief Inspector Phil McBride—Bridie to the family—
fixed it.

After my Leaving Cert. I took a year off and spent a few months in Oxford working as a waiter, to please Cressie. It was not a great success. She was stressed out all the time and my grandfather was always grumbling about poor little Katie May. It was like a madhouse, so I went to Germany with a couple of mates from school. After a few months we moved on to France, where I managed to get a job at a boat-yard in La Rochelle. At first I was just a general dogsbody, cleaning out charter yachts and doing general maintenance, but since I knew how to handle a boat—I'd been sailing with Frank in Dublin Bay since I was a kid—I was angling for a crewing job when my grandfather died. I had to go back to Oxford for the funeral, but I fully intended returning to France, where I was promised work with the biggest char-ter company in the Port de Plaisance.

But then, a strange thing happened at my grandfather's funeral. During the service I found myself wondering why I couldn't remember a memorial service for my father. I'd al-ways understood he drowned when his yacht ran aground during a ferocious storm and that John Spain died trying to save him. But somehow that story didn't hold together. Was he really dead? I sneaked a glance at Frank and my mother, who were both looking as tense and miserable as sin, and re-alised fully, for the first time, how little I knew about my ori-gins. It was as if I'd arrived fully formed, aged eight, as Gil Recaldo. How ridiculous is that?

As the vicar warbled on about Grandfather's supposed virtues, a great turbine was whirring in my head. That was my real moment of decision, though unconsciously I must have been travelling towards it for some considerable time, because my plan to return to France suddenly opened up all sorts of possibilities. What if I worked in the boatyard for a month or so, then sloped off to West Cork? I mean, if I was crewing, it would be hard to keep track of whether I was in port or at sea, so it wouldn't be too noticeable if I didn't keep in regular touch.

I more or less made up my mind to crew for a few weeks, then go walkabout. But when I got back to La Rochelle, someone else had taken my place with the charter company, and I was back to odd jobs, which meant I didn't earn very much, at least not enough to save anything. Then fate took a hand. One day while I was cleaning one of the charter boats a gang of Irish guys had thrashed, I came across a discarded copy of *Cara*, the Aer Lingus in-flight magazine. I was flicking through it idly when I spotted an article on *my* estuary. The minute I saw the photographs, I felt I was being sucked in. What was really strange was that one shot must have been taken from our garden. It was like travelling back in time, because it was exactly what I saw when as a child I sat on the dock, looking across the water. On the opposite bank was *that house,* where the American woman lived. Something exploded in my brain, and I knew the time had come. A week later, I hitched to Beauvais and got a cheap standby flight to Dublin. I told nobody where I was headed. As far as my folks were concerned, I was still in La Rochelle. Mobile phones are great that way.

four

E-mail from Arts Editor, *Dublin Daily News*
To: Fiona Moore

Ms. Moore, I like your outline and am pleased you
offered the project to me. I'd like a few days
to think about it—we're a bit snowed under at
the moment, but I'll get back to you for a chat
within the next week or two.
Sean Brophy, arts editor

WHEN CRESSIDA MOVED back to Oxford after eighteen years
in Ireland, she changed her name for the fourth time and re-
verted to type. Born Hollingsworth, she had taken the names
of her two husbands, first Sweeney, then Recaldo, but when
she went back to look after her elderly father, she found the
medical and social services people called her by his name.
She realised it was something to do with the way the old
man treated her, the way she acted out the dutiful daughter.
There was nothing in their relationship to suggest that in another place and another time she had had a life. Or, more ac-

curately, two lives, two husbands, two children. Even for a
while, something of a career. Within a few months of her
stepping into the open jaws of the paternal trap, in a de-
spairing gesture she only half understood, true to her char-
acter Cressida had begun calling herself Hollings—the
"worth" was deleted. It was an accurate description of her
state of mind.

Since his second marriage over twenty years before,
Colonel Piers Roland Hollingsworth had virtually ignored
his only child. He attended neither of her weddings and
never indicated the slightest wish to engage with either of
his grandchildren. Shortly after he and his second wife retired from Corfu to Oxfordshire, Cressida and Frank brought
nine-year-old Gil and six-month-old Katie May to meet
their grandfather for the first time. It was a dreadful weekend. The baby, sensing her mother's tension, howled
throughout, and the colonel seemed genuinely perplexed by
his daughter's association with a man he treated in turns as
an illiterate Spaniard or an Irish peasant.

Needless to say this didn't go down too well with ex–
Detective Inspector Francis Xavier Recaldo, a highly
accomplished Kerryman with a deadly line in sardonic
wit—which mercifully passed over his father-in-law's head.
The visit was never repeated, until the colonel's second wife
died and he took to writing and phoning Cressida with
alarming frequency. Then his health broke down. Having
had the devoted attention of women for all of his four score
and two, boyhood to dotage, when his health failed he was
determined to haul his daughter back to where she belonged.

With Katie May about to start school, Cressida had successfully applied for a job at a highly regarded Dublin art
gallery. However, while professing delight at her success,
Frank drew her attention to the difficulties that might ensue.
How would she manage when he was away researching his
books? When either of the children was ill? During the hol-
idays? The inadequate pay would certainly not cover regular child minding. "You know I'm really pleased for you,
Cress. It'll be wonderful for you to get back to work . . ."
The *but* was unspoken. They were both miserable. Frank be-

cause he couldn't rejoice for his wife's success and Cressida because she'd inadvertently brought to the surface the strains of the life they lived. In effect, they recognised that their relationship was too fragile to sustain change and this had a profound effect on them both.

So Cressida gave up the idea of returning to work, and things settled back to normal until Grandfather Hollingsworth fell ill. "Don't answer it," Frank said when the first letter from the Social Services arrived. It was followed several weeks later by an urgent summons from the Oxford hospital where her father was recovering from a stroke that had left his mobility impaired. The colonel had been deemed too old and frail for further treatment; there was little to be done, medically speaking. He was confused, though not incapacitated to any great degree, neither in body nor mind, but he did need constant care. He was coherent enough to refuse to consider a hospice, even if there was a bed available. Since there wasn't, he would have to be nursed at home.

"They're trying it on, and so is he. Keep cool, lovey, please. Don't rush over there. Once they get hold of you, they won't let go. What about the children?" And then the real problem. "For God's sake, darlin', we can't afford to have you traipsing back and forth to Oxford all the time."

The words were no sooner out of Frank's mouth than they were faced with real crisis. The hospital needed Piers's bed; he was about to be discharged. The following day Cressida flew over to Oxford and took her father home. What else could she do? But Frank was right; the mistake was hopping over too eagerly. When Cressie looked at the Elsfield house through the eyes of the social worker, she understood at once just why her father was thought to be able to afford around-the-clock nursing care. Small it might have been, but it was well appointed, cosy, and stuffed with valuable antiques. No use telling the authorities that the house and most of the contents belonged to his deceased second wife and would, when Piers died, revert to her son, who lived much less comfortably in what the estate agents described as "a compact artisan's dwelling" in Jericho, in the centre of Ox-

ford. He was, not unnaturally, deeply resentful of his stepfather's continued presence in his mother's house.

The couple of weeks Cressida had originally envisaged
she would need to sort out her father's care stretched and
stretched. Frank took the children to their cottage in Kerry,
where they ran wild and he finished the fourth of his travel
series, *Walking to Music around Ireland*. It was the first time
the couple had been parted.

Trapped in Oxford, Cressie felt let down by Frank, who
in turn felt she'd turned her back on him. They were running
two households when Frank's income from his writing was
stretched beyond its limit maintaining one. Eventually he
succumbed to the blandishments of his friend Chief Inspector Phil McBride and, without consulting his wife, agreed to
work, albeit on a part-time and flexible basis, at the Irish police headquarters in Dublin. Perhaps he hoped that returning
to his old job might force Cressida into looking at the reality of the situation into which she had plunged them, but she
was much too preoccupied even to think about it, being
more concerned with what to do about five-year-old Katie
May. September and the start of the school year was loom-
ing.

Frank and Cressida discussed the situation endlessly by
phone and letter, but since there seemed no easy way out,
they resolved to make the best of it. The idea that they sell
the cottage in Kerry was rejected. They assured themselves that it wouldn't be for long; the medical prognosis
indicated that Piers might survive a few months, a year or
so at most. At fourteen Gil was well settled in his Dublin
school, and Frank's work meant that he was needed in Ireland. So the temporary split took on a kind of permanence.
Frank and Gil remained in Dublin; Cressida and Katie
May moved in with her father in Oxfordshire, where the
little girl was enrolled at the village school.

For the first year or so, Frank and Gil squeezed into
Piers's house every holiday and half term, but even from the
start it never worked. The low ceilings were claustrophobic,
the bedrooms too few. Katie May had a tiny attic room, but
Gil had to make do with a put-you-up in the living room.

Cressida's bedroom barely held a small double bed, even when it was jammed up against the wall, and the space seemed to shrink further whenever Frank was in residence. Try as they might to make things work, the strain began to show, especially between Frank Recaldo and his father-in-law. As a veteran of the Second World War, the old colonel held an often-voiced contempt for Ireland's neutrality and its architect, Eamonn De Valera, whom Frank personified in his confused mind. It wasn't that Frank disagreed with these sentiments; he just couldn't stand his father-in-law's condescension. As senility kicked in, the old man got more and more abusive, thus isolating his daughter from her inconvenient husband and freeing her up to devote herself to her old pa. It was hard not to conclude that the whole ploy was deliberate. Frank, already prejudiced against the old man, never doubted the intended malice.

By the second year, Gil was refusing to tow the family line and preferred to spend his vacations with friends, while Frank's visits gradually became more widely spaced and briefer. Sometimes he took Katie May back with him to Dublin, or else Cressida dispatched her home by air as an unaccompanied minor. It felt hideously like déjà vu to Cressida, who watched helplessly as her family fell apart and her querulous father crowded in to fill the vacuum. As his health deteriorated, she grew too exhausted to do anything but struggle from day to day. What was intended as a temporary split in the Recaldo family lasted four long, weary years.

five

E-mail from Fiona Moore
To: Sean Brophy

Hi, Sorry to press you, but I've only just returned to this country and I need to start working pronto. I'd appreciate it if you could let
me have a decision ASAP? The *Independent* is very
interested, but I have old loyalties to the *News*.
I worked for the legendary Somerville for four
years. I'll hold the *Indie* off till Wednesday.
Fiona Moore

COLONEL PIERS HOLLINGSWORTH was buried on a hot late
June day in the Oxfordshire village of Elsfield, a week after
his death. As Frank Recaldo followed his family into the
half-empty church, he realised how little thought he'd given
to this much desired reunion. Little thought and absolutely
no planning. Taking his place in the pew beside his wife, he
squeezed her hand, and she returned the shy, diffident smile
that he loved. But he felt a dispiriting sense of loss. Where

had love fled? He knew he would find it very hard indeed to adjust to family life again.

From the moment he arrived the evening before, tension had bubbled to the surface, and he thoroughly upset Cressida by suggesting they move their bed into his late father-in-law's room. You'd have thought the deceased was still in residence from the way Cressie reacted. She refused point-blank, and they'd argued about it in whispers into the early hours, until she padded off to the kitchen to make tea, leaving Frank to fall into a fitful sleep. They had hardly exchanged a word all morning and were still not talking when they set out for the funeral service.

In some ways, Frank thought, it was like meeting his wife for the first time all over again. She was like a stranger. Five foot eight, she had always been slim, but she'd lost a lot of weight and was looking pale and ethereal. There were dark circles under her light brown eyes, and her faded honey-blonde hair, grown halfway down her back, was tied in a loose bunch at her neck. She looked, more than anything, in need of physical love, yet Frank suppressed an urge to fold her in his arms. She was dressed in a dull navy blue suit with a string of pearls at the neck, and black court shoes. By contrast, eighteen-year-old Gil looked athletic and vibrant in black jeans and white shirt, no tie. Just over six feet tall, broad-shouldered and tawny-eyed like his mother. His blond hair was unfashionably long to hide a tiny hearing aid in his right ear. Not quite ten-year-old Katie May was lean and leggy like her father, with the same intense blue eyes, pale skin, and a mass of blue-black curls. She was dressed in a navy-and-white striped Breton shift. Frank wore a dark grey suit and black shirt; he was six foot four and as spare as he'd been as a youth. The dark hair was now steely grey, but the blue eyes were still electrifying. They made a handsome group, when they were in good form, which was not the case on this occasion. Cressie was sick with apprehension, uncertain what to do or say. She shifted along the bench and gently stroked her daughter's hair. Katie May had always been a daddy's girl, but in their enforced exile, mother and child had become unusually close. Cressie wondered how she was ever going to be able to share her.

The funeral service was short and perfunctory, the locum vicar incompetent, which Cressie found mildly hysterical. Not so Gil and Frank, who were both fidgety with irritation. An almost visible barrier erected itself, splitting the family neatly down the middle, men to one side, Cressie and the little girl to the other. Alliances and loyalties formed during their enforced separation had, alarmingly, taken only a few hours to surface. Frustrations had matured with time, set, festered, and were about to explode. Cressida was so lost in thought that it was only when Frank's rich baritone was raised to "Onward Christian Soldiers" that she realised the rest of the congregation was standing. She glanced at Gil and saw his shoulders shaking, and when he turned and winked at her, his face was contorted with suppressed mirth.

"The colonel to the last," he mouthed. "Did you choose this?"

Frank stopped singing and looked from one to the other, and suddenly the four of them were giggling helplessly. *We could start from here,* Frank thought, as relief surged through him. He leaned across his daughter and whispered in Cressie's ear, "Why don't we all go out to lunch?" He only just stopped himself adding "to celebrate."

"Good idea," Cressie started, then bit her lip. "But what about this lot? They'll expect to come back to the house, won't they?" She whispered too loudly, not noticing that the singing had stopped. The vicar looked at her over his half-moon spectacles, cleared his throat, and began to intone a dirge for the dead.

"I've prepared sandwiches, just in case, and Grace brought some wine around yesterday. We can't just do nothing, can we?"

"Of course you can," Frank whispered. "How many of these people do you know?"

Cressie shrugged. "Some of them are relations . . . I think. Must be." She gave a nervous little smile.

"Come on Cress, you don't know a single one of them.

Where were they when you needed help? You don't owe them anything."

"But Grace—"

"Grace won't mind. Anyway, she can come, too." Grace Hartfield was a close family friend who could be relied on to calm things down. Frank glanced around but couldn't see her or her husband Murray Magraw.

"Oh what the hell," Cressie muttered. "Why not? Let's go into Oxford." Frank squeezed her elbow and put his arm around Katie May, who grinned up at him. "Pizza Express?" Frank nodded. "Thank God for that," Gil murmured. And for those brief moments, with the prayers for the dead as backdrop, the Recaldos relaxed.

After the service, while some people slipped away, the rest followed the vicar to the adjoining graveyard for the interment, which was conducted with almost unholy haste. Afterwards they stood around with an expectant air until Cressie apparently lost her nerve and invited them back to the cottage for tea.

"Tea? In the middle of the morning?" Frank said crossly. "God, give me strength. Why are you doing this?"

"Oh Mummy," Katie May moaned. "You said we could go out for a pizza."

"Shush," Cressie hissed. "It's OK. There's plenty of time. It's only half past eleven. They'll be all gone in an hour."

"Want to bet?" Frank's eyes glazed in frustration. "I believe there's an excellent lunch to be had at the . . ." he said sotto voce.

"The Abingdon Arms in Beckley—the next village," Gil came to his rescue briskly. "It's only a couple of miles away. Cheap, too. Real ale." Cressie stepped on his foot. "You all know where the house is?" she said politely, looking around at the mourners. "We'll go ahead. See you there in a few minutes," she added, and was appalled when, almost without exception, they took her at her word.

six

E-mail from Sean Brophy
To: Fiona Moore

I like your style. OK, I'll have a contract drawn
up in the next few days. I talked to Jez Murphy,
who's very enthusiastic about taking a selection
for *Jeu*, and Suzanne Philpott of *New England Review* also wants in on the act. I suggested she
contact you direct since you'll probably do a better deal for yourself. I disinterred some of the
stuff you wrote for this paper ten, twelve years
ago. What took you to the States? Look forward to
hearing from you.
Sean Brophy, arts editor

THE WAKE WAS not going well. A reluctant gathering no matter how you looked at it, Frank concluded, being more used
to the Irish variety, which usually contrived to be rather
cheerful. In Oxford, it seemed, things were ordered somewhat differently, and the hastily assembled guests were uni-

formly subdued and formal. Frank, made irritable from re-
curring bouts of angina, was in sore need of diversion. But
none was forthcoming. No amusing anecdotes, no awkward
belly laughs. Nobody falling down drunk. A heated argu-
ment or some other such little incident might have livened
things up, but the robust intake of wine had no obvious effect; the subdued remained impassively subdued. He'd
vaguely hoped someone might at least remark on Cressida's
years of filial devotion, but no one did. Instead, they seemed
to regard dear Piers's awkward daughter and her family as
species of alien.

An hour had gone by, and none of the guests showed the
slightest inclination to leave. What had seemed a sparse
enough gathering in the churchyard filled the small house to
overflowing. Frank made little effort to socialise, beyond
being frostily polite. In need of allies, he looked around anxiously for Grace and Murray, but couldn't see them. The
only light relief was provided by Katie May, who, every few
minutes, passed by the sitting room window, pulling mourn-
ful faces and making pleading gestures with her hands.
When that had no effect, she stood on her head and waved
her skinny legs in the air. These familiar antics usually made
her father laugh, but somehow he couldn't rise to it on this
occasion.

Gil was no help either. He slouched in the most comfortable armchair in the room with his nose buried in a book,
generating waves of resentment. "Why don't you help your
mother?" Frank said to him irritably.

"Why don't you?" Gil muttered back sullenly and wriggled back into the chair as if he wanted to disappear.

"Don't . . ." Frank began. Gil uncoiled himself furiously
and stood up. The two of them eyeballed each other.

". . . speak to you like that?" Gil growled. "That's what
you were going to say, isn't it? For God's sake, Dad, get off
my case."

"No, it isn't what I was going to say," lied Frank, hating
himself for being conciliatory when what he most wanted to
do was to tell Gil not to be so effing disagreeable.

Gil glared at him for a moment. "I'm off," he said and shrugged away his stepfather's restraining hand.

"Hang on, Gil, I want—"

"Look, I don't give a toss what you want. Or think. Or do. I traipsed all the way back from La Rochelle and got here two days ago. *You* couldn't manage to turn up 'til last night. So why don't *you* go and help my mother instead of standing there looking superior? She's shattered." He clenched his fists and stuck them in his trouser pockets. "Look, I don't suppose Mum wanted this . . . this . . ." He looked around wildly. ". . . excuse of a wake. I bet she wanted to have lunch with the rest of us. But he was her father, no matter whether we liked him or not. If he'd been yours, you wouldn't behave . . . Oh what the f . . . hell." His face was scarlet and his eyes full. He reminded Frank painfully of the damaged and vulnerable child he'd been when they first met. Frank felt thoroughly ashamed of himself.

"Gil, please," he started, but Gil ignored the plea.

"Why don't you bloody well look after her, Frank? What is it with you two?" He rubbed the back of his hand across his reddened forehead. "You're never around when you're needed." He twisted away and made for the door.

Two elderly women stepped apart in mock consternation to let him pass, then turned to glare accusingly at Frank. "Some kind of policeman," he heard one mutter, as he brushed past on his way to the kitchen.

"God give me patience," he murmured under his breath. "Can't these feckin' people get anything right?"

I'm a shit, he thought as he pushed open the kitchen door and saw Cressie was standing by the stove, staring into space, waiting for the kettle to boil. As she turned to greet him, a shaft of sunlight caught her face. *Sunflower,* Frank thought, *my heavenly sunflower.* He put his arm around her and drew her to him, surprised by a sudden surge of desire.

She went rigid. "Sorry, love, have to get on," she said distractedly and pulled away.

"Let me know if there's anything I can do, Cressida." Frank swivelled around to face a nonchalant young man he hadn't noticed when he'd come into the room—he was

standing almost behind the door, leaning against the kitchen
counter.

"Who are you?" Frank said rudely, caught by surprise.

"This is Dr. Ford, Frank." Cressie sounded flustered.
"He's been wonderful with Daddy."

"Just doing my job." The man came towards Frank with
his hand outstretched. Frank took it reluctantly. "Paul Ford.
I'm the local GP," he said confidently.

"Been here long?" Frank asked.

"In Elsfield?" Ford asked. It wasn't what Frank meant,
but he nodded. "About five years. I cover several of the vil-
lages around." An awkward silence followed until he added,
"I have to go, I'm afraid." He smiled charmingly. "Cressida,
you've had a tiring old time of it. Take care of yourself. If
you need to have a chat or anything, just give me a call or
drop round at the surgery. Nice to meet you, *at last*." He
nodded at Frank and left.

"Did I interrupt something?" Frank asked.

Cressie stared at him coldly. "Don't be ridiculous," she
said.

At that moment, the kettle let out a shrill whistle. Somehow the fact that it wasn't electric made Frank even more
twitchy. Cressida studiously rinsed out the teapot while
Frank leaned back against the counter and watched wearily.
She seemed unreachable. Passive, but definitely out of
range.

The doctor's "at last" stung him. He and Cressie needed
to talk before it was too late, before they forgot what it was
that had first drawn them together. Once, they couldn't bear
to be apart for an instant, but now, whenever he wanted to
make love, Cressida shied away.

He glanced up to see Katie May standing by the open
window, watching them. Listening, too, he told himself with
a sinking heart. Damn, damn, damn. Was it his imagination
or had the same sense of unreality begun to cloak even his
adored daughter? He registered, painfully, how she skirted
him when he came on his flying visits, which were often too
short for the ice to begin to crack, much less break. When
had this state of affairs become the norm? At first it only

amounted to a brief awkwardness as the little girl felt her
way into his affections, but recently there was a definite
sense of her consciously and obviously trying to get used to
him. It was even more humiliating watching her struggle to
shoehorn him into her world. Rage surged through him,
though he was at a loss on whom, beside himself, to focus
it. Usually he diverted his anger to his late and unlamented
father-in-law, but now it settled as a red mist of misery as he
confronted his tired, harried wife and watched her shy away.
Her first husband had battered her, mentally and physically,
and in that fleeting instant, to his absolute horror and ever-
lasting shame, Frank thought he understood why.

"When do you have to get back?" Cressida asked.

"Why?"

"For God's sake, Frank, what the hell's the matter with
you? I only want to know when you've to get back to the
film set."

You? It's supposed to be we. "Tomorrow or the day after.
They're trying to get as much done as possible while the
weather's good."

Frank's second novel was being filmed for television
when word came of his father-in-law's death. Relief that at
last they could get back their lives was replaced rapidly with
anxiety that his neat and ordered routine was about to be
shattered. For a wild and dizzying moment, he was tempted
to stay put and get on with his work. Frank brushed aside the
nasty little thought that his late flowering had happened during Cressida's sojourn in Oxfordshire. It wasn't that he
didn't recognise she would need his help in the aftermath of
her father's death. He wanted to give it, but he couldn't bear
the thought of being away from the action. He'd waited a
long time for success and with it, relief from perpetual financial strain. Why shouldn't he savour it?

"So soon?" she murmured, preoccupied. "Does it have to
be so soon?"

He folded his arms to stop himself from grabbing her
again. "Cressie, what ails you? You *are* coming, aren't you?
You need a break after what you've been through. You're

not backing out, are you? We can come back and clear this place when the filming's over."

She gave him an odd look, her mind elsewhere. She bit her lip. "When will it be finished? The film, I mean. Do they need you there all the time?"

Frank's temperature began to edge up, his heart raced. "Well they would, wouldn't they, seeing it's my book, my script. Yeah, they need me," he added laconically.

"Stop patronising me." Cressie's eyes held his until he was forced to look away.

"I'm sorry, sunflower." He hadn't called her that for years, but she didn't soften. "Please come. Waterford's beautiful, and for once the weather's marvellous," he said. "It'll be a bit of light relief, and we could use some of that, couldn't we? There's only a week or so left. Afterwards we could easily have a few days to ourselves—on the company. Just you, me, and Katie May. I found a great hotel near Ballyhack."

"Where's that?"

"On the coast, Wexford-Waterford boundary. It's lovely. But we could go down to the cottage, if you prefer. It's free now until the last week in August. Come on, darlin', how about it?" he pleaded, when really what he wanted to say was, *Why can't you be pleased for me? Or pretend to be?*

The name Frank Ventry was on everyone's lips. The production company making the film had bought the rights to his third and latest book, which was due to go into production early the following year. There was talk, too, of an option on his first. Business was booming, and as a result, the Recaldos were suddenly, and for the first time, in a seriously comfortable financial situation. Frank was disappointed that in the bosom of his family there was so little jumping for joy.

"I don't think I can," Cressie said softly, not meeting his gaze. He was distressed at how expert she'd become at avoiding confrontation. She looked now as she had when he first met her a dozen years before when she was being knocked about by her bastard husband and desperate to break free. Except older and frailer.

"Please, Cress? It would be like old times. I haven't had you to myself for so long."

Cressida looked away distractedly. "I have to get this place sorted," she mumbled. How expertly she wriggled free.

Frank flushed angrily. "It can wait."

She bit her lip. "I don't think it can. I promised Tim— Marjorie's son—we'd be out—"

"Promised?" he exploded. "Christ. It's always somebody else, isn't it?" He counted ten silently as he tried to calm down. "Tell you what, Cressida," he continued stiffly, "I'll take Katie May back to Waterford with me. That'll stop her mooning around the garden."

"What do you mean?"

"Look at her. The child is always on her own. She doesn't seem to have made a single friend since she came to this place. She's lonely."

"You think you can do better? Is that what you're saying?"

He felt thoroughly wound up. "Yes, Cressie, that's exactly what I'm saying." Though not, perhaps, what he intended to say.

"So, who'll take care of her? While you're working?"

"Oh, she'll be fine," he said loftily. "Two or three of the crew have their families with them."

"So the wives can look after her? Right?"

"Stop it. That's not what I meant. I *can* look after my own daughter. And there'll be other kids; she'll have company. Though I'm sure she'd prefer you to come. And so would I."

When she didn't respond, Frank picked up the newly filled teapot, turned on his heel, and returned to the living room. He refilled a few cups, then plonked the teapot on the table, noting, en passant, that the vicar was proving as inept a guest as he had been in church. The overplump young man was stuffing sandwiches two by two into his rosebud mouth, thereby single-handedly demolishing the half side of smoked salmon Frank had picked up the previous day in Dublin Airport. He felt a furious antipathy not just for the man and his greed. Had it been through stupidity or laziness that during the brief service, he had failed to grasp either Cressida's name or her relationship to the deceased? Thereby reducing her almost four years of devoted care to a mumbled "Mrs. . . . em . . . er . . . ," which, oddly enough, Cressie seemed to find unaccountably funny.

"Frank, darling?" Cressie came up behind him, unnoticed, and murmured in his ear. "Let's talk about it later."

Frank didn't trust himself to speak. He felt like kneeling down and banging his head on the floor. He touched his wife's arm fleetingly and went to open the window. The west-facing room was stifling in the afternoon sun. As he turned, Cressie was nervously plying the wretched clergyman with yet more food. Frank humbly embraced the shame of his own neglect of his small family. As his eyes followed his wife on her way around the room, he felt as miserable as she looked. Her isolation was almost palpable. He had not looked at her, really seen her, for a very long time, and he was moved almost to tears at how withdrawn she'd become. Lost.

Not knowing quite how to make amends for his jealousy at Cressie's obvious regard for the GP, he slouched against the wall and willed the wake to end. Long-distance relationships were hard to sustain, the thread binding even the closest of couples pathetically flimsy. Frank wondered sadly what there was left to save.

seven

Hi, Sean (or should I say Ed?). Second thoughts.
I've slightly broadened the range to include film-
makers as well as artists (as in painters/sculp-
tors) and writers (including drama). One thing's
for sure, there's a hell of a lot of talent
around. I've completed the first four, have done
the interviews for the following three, and have
drawn up a short list of eight from which to
choose the remaining five. Could we meet for a
chat?
Fi

WHO EVER INVENTED wakes? Gil wondered sourly. He lowered the book he was pretending to read and glared at a couple of old army types who were blocking his view while
they ground on and on about the inadequacies of the Labour
government. Gil worked the armchair forward, the better to

observe his stepfather while he flirted with Grace Hartfield on the other side of the cramped sitting room. Frank was looking a bit more cheerful, but then Grace always had that effect on him. Normally, Gil admired and liked them both, but today he wasn't so sure. Nonetheless, he had to admit they had a lot in common; the same reserved manner, the same way of not rushing to fill silences. Grace was easier to be around, though. She was less confrontational, didn't challenge every damn thing you said. Which Frank did, all the time these days.

Old habits die hard; Gil watched their lips. He couldn't catch everything, because they kept turning their heads away, but they were talking about Halcyon sure enough. "Oh pul-ees," he muttered and raised his book in front of his face. Some things it was better not to know. Or guess. Every time he thought about Halcyon, his heart sank and his head filled with questions for which there seemed no answers. He had been asking them ever since he discovered she wasn't just stupid but also deaf. Like him. Had she been bashed up the same way he had? And if not, how did that leave him? A genetic psychopath? The more he thought about it, the more terrified he became, but he kept it to himself. Festering.

His eyes moved from one conversation to another. It amused him to collect a word here, a word there, making little patchworks of talk. With a bit of practice it was possible to "hear" what people were saying before they opened their mouths. Yet deafness was both barrier and label. As soon as people noticed the tiny device he wore in his ear, they signalled that they "understood" by raising their voices. To everyone except his mother, it was *what* he was. While for Gil it was simply another factor in *who* he was—part of his personality. Cressie and Old John Spain taught him how to handle it, but later, when he had to accommodate himself to the improvements technology and, eventually, surgery brought him, he had to figure his own way through what seemed at the time to be thunderous changes to his perception of the world around him. For Gil, progress was often both intrusive and exhausting. Sometimes it appeared that the better he heard, the less he was able to understand the nuance of what people meant. Every step towards clearer sound seemed to erode his confidence, until the day he decided he'd had enough and switched off his hearing aid. He still wore it most of the time because he couldn't stand being nagged if he didn't. And it had its uses; it created a kind of protective no-go area. It amused him to notice how many people couldn't deal with the disability at all. Maybe they thought it was catching.

Gil let his book drop to his lap as the old men who'd been standing in front of him moved away, leaving his view over the room unimpeded. He liked the role of quiet, unnoticed observer; it gave him a sense of power, this ability to be on the sideline and yet in the thick of things. Excellent way of finding out what was *really* going on. There were better ways of hearing than with the ears—lips, eyes, and body language. He had absorbed all that when he was little and his hearing was almost nonexistent. This was no longer the case. Impaired was a more accurate description, but precisely to what extent almost impossible to measure. He presumed there must always have been a psychosomatic element to it though; sometimes, when he was under pressure or stressed out, silence enveloped him. As a child he had unconsciously used his disability to shut out the unacceptable, and he had never lost the knack. As he grew older, he became aware that he could switch off all sound at will. His use of sight and instinct was deft, so he missed little, and he was bright; his grasp of what was going on around him was acute.

At school he'd been nicknamed Cluedo. It started with a chance remark in his second year when one day a new guy asked him a question and Mullins said, "What are you asking that thicko for? He hasn't a clue what you're saying— he's stone deaf." Gil's mate Baz Phillips had butted in, "Don't you believe it—he lip-reads faster than you can think." Cluedo/Thicko? What was there to choose between them? But fortunately, Cluedo stuck and made his so-called disability acceptable to those who found it embarrassing. The silly nickname was only used at school, where it had one lasting effect: none of his schoolmates ever again equated deaf with stupid. It was OK to be bright.

Katie May stuck her head in the window. "Gilly? Why don't you come out in the garden? Please?"

"In a minute, Twink. I'll come in a minute. Promise," he said. His little sister turned away in disgust and ran off. Gil watched her. She didn't look like him, but somehow she awoke in him a memory of things that happened when he was her age. It was as if there was a volcano inside him, waiting to erupt. On the outside he acted just like every other adolescent; grumpy, withdrawn, and charmless. The sullen, inert exterior successfully masked his inner confusion.

He went back to his book and turned the pages listlessly, with one eye on the clock. People were beginning to leave at last. Gil snapped the book shut, edged toward the door, and slipped quietly out of the house. He went around the side to collect his bike; when things got on top of him, he cycled— in Dublin to the sea or the mountains; in Oxford he usually headed to Otmoor. It was not far, at most three miles by the winding country roads, but enough, on a hot day, to work up a good sweat.

Katie May was lying in wait, literally, stretched full length on the grass. She was making two straggly plaits of her fringe, incorporating coloured glass beads, which dangled over her eyes. It was something she did while she watched television or when she was particularly fed up. When she saw him, she jumped up. "Where are we going?" she asked and saw by his expression that he'd already forgotten his promise. "Please, Gil?" Her clear blue eyes looked suspiciously watery.

"Didn't Dad say he was taking you into Oxford for an ice cream?"

"Yeah, but where is he? I'm fed up waiting."

"He'll be out in a sec. The party's breaking up. People are leaving at last."

"That's what he's been saying for hours. And hours. Anyway it's not my idea of a party."

"Nor mine. What a shower."

"I'll get my bike."

"No."

"Please?" She pouted. Gil suppressed a laugh. She looked ridiculously like Frank. Slim to the point of emaciation with legs that seemed to start at her armpits. Gil, who adored her, reckoned that she was going to be a stunner—already was. She could normally twist him around her little finger, but not today.

"Sorry, Twink," he murmured. "Sorry, I just need to be on my own for a bit." He jerked his head at the house. "Ghastly, eh?"

Katie May shrugged. "I can keep up, Gil. I can keep up with you. Why won't you take me with you?"

"I'm going to see Jackman in the Radcliffe," he said. "Jackman" was Gil's version of Oscar Wilde's Bunbury, invented as a means of escaping his grandfather. He momentarily forgot that Katie May had worked out the ruse long since. "He's broken his arm." His sister's eyes widened. "When?" she asked, playing along.

"Now."

"No. When did he break his arm?"

"A few days ago."

"How do you know? You were in France."

"He rang me," he said hurriedly. "In France."

"Liar," she hissed. "I saw Jackman yesterday, and he looked OK to me." And with that surreal remark, she stuck out her tongue. "You think I'm stupid or what? There is no Jackman. Didn't you tell me so yourself?" She wrinkled her nose at him. "You just don't want me to come, do you?"

"No, I don't. Not today, Twink. Sorry," he said. "What are you doing out here, anyway?"

"Keeping out of the way, what do you think?" She sighed dramatically. "Why is everyone so cross? You. Dad—and Mum keeps blubbing. You'd think she'd be happy now we can go home, but she's not, is she?"

Gil shook his head. "I expect she's upset about Grandfather dying and that—"

"Why? He wasn't very nice, was he?" Katie May cut clean through her brother's piousness. "He was always

grumbling, telling me to shush." She wrinkled her nose. "I
shouldn't say that, should I? I mean sometimes he wasn't so
awful, he told me stories. Still and all, most of the time he
was a grump. Know something? Funerals make me sick. So
do you, Gil Recaldo; you're really mean. You've been away
for months and months, and now you just keep running off
by yourself. Bet you're after some girl."

"No I'm not," he said crossly.

"Well then why can't I come?"

"I'll be back soon. We could go swimming or something."

Katie May thought about this for a moment. "Don't feel
like it. Anyway the Stephenses are away, so we can't use
their pool." Her face brightened. "Grace invited us to a barbecue in her garden. We could go to the Ferry Hinksey pool
and go to Grace's house after swimming, couldn't we?"

"We'll see," he said. Katie May let out a yelp. "I hate
that. Why are *you* so grown-up and boring? Dad always says
that when he doesn't want to do something."

Gil turned his bike around and checked the tyres. "You're
right. Sorry." He gave one of her plaits a playful little tug.
"I'm a brute. Sorry, but I'll be back soon. Promise. Word of
honour, Twink. Trust me, I'll be back in an hour or so." He
went a few yards and looked back at her. "Could you do
something for me?"

"What?"

"Tell Dad I've booked Ryanair back to France tomorrow.
I'll need a lift to the Stanstead airport. See you in an hour."

"An hour or you're dead," she shouted. "No 'or so.' An
hour." And with that, she stumped off down the garden,
kicking the turf furiously as she went.

Gil wheeled his bike out on to the road.

The cottage was on the Oxford side of Elsfield, halfway
up the hill to the village. John Buchan's house, complete
with blue plaque, was about thirty-nine steps away from the
church. Grandfather Hollingsworth had a whole shelf of his
novels, which Gil had repeatedly tried and failed to read. As
far as he could see, the whole of Oxfordshire was littered
with the houses of living and dead writers. R. D. Blackmore,

the author of *Lorna Doone*, once lived in the next village of Beckley, where he was headed.

Shortly after passing the church, Gil ran slap into the first of four rather fierce, and obviously very recently installed, traffic-calmers. He careered into the ditch, where he lay, winded, for a few minutes. When he pulled his bike upright, he looked out over the plain to where the city was spread out below. The dreaming spires were shrouded in the shimmering heat, a fairytale panorama. Oxford was beautiful. Gil didn't often allow himself to think any good of the place that had robbed him of his mother. He remounted his bike and proceeded more cautiously over the succeeding sleeping policemen.

About ten minutes later, he fetched up in Beckley, which looked directly out on to Otmoor.

The first time Gil had visited his grandfather, an old neighbour told him that in ancient times the Roman army had marched across the moor, and the image struck and fired his imagination. Thereafter, whenever he went to Otmoor, he laid his head on the ground, certain he could feel the tramp, tramp of marching feet. It had a special magic that usually worked, but not today. It was too hot and sunny for illusion. On chill, damp days, the moor had a frail whiff of the sea, which helped him to project himself back to his mythical estuary—with the tide full out, of course. Otmoor had been drained for half a century or more, but because of an unusual volume of rain over the previous few weeks, there were still traces of surface water. When he made his eyes into slits, it was possible to imagine the water ebbing and flowing. A small flock of inland gulls added to the illusion.

He sat hunched against a low stone wall edging a pasture, his arms crossed on his knees, supporting his face. He wondered when the straggle of guests would finally leave, when it would be safe to go home without having to give account of himself to one or another of his mother's distant relatives. Old and dusty they looked, to a man. Just like Grandfather Hollingsworth, who'd never, in Gil's experience, taken the trouble to disguise his dislike of the young. Katie May had

come in for special distain. The miracle was that she somehow retained her joie de vivre, which was more than he
could say of himself.

The amount of grief their mother had taken from the old
man was something else. As far as Gil knew, his grandfather
had always treated her like that, ever since she was a child.
Yet the minute the old fascist announced he needed looking
after, she went running, poor little Twink in tow. Had Frank
not put his foot down, they, too, would have been trans-
ported. Surely there should have been some way for Cressie
to care for her father other than pulling her own family
apart?

Gil had to admit, if only secretly and to himself, that he
was grateful to Frank for digging in his heels about remaining in Dublin. He chuckled. Frank had probably been thinking only of himself, not that you'd know; he played his cards
so close to his chest. But at least it meant Gil hadn't been
forced to change schools, lose all his friends, and start ex-
plaining himself all over again. Most of all, they hadn't had
to squeeze into the Elsfield house and tiptoe around the bastard sickroom all the time. It was full of old-man smells and
funny chintzy furniture, built for cats.

The funeral was as grim as everything else. Cold, damp
church, the bloody vicar barely mentioning the corpse—he
couldn't even get Cressie's name right. Katie May and Gil
were referred to as "the em, er, ahm, great-grandchildren."
Brilliant. Then Cressie had to go and invite the sod back to
the house for tea. Gil wasn't sure whether or not the cucum-
ber sandwiches were his mother's idea of a joke.

He threw himself back on the grass and sniggered at the
memory of Frank's face when he saw Cressie piling his expensive smoked salmon on to Mother's Pride. "That'll teach
him, to come when he's needed," he muttered. But the satis-
faction of criticising his stepfather was lost as he contem-
plated the Recaldo family future. When he considered it,
Cressie, in Grandfather Hollingsworth's immortal words,
"had gone native." The old man had meant it to describe
what had happened to her in Ireland. But he was wrong. As
Gil saw it, Cressie changed when she returned to Oxford-

shire. In the process, he had lost his mother. He closed his eyes, the better to contemplate his grievances and only incidentally to plan the last leg of his gap year.

As he got to his feet to start his return journey, the idea of going back to the estuary had taken hold. He didn't know it yet, because his head was full of his forthcoming return to France, but the seed had been sown. The accidental sighting of the magazine article, when he got back to La Rochelle, was the clincher.

eight

E-mail from Sean Brophy
To: Fiona Moore

I do like your style. Sean will do fine. For now.
What about Monday, or do you insist on a day of
rest? We could have a lunchtime pint in The Liffey on Batchelor's Walk? Half one suit? If you're
free.
Sean

MEANTIME IN ELSFIELD, the remaining guests showed no
sign of leaving. "We just don't have the talent for it." Grace
Hartfield came up behind Frank, startling him.

"What?"

"For wakes. The English just don't *do* wakes."

"Oh, is that it? And there was I thinking it had something
to do with the corpse," Frank said irreverently. "Piers
Hollingsworth had a rare talent for putting the kybosh on en-
joyment."

"In death as in life, then," she intoned with a grin and

handed him a glass of red wine. "Have a drink; it might help."

"I'm not sure it will; I've already had a couple," he said, but took it anyway. "Excellent wine, Grace. Don't we have you to thank for it? Cress said you brought it around yesterday."

"Glad it came in handy," she said laconically. "But it was intended for you two. Thought you might both need cheering up." She smiled. Grace Hartfield was a general favourite with the Recaldo family. She and her American husband Murray were antiquarian booksellers of some repute, who ran the business from their vast Victorian pile in north Oxford. The two couples had first met in Ireland, more than a decade before, when Frank had been investigating the murder of Murray's cousin, Evangeline Walter. Not an ideal start to a friendship, but they had kept in touch over the years, mainly through contact with Evangeline's daughter Halcyon, but they had become much closer during Cressida's sojourn in Oxford.

Although she was in her early fifties, Grace was still a striking woman with an air of serenity that little seemed to disturb. She had strangely pale grey eyes that Frank always felt could see into his very soul, which he sometimes found a little uncomfortable. Her hair was white-grey, cut in a stylish bob, and her skin was pale and faintly lined, like parchment that had been crumpled then inefficiently smoothed out by hand. One of the things he most admired about Grace was her stillness. She also had a talent for observation; little passed her by. Most of all he loved her for her irreverence.

"I'm very glad to see you, Grace. Did you just get here? I missed you in the church."

"I was late; I slipped in at the back and halfway through, got so irritated with his reverence"—she glanced over at the hapless clergyman, who was still propping up the sideboard—"that I left, pronto, and went home to sort a few things. We sent out our latest catalogue a week ago, and if I don't keep up with the calls, we'll get swamped." She smiled ruefully. "Lousy timing, one way and another. I've only got here. I thought the party would be over. I was hop-

ing to persuade you all to come back to our place for a barbecue or something. Katie May's already agreed. I saw her
on my way in."

"Poor kid's bored rigid," he said. "A barbecue would be
lovely. Anyone ever tell you what an angel you are?" He put
his arm around her shoulder and gave her a little hug.

"Not much of an angel—I should have been here to help,
but I didn't realise there was to be a wake."

"Not sure any of us did. It just happened. Cressie felt she
had to offer, but we didn't really expect them all to take her
up on it. Is Murray around?"

"No, afraid not. He's in Ireland." She grimaced. "Tipperary."

"Halcyon?" He raised his eyebrows.

"Halcyon," Grace replied with feeling. Halcyon Walter
was Murray's brain-damaged ward who'd been institution-
alized since childhood and left to his care by his dead
cousin. The arrangement was a spectacular mess, which
Grace had stepped into with innocence and trust that even
now enraged her. The plan to make Murray, and by default
Grace, the girl's legal guardian had been hatched up shortly
before his cousin's death, without Murray—an entirely im-
practical man in every respect—having consulted his wife.
Grace could not recall, without shuddering, how she and
Murray turned up at Evangeline's invitation for the sole purpose of being introduced to her daughter, only to find that
Evangeline had died a couple of days before. During the
murder investigation, when it emerged that Cressie's then
husband, V. J. Sweeney, was allegedly Halcyon's father,
Cressida had offered to help care for the girl. But for that,
Grace knew she and Murray would never have managed. By
mutual if unstated agreement, the girls' putative relationship
to Gil was kept strictly from him; he knew her only as
Halcyon Walter, Murray's ward.

"I suppose Cressie filled you in on what's been going
on?"

"No, she hasn't said anything."

Grace sighed. "Sometimes I wonder if it will ever end,
Frank."

"What's happened?"

"What hasn't? Since Sister Angela died, the poor girl's been distraught. Violent." She drew in her breath. "I simply don't know how that good woman ever managed. A few hours of Halcyon, and I'm tearing my hair out," Grace said grimly. "Now the convent we moved her to in Clonmel is closing. And she's only been in it six months. Poor girl hasn't a clue what's happening to her. She's got completely out of hand. Missing Angela, I expect. If only she could talk to us."

"How long has Murray been over there?"

"Ten days. She ran away. Now she's in hospital with pneumonia." She held up her hand.

"Don't say it, Frank, just please don't even think it. . . ."

"I'm sorry, Grace." Frank touched her hand. "It's what you always feared, isn't it?"

"Yup. Murray's bringing her back with him," she said bleakly. "What else can we do?"

"To live with you? My God, how—?"

". . . will we manage? I've no idea. Murray assures me that it's only until she recovers. Heaven only knows what we'd have done if Cressie hadn't found a private home in Witney who promised the next available place. So let's hope. Meantime, Murray's stuck in Ireland until she's well enough to travel."

"Ever feel tempted to say 'I told you so?' "

"Constantly, but most of the time I desist," she said. "What's the point? You can't blame Halcyon. It's terrible for her. I feel really sorry for her. Mind you, she's been luckier than most with her condition; she had the same devoted caregiver most of her life. The only constant while one convent after another closes down. First in New York and then in Tipperary." She drew in closer and lowered her voice. "Sister Angela was always anxious about what would happen when she could no longer manage. She once told me that she'd hoped Evangeline would gradually take charge once they brought the girl to Ireland. Fat chance," she snorted. "Old Morticia only managed to have her home twice. Did you know that? *Twice?* In the six or seven years she lived in Ireland? That woman was something else."

"Morticia? Is that what you called her?" Frank chortled, then shuddered as the image of the dead woman's white face appeared in his mind, her chiffon scarf flowing in the wind. "I guess she had no real idea of the problems . . ."

"That's putting it charitably. It's one hell of a legacy. For us all, Murray and me, you and Cressie. I hope we can survive it," Grace said grimly, thinking of the impact it was having on her own marriage.

"Evangeline's Legacy?" the crime writer murmured. Good title. Frank pictured it across a book jacket. Could he? Could he possibly? "Evangeline's legacy," he repeated.

"You've an unhealthy gleam in your eye, Frank Recaldo. I've often wondered when you'd get around to it."

"I couldn't," he protested piously. "Wouldn't."

Grace wasn't fooled for a second. "No, I suppose not," she said. "Too gothic. Even for fiction. You'd be hard put to make her believable. And impossible to make her likeable."

Frank shook his head. "Too close, too involved." He changed the subject. "When does Murray get back?"

Grace shrugged. "A few days? Who knows? Poor man. Mind you, I'm not sure I don't envy him—looking around at this lot. Cheerful, aren't they?"

"As a roomful of undertakers. Have they no homes to go to?"

"I'm sure they'll be off soon," she murmured. "If we can just persuade Cressie to stop doling out the sandwiches."

"Maybe you should try; she listens to you."

Grace looked at him sideways. "And not to you? Since when, Frank?"

Frank passed his hand over his eyes wearily. "We had a bit of a barney last night."

"Cressie's worn out, Frank," Grace spoke urgently. "She's grieving. Don't look at me like that, it's true. She tried so hard. For heaven's sake, she only wanted what everyone wants—for her parent to love her. And as we know, Piers was pretty miserly with his affection. I don't honestly know how she kept going. You should take her away for a holiday, just the two of you."

"I've already asked her, and she's refused." He ran his fingers through his hair. "At least I think so," he added dubiously.

"Try again, Frank. Katie May can come and stay with us. Gil, too, of course. If he likes—"

Frank gave a snort of laughter. "If he likes? Hard to know what Gil likes at the moment. He seems to think I was put on earth specifically to blight his life. He's furious at having to come back from France. I'm not sure which of us is the baddie—me or his mother—but either way, he's being a royal pain in the arse."

"Oh come on, Frank. He's a nice boy. . . ."

"Indeed he is—if you don't have to put up with his moods."

"Really?" she said innocently. "But he's been away for months."

"OK. There's a pair of us in it." Frank held up his hands in mock submission. "He's heading back to La Rochelle tomorrow. Cressie's upset—she thought he'd come home to Ireland with us for a bit of a family holiday, but he's having none of it. I'm not sure I am, either. He's so far up his own arse there's no talking to him."

"What's gone wrong, Frank? You two used to get on really well."

"Used to, before the testosterone kicked in," Recaldo said wearily. "Not so much adolescence as obsolescence—mine, I mean. For the past couple of years everything's a battle." He felt the hideously familiar but almost forgotten pang of parental outrage, just as he had first time round, when his two sons from his first marriage had reached the same state of sullen inertia. It had affected his marriage then, and he was alarmed to find himself once again in the same position. Or was he simply using Gil to shield other problems?

"That bad, huh?" Grace asked lightly. "Anything I can do?"

"It'll pass, I hope." He turned his head to the window because he couldn't bear to admit that his frustration with Cressida was getting on top of him. They had been so close once, so happy before the upheaval. Lately Frank found himself wishing that neither of them had the baggage of previous marriages to spoil their joy in what they'd found together. Would Katie May, in time, also crystallise into another fly in their ointment? It seemed hard to believe, watching her clowning around the garden. When she saw him, she waved and began making faces. "Daddy, when are we *going?*" she mouthed.

"Hang on there, I'll be out in five minutes," he called to her out the window, then shut it with a bang. He debated whether he would tell his wife where he was going but decided against it. He looked around the half-empty room. Gil had disappeared, and Grace was heading for the kitchen. He strode purposefully to the door, and his sudden movement must have at last signalled that the party was over because the stragglers began to work their way, crabwise, towards the hall. Frank practically galloped out of the house and around to the back garden where Katie May was waiting impatiently.

"Seen Gil?" he asked.

"Yeah," she replied, keeping faith with her brother. "He's gone to the Radcliffe Hospital to see his pal Jackman." She smiled innocently. "He told me to tell you he booked a flight tomorrow morning and wants a lift to Stanstead airport."

"Did he now?"

"Yeah. He said the wake was too much for him."

Frank grinned down at her. "For me, too, baby," he said with feeling.

nine

E-mail from Fiona Moore
To: Sean Brophy

Sean, Thanks for the (unexpected) lunch as well
as the compliments. I didn't know where to put
myself, but I'm really pleased you like the first
three profiles. I've certainly developed a taste
for it. As the man said, you meet such interesting people. I was thinking over what you said
about including a few newcomers, and I like the
idea. I'll dig around and see what I come up
with.
Fi

WHILE FRANK WAS in the garden with his daughter, Grace
went to look for Cressie. She found her sitting on the floor,
just inside the kitchen door, her head cradled in her arms.

"Cressie, for heaven's sake, what are you doing?" Grace
asked.

Cressida looked up and made a moue. "Keeping out of the way. Have they gone yet?"

"Almost, so don't start distributing food again. Just stay where you are for a few minutes, then we'll catch them in the hall to say good-bye." Grace sat down beside her friend and put her arm around her. "I'm sorry Cress, was it awful for you?"

Cressida bit her lip. "Yes. Much worse than I expected. Somehow I thought I'd be relieved. You know, start my life over . . . but now . . ."

"Cressida?" One of the guests put his head around the door. He was a small, plump, middle-aged man with bushy eyebrows and bad teeth. He looked at the two women on the floor and shook his head impatiently. "We're off now. I'll see you tomorrow morning at eleven o'clock."

Not a word of thanks, Grace noticed.

Cressie struggled to her feet. Her skirt was crumpled and had a grease stain down the side. "Oh? Tomorrow? Oh. Can't you leave it for a few days, Tim? I haven't been able to talk to my solicitor yet. She's been away," she added lamely.

"That's most inconvenient. We'll have to manage without her," he said rudely, but it seemed that Cressida wasn't about to be pushed around. "Tomorrow isn't possible," she said, then spoiled it by adding, "Sorry."

Grace, who hadn't a clue who he was or what was being discussed, wondered if Tim would have apoplexy on the spot or if he'd have manners enough to wait until he got outside. There was a moment's standoff before he pulled his diary from his jacket pocket and leafed through it irritably.

"Saturday?"

"I'm not sure solicitors work on Saturdays, do they? Mine won't be back till next Tuesday, I'm afraid."

"This is a damn nuisance. Don't you realize—"

Cressie drew herself up and pushed her hair back from her eyes. "I don't want to discuss this," she said fiercely, "at my father's funeral."

"A week tomorrow then," he said with finality. "Ten o'clock. It's time for closure," he said loftily and withdrew.

"Time for what?" Grace stifled a laugh and raised her eyebrows. "Who dat?" she mouthed.

Cressie peered out into the hall before replying. "That's the blessed Marjorie's son. You know, my late stepmother." She wrinkled her nose. "Not sure what that makes us—darling Tim and me, I mean. He's a terrible fusspot and," she added with a surprising show of spirit, "he has dreadful breath. He can't wait to get rid of us."

"Rid of you? Now you mean?"

"Well, this *is* his house, and he wasn't best pleased that his mama left it to Daddy for his lifetime." She chewed her lip. "Yesterday, he served notice on me to quit."

"Yesterday? I don't believe it. That's obscene. And he had the gall to come back here and stuff himself with your food? Cheek."

"Yeah well, it's his house and I guess he was checking up on us. He's probably afraid I'll run off with the contents," she snorted, "which he seems to think belong to him."

"And do they?"

"Most, but not the few important bits and pieces. That reminds me, Grace, there are some prints I want you to look at. Could you? Lovely watercolours, too." Her eyes filled with tears.

"Of course, any time. I may not be any use, but I can put you—"

". . . in touch with a man?" Cressie finished and managed a wan smile. "Thanks, Grace."

"So when *are* you moving out?" Grace asked, but instead of replying, Cressie said she'd better check on the guests.

"Back in a tick, Grace. Don't go."

Grace had almost finished tidying up by the time Cressida returned. "All gone, thank goodness." She poured a glass of wine apiece, and they sat down at the table. "Gil seems to have disappeared."

"Yes, I forgot to tell you; he's gone out for a spin on his bike. Oh, and Frank's taken Katie May into Oxford for ice cream or something."

"Yes, I caught them as they left." Cressida picked up her glass and took a long draught of wine. "Well, thank God that's over. I've no idea who any of those people were. What did you think of that vicar?" She giggled. "Wasn't he something else?"

"Lazy sod, he might have got your name right." Grace glanced at the clock. It was nearly five. She was expecting a call from a customer in New York, and she couldn't remember if she'd diverted her calls to her mobile. If not, he'd just have to ring back, she decided. Cressida had finished her wine. Grace refilled her glass and topped up her own. "Cress? Do you want to come and stay for a few days?" she asked and looked around the cramped kitchen. "Frank can't stand upright in this place, or Gil, for that matter. They both look bloody miserable," she said, then added quietly, "and so do you. D'you want to talk about it?"

Cressie looked away and changed the subject. "Murray isn't back, is he? What's happening with Halcyon?"

Grace sighed. "She still in hospital in Clonmel. Murray's staying nearby, visiting every day."

"He's very good," Cressie said. Grace looked as if she might not agree but held her tongue.

"They managed to keep her in bed then?" Cressie gave a little snort. "That'll be a first."

"Oh yes. She's not at all well, Cress. I didn't want to say anything until all this was over. Both lungs are affected, and she doesn't seem to be responding to the antibiotics."

"Will she . . . will she be OK?"

"Murray seems to think so. At least if she's in immediate danger, he hasn't said so to me. But then . . ."

"He would say, wouldn't he? D'you think Gil should see her?" Cressie bit her lip. "He's going back to France. We could go over to see Halcyon together, and he could get a flight from Dublin. Or Cork. Couldn't he?"

"I suppose he could, Cress, but I think I'd be a bit careful, honey. For one thing, Frank would have a fit. He hasn't seen her for years, has he? You said yourself that it was better that way."

"He should see her."

Grace wondered if her friend was having a breakdown. She never figured out why Cressie persisted in visiting the girl down the years, much more frequently than Murray did. "Val abandoned her, so I have to take some responsibility," she'd said all those years before, and she'd been good at her word. Even while she was in Oxford, she made time to see the girl on her rare visits home.

"But Gil doesn't know she's his sister, does he?" Grace said impatiently. *Half sister,* she corrected herself silently. "So what's the point?" In her view, Cressie was acting very oddly. Halcyon, who could neither talk nor hear, was locked in a strange half world of her own. She rarely recognised even her most frequent visitors, and when she did, she was often aggressive and violent.

Until Grace knew Frank well enough to ask, she'd always wondered how he coped with Halcyon. "Visiting's one thing," he'd burst out. "But trying to integrate her into a family with more than enough emotional turmoil already to cope with is a step too far." And so it had proved. When Katie May was a toddler, they stopped having Halcyon to stay, and from then on, Cressida visited the girl alone. Grace didn't know what straw broke Frank's back, or even if there was one, since neither he nor Cressie offered an explanation. Why should they? The girl was Murray's ward, after all, his responsibility.

At that point Grace didn't admit to Cressida that she and Murray were having their own communication problems. They rarely discussed what Grace called the Halcyon situation, but there was little doubt that the girl had become an increasing bone of contention between them. Its latest manifestation was that Murray, who had slipped over to Ireland for a few days, seemed curiously unwilling now to return. Something peculiar had happened to him. When he rang, he talked nonstop about how beautiful and peaceful Halcyon was: "She looks just like Evangeline did at the same age. She's so pleased I'm here. Do you know, Grace, she won't let go of my hand, poor baby." Grace shivered.

"Why not just let Gil go off for the rest of the summer, Cress? He'll be back in October. He can see her then, can't he? By the way," she added, keen to get off the subject, "what's he going to read at university?"

Cressie hunched her shoulders. "You tell me. One moment it's marine engineering, next languages. He either wants to build boats or become a writer—take your pick."

Grace laughed. "He could easily do either. Or both, couldn't he? Wonderful, isn't it? At that age they can conquer the world, do anything they want." She smiled at her friend. "Gil's a lovely boy, Cress. And don't worry about Halcyon. She's very strong; she'll recover."

"You're right." Cressie replied. "I'll go and see her as soon as we get back to Dublin. Did I tell you Frank's all on for leaving at the weekend. He wants me to drive to Fishguard and take the ferry, after Gil leaves." She pursed her lips.

"And is that what you want?"

"I don't know what I want." Cressie ran her hands through her hair. "I thought it would be all simple once Daddy died. I thought . . . Oh Christ, Grace, I'm in a terrible muddle. I don't know what to do."

Grace refilled Cressie's glass, which she'd already emptied twice to no noticeable effect. "It might help to get it off your chest. Frank's is in a bit of a bate, isn't he?"

"He seems to think I'm too cosy with Paul Ford. He came into the kitchen while we were talking and was so rude. I was furious."

"Paul *does* hang around a bit. . . ." Grace began. It had been obvious to her for months that the GP was making a play for Cressie.

"Oh for heaven's sake, Grace, don't you start. I like Paul, and I don't know how I'd have managed Daddy without him, but I've never fancied him. Never," she added emphatically. "He's easy to talk to, though." She made a face. "I'm making a frightful mess of everything."

"Oh, for God's sake, Cressie, why do you always take the blame on yourself? You've had a hell of a few months. Few years, when you think about it. Your father was very, very demanding." The minute Grace said it she knew she'd made a mistake. Cressida's expression was a mixture of hurt and anger. She clasped her hands together and leaned across the table.

"We got on all right. Well, better and better, in fact. He was quite sweet to me towards the end. Which is something of a first. Every other relationship I've ever had started all right, then went steadily downhill."

Grace could hardly believe her ears. That Piers Hollingsworth had undoubted charm she could not deny, but he had also been completely self-centred and made an absolute slave and skivvy of his only child. Not even little Katie May was allowed to take precedence over the old man's demands. Grace, being Cressida's only real friend in Oxford, had witnessed the household on a day-to-day basis, and she was an unsentimental woman. In her view, Colonel (retired) Piers Hollingsworth was a born murderee. She didn't understand how he had been able so easily to bewitch the daughter he had neglected for most of her life into devoting herself utterly to him. And surely Cressida was right to blame herself for so casually relegating Frank to a poor third after the children, when they didn't get much of a look in either? No wonder he was fed up.

"Is Frank well, Cressie? He seems very lethargic, and he looks awfully pale."

Cressie seemed not to hear. "I don't want to leave," she whispered. "I don't want to leave Oxford."

"But I thought you hated living here; you couldn't wait to get back to Ireland."

"That's what I thought, too. But now that I can, I'm suddenly terrified."

"Are things that bad between you and Frank, Cressie? Is that the problem?"

"No. Yes. Well, only partly." Cressie leaned closer to Grace, but didn't meet her eye. She licked her forefinger and began to trace circles on the table. Then it all came out in a rush. "Once Frank started hassling me to go back with him, I realised that I feel safe here. It's where I grew up, near enough. Cressida Hollings. Not Cressida Sweeney or Cressie Recaldo. I can pretend there is no past. Nobody knows about the murder or Val or any of that. I'm not perpetually looking over my shoulder, wondering when someone will blurt it out to Gil or Katie May."

She bit her lip. "It wasn't Ireland I was so struck on, you know? It was Coribeen, Gil and me together in Coribeen. I hardly remember what Val looked like anymore. Anyway, he didn't matter. I was happy in Coribeen."

Happy with a murderer who abused her and her child? Some happy. Grace took Cressida's hands in hers and held on tight. "But my dear, when I first met you, your poor face was covered in bruises, one eye was closed, little Gil's arm was broken. Cress, Val was being hunted for murder. He abused you, darling. Knocked you and Gil about. Frank was the guy looking after you both. Frank was there for you. He's a lovely, good, kind man. Cressie?"

Cressida dropped her head, but her finger continued to move frantically in an endless circle. "Yeah, a bloody saint. Don't you see?" she cried. "That's the whole damn problem. With Frank I can't get away from the past, can't forget. I hate being an object of pity. Someone to be kind to. It's pathetic." She began to weep softly. "Oh Grace. I think I was happiest when it was just Gil and me. When we were on our own. Not being told what to do all the time. I should never have left the estuary."

Grace sat quite still. *And now, God help us, it's you and Katie May,* she thought sadly. You don't want to share her. She almost gagged with the pity welling up in her. And the disquiet.

"Will I see you later, Cressie?" she asked gently. "For supper?"

Cressie got up and hugged her. "Thanks for letting me get all that stuff off my chest, Grace. Thanks for listening. Thanks for everything. I'd love to come." She smiled. "Matter of fact, I told Frank I'd meet him there. I'll just wait for Gil, then we'll come straightaway."

On cue, Gil put his head around the door. "Hi. Where's everybody?"

Cressie turned to him with a smile. "Dad's taken Katie May into Oxford. They're meeting us later at Grace's house for supper."

"When?"

"As soon as I'm ready."

"Are we coming back here tonight?"

Grace looked to Cressie, who said, "Afraid so."

"Right. Did Dad tell you I got a flight for tomorrow?" he asked then bolted.

Cressie threw up her arms. "Nobody tells me anything," she said. But she didn't seem too put out about it. "Give me five minutes, Grace?"

"That was a bit of a thunderbolt. Will you be all right, Cress? With Gil going so soon?"

Cressida looked thoughtful for a moment. "Yes," she said in a surprised voice. "I think what I need is a bit of time. Funny how you don't realise what you're feeling till you say it out loud, isn't it?"

"What do you mean?"

"I don't want to go back to the way things were—with me and Frank, I mean—me the dependent one, him the tower of strength. I'd prefer something a bit more grown-up, to tell you the truth. More equal. Frank's just going to have to hold on until I work out a way of achieving that."

"Good for you," said Grace faintly.

Somehow or other, her chat with Grace seemed to clear the air for Cressida, and things began to improve between her and Frank. This was partly, though inadvertently, due to Tim Wallace, who rang next morning just before Frank left for Standstead with Gil and tried to renegotiate the deal he'd made with Cressie the previous day. Now he insisted she vacate the house over the weekend on the pretext that his builder was suddenly free to start the restorations the following week. Cressie was unwilling to give in to his bullying, but Frank suggested mildly, since Tim's urgency matched their own, they could cut a deal. She responded by listing off what had to be done: appointments with the bank and the solicitor, her father's clothes sorted and sent to Oxfam, NHS equipment returned to the hospital service, furniture to be put in storage, papers gone through, the house cleaned. The list grew and grew. "Bugger the cleaning," Frank said robustly. "If Wallace is so damn impatient, I don't see why we should bother about cleaning the blasted house—specially with the builders coming in."

"I don't believe there is a builder," said Cressie and was about to add that whether there was or not, she couldn't leave the house like a tip, when Gil took her by the shoulders.

"Look, Mum, stop being such a martyr. Haven't you done the slave bit long enough? Leave it. The house looks fine."

"Why don't we just divide what's to be done between us?" Frank suggested. "I'll sort out Piers's wardrobe, then ring Mallam's and ask when they can collect the furniture for auction." He put his arm around Cressie's shoulders. "The sooner it's done, angel, the sooner we can get home."

Still Cressie demurred. "I don't think we can sell anything until the will's gone through probate."

"No, but surely the auctioneer has storage space? There are only a few items."

"But his papers are stored in that tallboy. . . ."

"Oh Mum, we can box them up, then you can go through them at Grace's house," Gil interjected impatiently. "Or at home. I bet most of it is junk anyway."

Cressie smiled. "No," she said triumphantly. "One of the drawers is bung full of watercolours and prints. I haven't been through them all, but there's a few good names, and Grace has promised to look them over with me."

"Sure they're your father's?" Frank asked. "Wasn't Marjorie an art dealer? They might have belonged to her."

"No," Cressie said firmly. "They were my mother's. I remember them from when I was a child. They've always lived in that chest. Anyway, my father left them to me."

"You've seen the will?"

"No, Daddy mentioned them a few months ago, and I rang the solicitor when Tim started agitating, just to check. I wanted to be absolutely sure what belonged to me. Daddy lodged a list with Stephanie—his solicitor—when they moved back from Corfu."

"Bit of luck, that," Frank said. "Careful, wasn't he?" Somehow or other he made it sound like an insult. It occurred to him that the contents of the drawer might have been sold to help pay for nursing care, but he held his tongue. The situation was already fraught enough.

"We've got to get out of here, Dad," Gil said. "Or I'm going to miss my flight." He hugged his mother. "Stop worrying about everything, Mum. And stop worrying about me. I'll be back in a couple of months."

"Let's talk it over when I get back, Cress?" Frank shouted out the car window as they drove away.

_____regression 3

ten

Duncreagh Listening Post

(archive discovered by Gil Recaldo)
Local garda investigating mysterious river death
have been joined by detectives Superintendent
Peter Coffey and Phil McBride from Cork City.
Supt. Coffey leads the investigation.

AFTER I LEFT France, I didn't go home or contact my parents. I worked in a Dublin city hotel for a couple of weeks to top up funds then hitched south early one bright Monday morning. That was the easy bit. Cork to Duncreagh was trickier. The bus was a real old boneshaker that stopped at every village en route. My plan was to go straight to Trianach, but when I got off at Duncreagh and asked a passer-by the way, he said it was a good six miles off, but that I was sure to pick up a lift along the road. The extra bit of information was nice, but somehow or other I didn't really fancy hitching, and it was a bit late in the day for such a long walk. I hadn't intended working in Duncreagh—time was too short—but I suddenly lost courage. My quest seemed silly and pointless. I wasn't sure what to do.

I was wandering around the town aimlessly when I spotted a card advertising a temporary vacancy in the window of a jazzy-looking restaurant called Provender. A woman standing at the bar waved at me when I peered in. The tables were all set for dinner, but it was too early for customers. I went inside, applied for the job, and showed her the references from my various gap jobs that I carried around with me.

"You're well prepared, anyway." She laughed. She looked a bit like my mother only smaller and jollier. She made me do a practice run with plates and glasses and all that stuff. It was a doddle, but then anything would be after the months I'd spent doing silver service. "The lad working for me had to go home to Cork—to train for some athletic event, if you please," she said. "He won't be back for a fortnight, so if you promise to stay that long, the job's yours."

Twenty minutes later I was being shown a small room, painted lurid pink, at the top of the house that seemed to be part of the deal.

"If I've learned one thing, it's that we can't keep staff unless we provide accommodation and three meals a day," Mrs. Cronin told me cheerily. "The condition is that you stay for the whole two weeks, mind. If you don't, then I'll charge you for the room. Deal? We close on Mondays, but otherwise it's a split shift every day. Sorry, but there it is." She was nice but quite firm about what she would and would not tolerate. She talked a mile a minute but apart from a cursory look at my references, didn't seem to need any personal information. Suited me.

The restaurant was consistently busy; about forty covers at lunchtime and the same in the evenings. The menu wasn't vast, but the grub was good—nothing special but plenty of it. On Fridays and Saturdays, a jazz trio played in the evening. I'm not musical like Frank and Katie May, but it seemed to be quite a draw, because the place was packed on those evenings. Duncreagh people were friendly and great tippers; I earned much more than I had in either Germany or

France. Trouble was, I worked so hard, I was completely knackered and spent most of my free time sleeping. During the whole fortnight, I never made it to Trianach. I don't think I was ready, somehow. Sad.

There was one advantage to my fortnight in Duncreagh and one disadvantage, neither of which I realised until later: I could come and go in the town without comment, but I had no idea who among Provender's customers might be from Trianach. I suppose, in my innocence, I assumed that being a waiter made me kind of anonymous. The first thing you learn in the job is how to avoid looking at the customer directly. You're the guy taking the order—nobody really notices you. Unless you spill the soup in their lap, of course. But I'm a bit better than that.

I had one definite bit of luck. The office of the local weekly newspaper, circulation around three thousand, was two doors down from the restaurant. It was called the *Duncreagh Listening Post,* and it took itself very seriously. My mind must have been working at half speed, because it was a couple of days before it occurred to me that newspapers are likely to have archives. The woman at the front desk was gullible enough to believe me when I told her I was doing a project for my English course at Oxford—she must have been impressed because she couldn't do enough for me. She was really nice, and I felt mean for lying—or nearly lying.

In the following days I popped into the *Listening Post* for a browse whenever I could. I had assumed the back numbers would be on microfilm or microfiche, but in fact they were all loosely bound in huge folders, month by month, year by year. That, of course, slowed my search. It was easy to get sidetracked, reading about the local antics. Nothing remotely interesting turned up until I stopped messing, retired to my pink bedroom, and worked out a plan of attack. I stopped going through back issues randomly and became rigidly systematic. First, I tried to work out when we left the estuary. Using my birthday in March, as reference point, I thought I could make a stab at an approximate date. It took several visits for me to find a little article about John Spain's death on the Baltiboys Rocks. The only reason I knew it must be Spain and my father was because it mentioned "A fisherman who went to the rescue was drowned." Neither man was named. That was odd in itself because elsewhere in the paper names and vital statistics were scattered all over the place. I sat very still and felt a draft of freezing air swirl around my head. No names. No clues to guide me except the improbability of the same sort of accident in the same year, much less the same month.

I began to trawl through the two weeks on either side of the drowning. But anything remotely relevant was confined to just three issues, one before and two after the accident. I know it was only a local rag and a weekly one at that, with more interest in agricultural shows and pictures of local dignitaries than anything else, but I'd say there was something very, very fishy happening around Duncreagh in late September ten years before. Or so I thought, until I checked the old reports against more recent ones and realised that the *Listening Post* was a far cry from national tabloids: no sensationalism, not even vague excitement. It seemed to worry about people's reputations. I suppose that if you live all your life in a small place, that would be important, since everyone knows everyone else. According to Mrs. Cronin, "Around here they know what you're having for breakfast before you open the refrigerator." If that was true, then it probably wasn't necessary to print names or lurid details. Still, a report of a woman found dead in her garden that gave neither name nor location did strike me as pushing respectability just a bit far. But I was definitely intrigued. During that week, and once or twice later on, I photocopied bits and pieces I thought might be relevant and took them away to mull over. Amazingly, most of them turned out to be like little parts of a jigsaw that gave me plenty to worry about.

Before I knew it, my two weeks at Provender were up. I said good-bye to Mrs. Cronin and while there was still juice in my mobile phone battery, I left a little flurry of carefully phrased messages for my parents and my little sister. Fortunately, they didn't answer the phone personally, but that might have been because I rang at 5 A.M. I was feeling guilty that I hadn't sent Katie May any postcards and hoped that

Thierry, one of the guys at the Port de Plaisance, had kept his promise to send one every few days from a bundle I'd written. I didn't hold out all that much hope. He was a nice guy and all, but generally spaced.

While I was at it, I checked my text messages. There were two from Katie May, the first saying I was a dead loss for not writing (thumbs-down for Thierry, or maybe he didn't understand my Franglais?), and the second, a very excited one telling me that Dad had finally caved in and promised to buy her a puppy, one day soon. Dear little Twink. There were none from my mother, but then she'd never managed to get to grips with texting. She left messages on my voice mail: the usual stuff about the weather, eating properly, getting enough rest, when was I coming home. I ran through them but didn't really listen. I felt cut off from home and the family. Drifting away without a thought of how I might ever get back.

Duncreagh had one more little shock for me. I picked up a few groceries and stuff before I set out, but only what would fit in my overstuffed backpack. As I wandered from shop to shop, I passed an estate agent, and in the window was a picture of a heart-stoppingly familiar house with a For Sale sign plastered over it. Monday closing seemed to apply to estate agents as well as restaurants; they were shut. I felt sick. I didn't know whether to go on or throw myself at Mrs. Cronin's mercy and ask for my pink room back. When I left, she told me I could have a job in her restaurant any time, and I promised I'd return the following summer to work for her. I felt like running back and saying, "Take me back. Now, now, now."

I had done little to prepare for the next bit of the adventure—if you could call it that. In the cold damp light of day I decided there was no point to the whole mad escapade. My father was gone; Tar was dead. Who would know me after so long, or remember anything that had happened? I was a stranger in my own birthplace yet I hadn't really taken that on board until the jazz band in Provender struck up that first Saturday night and people began to dance. They didn't slouch around, the way guys my age do; they really went for it—holding each other, laughing, singing, having fun. They looked so carefree and happy. An illusion? Maybe, but one I'd never experienced. It seemed unlikely that any of them would give a second thought to the grim stuff that preoccupied me. I made up my mind to go and take one good look at the estuary and then give up.

It was a fine afternoon when I set out on the six-mile tramp, with a fresh wind that smelt faintly of seaweed. One of the first things I'd noticed in that part of the world was how quickly your skin tasted of salt. I suppose it got carried in on the rain—and it rained a lot, which made my hair crinkle up in a tangled mop. Weird. I looked like a sixties hippy.

One or two cars stopped to offer a lift, but I preferred to walk. Every step of the way seemed to carry me further and further from reality. I felt detached from past and present, everything was fuzzy and blurred, but I pressed on like a robot. I'd gone about three miles when the sea mist rolled in, and everything disappeared. I was marooned in space until a passing delivery van almost ran me down. "For God's sake, you put the heart across me," the driver shouted. "D'you want a lift?" This time I hopped in gratefully. Ten minutes later I was in Passage South, simply because I didn't want to tell the driver exactly where I was headed. While I was there, something happened to make me revert back to my original plan.

Passage South was crawling with foreign students. The man in the pub spoke to me in German. The fair hair, I suppose. I answered before I even thought about it. I'd done German at school for a few years, so we were about even linguistic-wise. I mumbled something about waiting for a ferry to the islands. It made things less complicated if everyone thought I was a stranger passing through. When I asked—*auf Deutsch naturlich*—for a pint, I thought the barman was going to challenge me about my age, but in the end he pushed the brimming glass across the counter with just enough hesitation to make sure I knew he doubted I was old enough. I just grinned and said, "Cheers."

There was an old codger in sunglasses and a tweed cap sitting further along the bar chatting up a woman wearing

leather trousers (fat bum) and a dark grey sweater with loads
of silver jewellery. I nearly burst out laughing at the sight of
them. She was all over him, and he was gagging for it,
which surprised me a bit, because with his getup, I'd have
put him down as gay. They didn't take any notice of me.

The walls were covered with framed sea charts. One even
had tiny flashing lights along the coast, that came on in ro-
tation, marking the lighthouses. As my eye moved inland, I
found myself staring at Trianach and realised I must have
passed the causeway without noticing it before the van
picked me up. For some reason that excited me. I finished
my drink and checked the name over the door as I left. M.
& J. Hussey didn't ring any bells. As I set off back up the
road, the mist lifted, and I was spooked by how familiar the
fuchsia hedgerows suddenly seemed. Or was it the scent of
the wild woodbine? Something vaguely remembered
twitched in my nostrils. I half expected to see the nameless
faces that crowded my memory, but I recognised no one, and
I could have been invisible for all the attention anyone paid
me. I suppose I looked like all the other scruffs about the
place. Another anonymous backpacker passing through. I
really thought I was invisible.

All over Trianach, newly built houses spread like a rash
across the landscape. Plenty of cars passed me, most of them
new and flash, but it was eerie how few pedestrians there
were. Tar's tumbledown cottage stood apart from the other
houses in the settlement, still miraculously not overlooked.
It took me a while to locate it. I couldn't find anything that
matched the picture in my head until I went down to the
shore and found the little inlet where he had kept his boat. I
stood at the water's edge, and it all came flooding back, as
if someone had switched on a zillion-watt bulb. We'd
trudged up that little path so many times, lugging the fish
basket behind us, that my feet seemed to know the way, and
I found the garden without any further difficulty. It was
completely overgrown in front, but the area behind the
house was exactly as I remembered; mostly bare rock and
natural sandstone paving. The track to the rotting back door
was clear.

The sour smell of mice hit me as I entered. They had eaten most of the curtains and the stuffing spilled out of Tar's battered old sofa. I could hear them scuttle away when I sat down—a hungry cat would have been useful. There were bits of old boat engine on the table. I had to laugh when I saw that. It threw me right back. Poor Old Tar. He was forever tinkering, but he could never get anything going again; if it was bust, it stayed bust.

I wondered why none of the neighbours had cleaned the place up. Had it lain empty since John Spain died? Besides mouse, it smelled of mould and damp as well as something else I thought I recognised. There were large stains on the ceiling where the rain had leaked in. There was no electricity and stupidly I'd brought no matches, but in any case, although there was plenty of turf in the outside shed, I didn't want to attract attention by lighting a fire. I downed a can of beer and ate the squashed sandwiches I'd picked up in Duncreagh. By now it was growing dark, and the cottage was chilly, so I went into the little bedroom at the back and stretched out on the remains of John Spain's bed.

That was when the events of that last night on the estuary began to roll in my head like a faded film, and my memory came back with a vengeance. Because, you see, I had slept on that bed before.

eleven

AFTER GIL LEFT, Frank, Cressida, and Katie May went to
stay with Grace in North Oxford, where, after a little further
nagging from her husband, Cressida caved in and agreed to
go back to Ireland with Frank. She scribbled a note to Tim
Wallace, promising to return at the end of the following
week. Then she would also go through the watercolours
with Grace and tie up whatever loose ends remained. Three
days later, the Recaldos flew to Dublin, collected Frank's

car from home, and drove down to Waterford for the last day of filming. After it was all over and the crew dispersed, they went to a country house hotel near Ballyhack, on the Wexford side of the Barrow River, for the weekend.

The glorious weather held up and with it their spirits. "Why don't we live here?" Katie May innocently asked one afternoon as the three of them strolled by the river.

As she ran ahead, Cressie and Frank looked at each other enquiringly.

"You know, I was just thinking that myself," Frank remarked. "Here, or somewhere like it. We don't really need to stay in Dublin now that Gil's finished school, do we? If we sold the house, we could afford quite a nice place in the country."

Cressie's response disappointed him: "You really think we'd get that much for the house?"

"At least. And my income is only going to improve, surely."

"Oh Frank, of course it will." She smiled at last. "It would be wonderful. I've been dreading going back to the house. Let's do it. As long as there's a school nearby for Katie May."

"We could start looking now, if you like," Frank said tentatively. He hoped it wasn't just the house she was dreading. "List your preferences."

"You first."

"Somewhere on a river."

"Estuary," Cressie cut in. "It has to be near the sea, too."

Frank raised her hand to his lips. "Nothing I'd like better, love." He hugged her to him, and for the first time in ages, she responded warmly.

"Garden. Big garden. I could grow herbs."

"Big kitchen."

"Big dog," Katie May shouted. "Like Finnegan." Finnegan, their red setter, had lived to a great age and died just before Cressie went to Oxford. "And a massive bedroom with yellow curtains." Yellow was currently her favourite colour.

Cressie brushed her hair back. Her eyes sparkled. "Oh Frank, oh darling, wouldn't it be fine? Let's do it."

He grinned down at her. "Right, we'll decide exactly what we want and then start the search. If we aren't too particular which county, then we should have a good choice. It'll have to be near enough a town for shopping, library, bookshop. A train link with Dublin would be good. Anything else?" He linked Cressie's arm. "As long as we're all together again, my own darling, I don't give a damn where it is. Wicklow, Wexford, Waterford, Kerry, Clare, Galway, Donegal." He skipped around the Irish coast with agility but neatly missed out Cork, though it was in both their minds. "Of course, we could always extend the cottage," he added thoughtfully.

"Oh, no. I like it as it is," Cressie demurred. "Anyway it's too remote for all the year round." This was true; the cottage near Castlebrion in County Kerry was at least seven or eight miles from the nearest school. They'd originally bought it to be near Frank's family. "I think I'd like to get a job if I can," she said. "Now that Katie's in school."

"That would be great," he said and meant it. He cupped Cressie's face in his hands. "I feel a right pig for being so mealymouthed the time you were after that gallery job. I'm very sorry about that. Ashamed. I wake up sometimes and feel sick at how stupid I was."

"It was the wrong time, love." She smiled ruefully. "No, I mean it. It really was the wrong time, when you think what the next year brought, my father and everything. I'm glad it's over," she added quietly. "But I'm also glad I did it. Looked after him."

"You are a kind and thoughtful woman, Cress. I hope . . ." He trod carefully, knowing how touchy she could be on the subject of her father. "I just hope he showed some appreciation."

Cressie shrugged. "Appreciation wasn't exactly his forte. I did it for me as well, you know."

"Yes, I know. Have you anything in mind, jobwise?" he asked lightly.

Cressie laughed. "Well, not nursing, I can tell you that

much. I've had it up to here with bedpans. I'll keep my eye
open. But if we're going to move from Dublin—" She
stopped suddenly. "Frank? What about Phil McBride?
Won't he be upset if you jack in your work at the Phoenix
Park?"

Frank gave her hair a little tug. "Or is it my plots you're
thinking of? Think my inspiration would dry up if I didn't
keep my detecting hand in?" he teased. "I've hardly done
anything for Phil this past year," he added carelessly and
could have kicked himself. One of the fictions he had main-
tained after Gil finished school was that his part-time job at
garda headquarters kept him in Dublin.

It might just have been a passing cloud that cast a shadow
on Cressie's face, but the atmosphere chilled a little. She
glanced at him sideways but said nothing. They caught up
with their daughter, and found a small, secluded beach at the
mouth of the river where the three of them went for a cold,
swift, silent swim. For the time being, there was no more
talk of moving house.

The following day Murray Magraw drove over from Tipperary and joined them for lunch. Afterwards Cressie went
with him to Tipperary to visit Halcyon, who was still in
Clonmel hospital. From there, she planned to travel by train
to Dublin and on to Oxford while Frank and Katie May went
to the cottage for a few days. She promised to be back in
Dublin at the end of the following week.

As soon as she left, the atmosphere lightened, but Frank
felt guilty and disloyal for even thinking it. He and his
daughter drove across country to Kerry. He was feeling distinctly unwell, but Katie May was in her element. The heat-
wave continued, so she swam and played with her cousins
who lived a couple of miles away, while Frank tried and
failed to come up with a schema for his next book. Usually
he never lacked good ideas, but somehow, this time inspiration eluded him. He half wondered if it was divine interven-
tion, chastising him for the hubris of his claim that he could
devise plots independently of his police work. Or, more
likely, for fibbing. Either way, coming up with a worthwhile
plotline proved unaccountably difficult.

Having Katie May to himself was compensation, and he had time at last to become easy with the little girl—or rather her slave. She'd had a solitary time of it in Oxford, and she adored having her father to boss around. The Castlebrion cottage was in the township of Dunquin, in beautiful, rugged country, where he'd set the first of his travel series. On a good day it was possible to get a boat to the Great Blasket island, but though it was warm and sunny, there were gusting winds, so the boat wasn't running. Katie had been promised a trip but didn't seem unduly bothered when it fell through. Soon it was as if they had never been apart, and he found himself wishing that the hiatus would last forever. He had always been at his best one to one.

Cressie phoned each morning from Oxford and promised she'd soon join them. When? When everything was sorted. The list of hitches inexplicably lengthened: the solicitor delayed coming back from holiday; the insurance company questioned the cost of the funeral; Grace had advised her to have some of the watercolours valued at Sotheby's; Marjorie's son Tim was being stroppy about everything— the inventory, the state of the house, the neglected garden. "He's threatening to get it all put in order professionally and bill us, Frank. It'll cost a bomb."

"Tell him to go to hell," Frank said dourly. "If you don't, I will."

"I already did. I completely lost it yesterday. We had a screaming match in the garden in full view of the neighbours."

"That must have livened things up for them."

"He wouldn't let me in the house. Said I'd taken stuff that belonged to his mother. Fortunately, I'd arranged for Stephanie to come. She sorted Tim out, pronto."

"So what good are you doing over there? Why don't you leave the pair of them to it and come home? We miss you."

"Well, I would, except the car broke down. The bloody clutch cable needs replacing. I've booked it in for Monday. So I should be all set for Wednesday—Friday at the latest." For once she didn't apologise, Frank noted. He didn't believe a word of it. Whatever was keeping his wife in Oxford, he doubted it was the clutch cable of a three-year-old Volkswagen Beetle, the one thing her father had provided for her. He felt resentful and confused, wondering if the good-looking, *healthy* doctor had something to do with her reluctance to leave Elsfield—then squashed the idea. Cressie was too disengaged to be open to falling in love. Wasn't she? *Heigh-ho,* he thought, *one step forward and two back.* His emotions had been in turmoil since his father-in-law's death. The brief, happy rapprochement in Waterford rapidly faded into confusion. Had the idea of moving released her old demons? Made her think of the Glár Estuary again? He knew her heart was still there. Yet somehow, on that glorious day in Ballyhack she'd been able to voice her preference for an estuary—any estuary—without strain. Or had he imagined it? His increasing angina attacks terrified him. He desperately needed his wife. *She has to come of her own accord,* he kept telling himself. *She has to want to be with me.*

Poor Frank was too busy feeling martyred to realise how irrational he was being. Had that chance remark about giving up his police work rekindled her resentment at his refusal to move to Oxford? Once upon a time they had discussed everything, but separation had encouraged their natural inclination to withdraw into themselves. They were both very private people with a fragile hold on trust.

Why is marriage such a roller coaster? he asked himself angrily, feeling aggrieved and not a little hard done by.

_____regression 4

twelve

Duncreagh Listening Post

(archive discovered by Gil Recaldo)
Murdered woman was international art expert. She
was recovering from recent surgery when she was
felled. A number of people are helping gardai with
their enquiries. No one has yet been charged.

I SLEPT FOR almost sixteen hours, until the sunshine woke
me around six the next morning. I lay on the bed, trying to
ignore the smell of decay, and willed myself back into the
mind-set that had led me so far. I was pleased I hadn't given
up. I had enough provisions to last me a few days, if I was
careful. My time was my own. I got up and began my ex-
ploration. That's when my problems really started.

The actual landscape was nothing like the version in my
head. The real thing was a distortion of my childhood
dream, which was uncluttered: bright green grass, grey
rocks, brown and purple hills. I had a clear picture of individual houses because there had been so few. Now there

were buildings scattered all over the place, obscuring my landmarks. What I remembered was simple, almost abstract beauty, empty except for the three or four buildings that seemed so monumental I hadn't even thought of the possibility of missing them. Now, either they didn't exist or were lost among the bright new houses scattered randomly like pebbles.

I wondered if it was because I'd approached Trianach from the land. Even after tramping every inch of it, endlessly retracing my steps up and down the waterline and the lanes in search of familiar sights, nothing seemed to fit. Fences had been thrown up, hedges planted, and bog-roll trees marked out the boundaries. The contours of the land were not so crisp or clearly defined, but then, maybe they never had been? The mountain backdrop, when it was visible through the mist or the lashing rain, was smaller in scale, not nearly as impressive as I recalled. I was looking for something huge, and I didn't find it. In my dreams I saw myself wandering through familiar haunts with Tar, but when I woke, the sense of belonging evaporated, and I felt like a stranger, alien in what I'd hoped would be my refuge.

The river was different, too. I'd pictured myself gliding over it so many times, facedown on the glassy surface. There was no glassy surface now—had there ever been? Each day brought a change of weather; strong sea breezes freshening to downright gales were the only constant as I tramped endlessly up and down the roads and the riverbank until I was completely confused. And lost.

I couldn't bring myself to go into Passage South, and there was no way I was going to walk to Duncreagh. I got more and more depressed. The squalid business of surviving seemed to take up most of my time. I slept later and later in the musty old bed, only getting up when my growling stomach woke me. Hunger was ever-present; that and a deep chill that settled on my clothes until I began to wonder if I was carting the dank cottage around on my back like a snail. The smell of mould stuck in my nostrils like rotting cheese. My brain became so sluggish that the idea of shifting my landmark search from the river evaded me for four days. But once the idea struck, I knew it was the only way any of it would make sense.

When I was a child, I was always in some boat or other crossing and recrossing the estuary. Occasionally on my father's yacht, *Azzurra*, but more usually I was with Tar. Cressie was never keen on boats or being on the water. What she liked was looking at the river, living and walking alongside it. But like a true country-woman, she kept her distance. She never swam, and she loathed the yacht. Somehow I was aware that it wasn't just fear of the sea that guided her, more fear of my father. I didn't like being on the yacht either. It was only in the hours and days when he was at sea—and out of the way—that we were truly happy and relaxed. Did I contribute to this state of affairs? Apart from kneeling by my bed each night and praying that my horrible father would leave us in peace. Forever and ever. Amen.

Alone in Spain's cottage, this uncomfortable thought disturbed my fixed sense of things. Until now I was certain my unhappiness was a result of the parents not getting on. They had avoided each other, and it really bothered me that I couldn't recall ever seeing them smiling and happy together. I had only a very hazy memory of when the violence had started because nothing much then had penetrated my silent little cocoon, but, sure as hell, once it did, Coribeen was filled with fear, which I was certain I could see and feel, even touch. Cressie must have felt it, too, because, towards the end, whenever we went into the house, the two of us would stand in the hall, holding hands and sniffing the air just the way our dog, Finnegan, did. Holding our breath, waiting for the next explosion. If my mother knew how much I remembered and how much I've discovered about us, the Sweeneys, she would die. *Gil Sweeney, murderer's son.*

Why or how did the marriage become such a nightmare? I'll tell you something for nothing: all my life I held Sweeney responsible and blamed him and him alone. Now that I was back where it all started, that seemed too neat. Too juvenile. Did couples turn savage for no reason? Was Cressie only a victim? Helpless, as our family fell apart?

That was certainly how I saw it as a little boy when I gave her my absolute, total, unquestioning devotion. But in the couple of days around grandfather's funeral, as I watched Cressie and Frank circling each other, saying one thing and looking another, I wasn't sure of anything anymore.

When I was small, Cressie was my heroine. I thought she was a goddess. She was, without a doubt, the most important person in my life. My father was a marginal figure, and until he turned vicious, hardly impinged at all. In the glory days when the business in London was booming, there were parties in the house all the time. Sometimes, I'd wander downstairs to find the dining room filled with big, red-faced men and women who puffed at cigarettes while Cressie danced attendance. I remembered them as legs; long corduroy legs, brown brogues, shiny black stockings on slim calves, the women's high heels dangling in my face when I hid under the table. An occasional face would bend to smile or pinch my cheek—playfully—but taking my cue from Cressie, I ignored these tentative overtures, fearful of entering the enemy camp. Once Sweeney and the gang were safely aboard the yacht, Cressie and I would take off, sometimes to see John Spain or else to a town, to a gallery of some sort, with big bright pictures on white walls and a huge piano in the centre of the polished floor.

In retrospect, those times were coloured in a rosy glow of safety and contentment. Although I searched, I didn't find anything like the gallery around Duncreagh. Maybe it's in Daingean, another town about ten miles further on. Not that it mattered; there were other places I was more anxious to find.

I haven't a clue why I didn't think of a boat first. Except for money—or lack of it. I'd recently worked at a marina, so I knew how expensive they were to hire, and then of course there'd be all that identification stuff to go through. There were a few aluminium tubs lying facedown at the cove I thought of borrowing—and probably would have done had I been able to find a decent pair of oars. I remembered seeing a boatyard as I tramped from Duncreagh to Passage South—at least I was sure I had, though it wasn't

marked on the faded old map I found in the cottage. I had a
vague idea it might be near the old bridge where the river
comes closest to the road, but that was a fair step away, three
or four miles from the Trianach causeway along the Duncreagh road. Easier to investigate nearer possibilities before
traipsing all that way. There was certainly a yard near the
marina in Passage South, but somehow that was a bit public, too full of people. I didn't particularly want to explain
myself at this stage. Not at any stage for that matter. I
couldn't bear the thought of people rattling my family skele-
tons or knowing my story before I knew it myself. I suppose
I was scared of what I might discover about my background.
There's some advantage in anonymity. I kind of relished the
sense of freedom. Anyway, it was teeming with rain for the
first three days. Unbelievable. It just poured down, hour
after hour. I suppose it must have rained like this when I was
a kid but, funny thing, I only remember the sun.

It was hunger rather than curiosity that eventually got to
me. Tramping across the causeway from Trianach one late
evening in search of something to eat, I noticed the lights of
a wayside pub I missed while I first searched for John
Spain's cottage. There was a black Mercedes parked outside. Inside there were only a few people in the bar, but it
was so small and dim that it looked full. A guy at the bar and
two men at a side table deep in conversation. A chalked
blackboard offered fresh mussels and chips. I asked for a
double order and a pint of lager and sat by the fire to wait.
The man at the bar left, and as he passed me, I recognised
him as the same guy who'd been in Hussey's bar the first
day. I ignored him. No sign of the girlfriend, but he was still
in the cap and dark glasses. Bit of a dresser. He had a leather
coat draped around his shoulders. *Ve haf veys of making you
talk.* Posy git. The two tough-looking men at the table continued their conversation, which, as far as I could make out,
consisted of a series of amiable grunts. They had about six
teeth between the pair of them.

I was halfway through my plate of mussels when one of
them left and, after a minute or two, the other man, the

wirier of the two, pulled his chair nearer my table. "Did ye enjoy them things?" he asked, pointing at the mussels.

"Yeah," I said. "Don't you?"

He gave a loud guffaw. "Wouldn't touch them—well, apart from handling them. Myself and the brother"—he nodded his head at the door—"own the mussel beds at the mouth of the estuary. Those are some of ours. Are they all right, then?"

"They're good. Great," I said, and he looked pleased. I suddenly had a brilliant idea. "D'you have any work going? Casual? Part-time?"

"There might be, then. For how long were you thinking of?"

"Couple of weeks? I'm staying with friends; I like to pay my way," I said, not sure he believed me. In fact, I'm certain he didn't. He looked like an inquisitive ferret.

"Not permanent and pensionable, then? By gor, that's a relief. Would you be up at the university?"

I was going to say something snippy like, "In a manner of speaking," or, "Mind your own business," but he had something I wanted the use of, so I told him the truth. "Not till October."

"Ye look like a strong lad. Can ye handle a boat? It gets rough out there."

"Yeah. I sculled at school, and I can sail a dinghy. My dad taught me," I added winsomely to add credibility.

He took hold of my hand and turned it over. "You'd find it hard on those soft hands," he said. "The old shells'd cut the fingers off of ye. What do you think?" he asked, his sharp little eyes twinkling furiously. Test question.

"I could wear some kind of gloves, couldn't I?"

He threw back his head and laughed. "Well now, young fella, you could indeed. I'll find something for you. You're in luck. My nephew that was helping out for the summer walked off the job this morning. The ungrateful scut," he added, and I wondered what I was letting myself in for. Too late.

"I could give a week's work, that's all. Four hours every morning. That OK? One week certain. After that, the tourist trade begins to fall off, and me and the brother can manage on our own. Six quid an hour, old money; you'll have to work out what that is in Euros yourself. I've as little as possible to do with those things. So if you want to try it, meet me tomorrow morning, and we'll see how you get on. The old slipway at six o'clock sharp. You know where that is?"

"I can find it," I said a bit dubiously.

"Fine so. See you then." He pushed back his chair and stood up, his face wrinkled in an impish grin. "What's you name, young fella?" he asked, not quite catching me by surprise.

"Hollings."

"Oh? Hollings? Right so." He held out his hand. "Mick Sullivan—the brother is called George. By the way, the slipway's up beyond The Old Corn Store, and that's about a mile downriver from Spain's Cove." He chuckled. "You can walk it in low tide; otherwise you'll have to go by the road. You know where it is, don't you?"

I hoped he didn't notice my jaw drop.

thirteen

E-mail from Sean Brophy
To: Fiona Moore

Fi, Someone dropped off two tickets for Tom Murphy's opening at the Abbey tomorrow night. Any
chance you could come? I think we should talk some
more about this great new idea of yours, don't
you? Any luck with that old geezer in West Cork?
Also short discussion required on *jeu d'esprit*
versus *coup de foudre* with your conclusions on
same. Or am I being a bit previous?
Sean

"HOW ILL IS she?" Cressie asked Murray as she settled into
the car. "Bad. Both lungs are affected now." His soft American drawl betrayed no sign of his long years in Oxford. In
normal times, when they saw each other on a regular basis,
Murray was affability itself, but on the cross-country drive
from Ballyhack to the Clonmel hospital, with Halcyon's future in the balance, they were both preoccupied with much

the same thoughts. If the girl lived, there would be the continued strain of ensuring proper residential care for her. If she died, relief would be tempered with guilt but even so, it would be easier to live with. Cressie desperately wanted to talk it over, but Murray wasn't his usual garrulous self; she could hardly drag a word out of him. She stopped trying, and they fell into gloomy, uncomfortable silence.

Something had changed in Murray. He had no wish to discuss nor analyse his feelings—he got enough of that from Grace. He blamed V. J. Sweeney for the plight he was in, and by default, Cressida. He knew it wasn't fair, but he couldn't help himself. The fact that she tried to atone in some way for her late husband's cruelty to and neglect of his natural daughter didn't altogether wash with Murray. Never had. "Cressie's not to blame," Grace always protested. "You can't lump her with Sweeney. Think how it must have been for her."

In truth, from the beginning, Cressida, without meaning to, made Murray feel unworthy. He resented the way, without any prompting, she took on the burden of visiting Halcyon while he only did so because of the vow his murdered cousin had wheedled out of him. Over the years he gradually began to admit, grudgingly, how much of the burden Cressie had lifted from his shoulders. His present irritability was petty: while he had failed to find suitable care for his young cousin, Cressida had found a vacancy in a home right on their Oxford doorstep—just as she was bowing out and returning to Dublin. "And you think that was deliberate, do you?" Grace had asked tersely. "For God's sake, Murray, get real. You've been trying to find care for her in Ireland for months. You said yourself it was hopeless. Look at you; you're worn out flying backwards and forwards." Mercifully, Grace stopped short of asking him why, if he was that fond of Halcyon, he'd kept her in her mountain eyrie for so long, out of the way and out of sight.

"What happens if it doesn't work? I really couldn't bear to have her living with us," he said plaintively. "I think I'd have a nervous breakdown."

Grace gave him one of her clear-eyed stares. "Just you?"

she asked quietly. "I think you're forgetting, Murray, that we will *both* have to deal with her." They did not refer to Grace's long anticipation of such a crisis then or at any time, though it hovered like a sword between them. Grace, who had never had a good word for Evangeline, always claimed that Murray's cousin had taken unfair advantage of his good nature, but what she meant was that neither of them had had the courtesy to ask *her* opinion of the arrangement.

Evangeline hadn't liked Grace, but then she'd not liked Murray's first wife or any of his girlfriends. In dark moments Murray secretly wondered if his cousin had consciously intended the strain she'd put on his marriage when she reclaimed him as her slave by bequeathing him the child she could not cope with herself. Perhaps she was reenacting the relationship they'd had as adolescents when she had always dominated him. The worst thing of all was that, as time went by, he was less and less inclined to discuss his disquiet with Grace.

Murray looked at Cressida out of the corner of his eye, marvelling that he had never before noticed how beautiful she was. But remote. She was miles away, in a world of her own. He wondered what dark thoughts were passing through her head. Though she and Frank had appeared to be in reasonable form over lunch, he had sensed an underlying tension between them, particularly when Frank mentioned that they were considering moving out of Dublin. "Now that our boat has come in," was how he put it. "We prefer the country, preferably near the coast somewhere," he added and went on to describe the sort of house they were looking for, and the location. It sounded exactly like the Glár Estuary to Murray, but as he could see Cressie growing agitated, he didn't remark on it. And the same disquiet stopped him mentioning that he had run into Rose O'Faolain, an old friend of hers, at an auction near Thurles the previous week.

Halcyon had had a bad night, and he'd only gone to the auction because Grace phoned to say that she'd received the catalogue, and it might be worthwhile taking a look at a small number of books of Irish interest included in the sale. Murray couldn't resist. When she added that since the late

Alex Mure Robertson was chiefly known for his art collection, it was safe to assume that few booksellers would consider the sale worth the detour. And thus it proved; there was only a handful of book people among the stampede of art dealers attending. But as it happened, Murray was barely there five minutes when he recognised a face from the past.

Some months after Evangeline's death, a colleague of hers, Rose O'Faolain, arranged a simple memorial service in Daingean, where she had an art gallery. "Evangeline did a lot of catalogue notes for me over the years. I feel I'd like to do a little something in return," she said. Murray was deeply touched, but apart from an effusive letter of thanks, he had not kept in contact. However, the art dealer was not easily forgotten.

The passing years had done nothing to subdue Rose O'Faolain; if anything, she was larger and more flamboyant. Murray didn't think she'd recognise him and was shy of coming forward. He didn't have to. "Well, if isn't Mr. Magraw? You *are* the bookseller, aren't you? Evangeline Walter's cousin?" She held out her hand. "What a very nice surprise. Mure was a great admirer of Evangeline—did you know?" she gushed. "A great admirer." She looked around. "Is your wife with you? No? That's a pity." She held her face to his conspiratorially. "I suppose it's the books you're after?" She laughed merrily. "How is Grace? I remember her well—lovely woman. I'm delighted to see you after all this time," she said breathlessly, then patted her capacious bosom. "I'll have to give up the old smoking," she wheezed. "Or it'll be the death of me. How *are* you?"

Murray smiled. "I'm well. And very pleased to see a familiar face, Mrs. O'Faolain."

"Oh dear me, that's much too formal. Rose, remember?" They shook hands.

"Murray," he mumbled, a little overwhelmed and even more so when she said, "Still in Oxford?" But then he hadn't realised that Grace and Rose had kept in touch.

"Yes, although we don't have the shop anymore; we work from home." He smiled. "I guess we've downsized."

"Aha, same as myself. It's easier on the nerves, isn't it? As well as more economical."

"Sure is. And you don't have to get up so early in the morning."

"Isn't it true for you?" She had another coughing fit. "What about a spot of lunch? I've got more or less everything I earmarked, and the books don't come up 'til about three o'clock, so we've a bit of time for a chat. There's a buffet downstairs." This was news to Murray, and he followed meekly in her footsteps.

"Buffet" was stretching it, but there were heaped plates of sandwiches and opened bottles of wine on a long refectory table in the medieval dining room. Rose and Murray settled themselves at a small table by the roaring fire, a glass of cheap burgundy apiece. They chatted about the collection, their businesses, this and that, and Murray only gradually became aware that Rose was steering the conversation around to Cressida.

"Do you have anyone working for you? Or do you and Grace manage the business on your own these days?" she asked absently.

"We have secretarial help and a bookkeeper; the rest we manage. Or did. For the past few years, a friend has been giving us a hand—mostly Grace's end of things—you know she's interested in ephemera with a regional slant? These days she likes good illustration—chapbooks, pamphlets, prints, that kind of thing—which very often turn up in lousy condition. Grace used to do her own conservation and was able to . . . er . . . train her up." He looked up and gave his goofy, rather charming smile. "Turned out very well, all round, but she's leaving Oxford soon, so I guess we're back to square one. We'll miss her."

"That wouldn't be Cressida Recaldo, by any chance?" Rose asked innocently. Murray put his head on one side and gave a loud guffaw. "The very same. You knew she was in Oxford, I take it?"

Rose covered her face with her hand. "Sorry, I'm not very subtle, am I? Yes, I'd heard on the grapevine. She used to work for me, you know? I was very fond of that girl. Such a dreadful business. I think it's great you've managed to become friends. I congratulate you. It can't have been easy for you, one way and another. Or for Cressie and Frank." And for the next half hour, Rose pumped Murray for news of her "young friends," but it was only as they were about to part that she mentioned that Cressida's old home had recently gone on the market again.

"And considering house prices these days, it's a bargain. Though mind you, it's been empty since Cressie left and allowed to moulder and what with the damp and everything. . . ."

"You've seen it?"

"Well, yes," Rose admitted with a faint blush. "I drove over yesterday, as a matter of fact. Curiosity got the better of me." She grinned. "To be absolutely honest, it wasn't just curiosity. Marcus Brady's an old friend," she half pointed at the auctioneer, who was deep in conversation at the other end of the room. "He told me he'd sent you the sale catalogue, so I hoped either you or Grace would be here. . . ." She shrugged. "Oh, all right, I'll come clean. I asked him to send it to you, so I was looking out for you. Amn't I the terrible old meddler altogether?" she said archly.

Murray raised his eyebrows. "Well, Rose, I wouldn't say that, but I'm not sure why you're telling me all this," he said innocently. "*I* quite liked the estuary, but not Grace. It spooked Grace completely. But that's another story."

"Hmm," murmured Rose softly. "You have me all figured out, haven't you Murray Magraw? As a matter of fact, I was really thinking about Cressie. Is her father still to the good?"

"You're remarkably well informed, Rose." He chuckled, then put on a solemn face. "No. As a matter of fact, he passed away a coupla days ago. Cressie was with him to the bitter end. Four years she's been waiting on the old tyrant, hand and foot. Frank's pretty browned off with the situation."

"They *are* still together, aren't they?" she asked in some alarm.

Murray shifted uncomfortably in his seat. "Grace thinks

they'll work it out," he mumbled. "But I wouldn't want to bet on it." He looked up. "Frank's doing very well—as I'm sure you know. One of his novels is being filmed."

But Rose wasn't to be sidetracked. "Look," she said gently. "I'm not just being nosy. I know—knew Cressie better than most. She worked for me for years, and I became very attached to her and the little boy. After the murder—" Rose put her hand to her head. "Oh dear me, my big mouth. I keep forgetting Evangeline is . . . was . . . I'm sorry." She rubbed her hand over her chin. "How is her daughter? Halcyon, isn't it?"

"Yes." Murray nodded slowly. "Poor kid's in hospital in Clonmel. That's one of the reasons I'm over here right now. You knew she was in a home—cared for by the nuns—not far from here? Near Twomileboris? Well, that was closed down. They haven't had any vocations for years. Halcyon and Sister Angela, the nun who cared for her, moved on to a smaller convent in Clonmel, but then the poor woman upped and died a few months ago. Hally completely fell apart. Refused to eat, cried all the time. Poor kid's pretty ill."

"That's terrible," Rose said. "I don't believe I ever saw her."

"You may have, without realising it, you know," Murray cut in. "She was at John Spain's . . . er . . . funeral."

"Oh? Was she?" Rose frowned. "That wasn't the girl Cressie was minding? I thought at the time she looked a bit like Gil."

"Oh? I don't think so."

Murray's tone was sour. "Hally has a habit of tagging on to the youngest in any company—I guess it was that. In fact, she looks remarkably like Evangeline did at her age," he said tenderly. Had he looked up, he would have seen Rose gazing at him pityingly, "I've grown very fond of her. We have no kids of our own, y'know, Grace and me. Hally is the nearest we . . . *I* have to family. I see her as much as I can. She used to be hard to manage, but now, just in the last little while, she's really sweet. Cute, too. Grace and I talked about having her at home with us, but Grace doesn't care for the idea." He looked at Rose for sympathy but received the same vague stare.

Rose was feeling a bit of a fraud. Cheap, and didn't quite know what to do about it. Should she come clean? Murray obviously hadn't a clue that his wife had met her on a couple of occasions when she had been over *alone* to see Halcyon Walter. Rose knew all about the circumstances of Grace's first meeting with the girl, two days after Evangeline was murdered. Halcyon had been seventeen or so at the time but with a mental age of three or four. Murray had not told Grace that he had agreed to become her legal guardian—in fairness, he probably thought Evangeline would outlive him, but she'd omitted to tell him she had terminal cancer: she was already dying when she was murdered. So the Magraws had arrived to find Evangeline dead and responsibility for the girl neatly dumped on them. As Grace herself said, "I was flabbergasted. I had no idea how to manage her, and Murray hadn't a clue either. God knows what we'd have done if Cressie hadn't stepped in."

"Cressida helped out with the girl, didn't she?" said Rose softly.

"Yeah, for a while. Until she had her own daughter. Hally used to go to them weekends sometimes, that kinda thing, but it all stopped when she came over to Oxford to nurse her Dad. I guess it was down to me after that."

"Oh?" said Rose. The story was turning into a nifty little three-decker with Murray self-cast as hero. Worse, a repetitious, self-congratulatory hero. Rose was disappointed, since she'd had him down as the easygoing, humourous type.

"Everything was hunky-dory until Sister Angela passed on. Hally just turned her face to the wall. I've been back and forth almost every week for the past four months or so. She caught pneumonia, and she's not responding to antibiotics, poor lamb."

"Oh, I somehow thought . . ." But Rose didn't disclose what she was thinking. "I hope she'll be better soon," she said kindly and out of habit couldn't help adding, "Is there anything I could do?"

Murray looked at her. "Thank you, Rose," he said. "I'll never forget how you managed that memorial service for Evangeline." He leaned toward her. "Nobody else did a thing, y'know? Even her great pal O'Dowd walked away. I hope you know how much I appreciate your efforts. Perhaps," he hesitated. "If anything . . . if poor Hally . . ." He ran his fingers through his thinning hair. "If Halcyon . . . You seem to know how these things . . . funerals . . . work."

"What about the nuns? They would—"

"Like I said, the original home's closed down. The nuns in Clonmel—the few that are left—hardly know her. No, I think we'd have to do it ourselves."

"Oh, well, in that case, Murray, just give me a call." She passed him her business card. "Any time. You can count on me." She got up slowly and fetched herself another glass of wine.

When she got back, Murray was in contrite mode. "Rose? I'm sorry for sounding off. Stress, I guess. Cressie's done a lot for Hally, and I'm really grateful. It's just that since her dad's illness . . ." His voice trailed off. "You know how it is. We're very close to Cress and Frank." He gave her a shame-faced grin. "Some friend I am, huh?"

"That's OK, Murray. It happens to us all from time to time. You're looking a bit worn out, if you don't mind my saying so."

"I *feel* worn out." He grinned again. "So, you think Frank and Cress would be interested in the house on the estuary?" he asked.

"I'm not sure, but Coribeen was more than a house to Cressie. She adored the place. I used to wonder how a young woman could live in such isolation—but then being alone never bothered Cressie." Rose leaned closer. "Val Sweeney was brutal to her, you know, and the child as well. I always had the feeling that Gil's disability . . . V. J. was a big man, athletic and strong . . ." Rose drew herself up. "I'm sorry. I shouldn't be gossiping like this."

"So why would she go back? The place must be full of bad memories."

"It's all a very a long time ago. Very few people would remember anything about it."

"I understood Jer O'Dowd bought the house. Wasn't there to be a golf course or a marina or something?" He scratched his head. "Funny guy. Never could quite figure him."

"It seems he couldn't get planning permission. That's what I was told, anyway. If it's true, it would have been a first." She gave a derisive little snort. "They say the life went out of him after Evangeline was killed." She didn't add her informant's other remarks: that he and Evangeline were like a pair of old queens—the one as camp as the other. That Smiler had never managed to come out of the closet and continued to make a right eejit of himself chasing after married women, usually blow-ins. "Poor old sod," she murmured half to herself.

"You know him well?"

"Not directly. But a couple I know live on Trianach. As a matter of fact, they bought Evangeline's house from O'Dowd a few years ago and run it as a guest house. Cressie knows them; Marilyn used to char for her.

"Ah. The Donovans. They bought Evangeline's furniture as well." He raised his eyebrows. "Not so much bought as obliged me by taking the stuff off my hands. Real sharp, they were," he murmured, suddenly repelled. At the same time, pity for Cressida stirred in him. So much was known about her; all her private misfortunes gossiped and gloated over. Rose had only just stopped short of blaming Sweeney for Gil's disability and, by inference, Halcyon's—something that Murray had secretly agonised over for years. He didn't wonder Cressie had done a runner. How could she possibly have protected Gil if she had stayed? Or lived down the rumours about her husband? Or that the investigating policeman was her lover—which he and Grace assumed to be the case from the first moment they saw the pair together, three days after poor Vangie was killed. Rose claimed that people would have forgotten the scandal after all those years. Not so you'd notice, Murray thought wryly, as he listened to her prattle.

He stood up. "Time to go, I guess. Look, I'm sorry Rose, you're going to have to tell Cressida all this yourself. I really don't want to get involved. I wouldn't like them to know I was, er, discussing their business. I'd be ashamed. But say, I sure as hell wouldn't go back—if I were her."

"No? Perhaps you're right. But she and Frank were very well liked. Everyone knew Cressie wouldn't harm anyone. Nor Frank. He's a decent man. I've heard it said many times." And with that, the two fell silent.

Afterwards Murray wondered what exactly Rose meant when she claimed that Cressie and Frank wouldn't harm anyone. He wondered about it again, as he and Cressie pulled in to the hospital forecourt, but he kept his troublesome thoughts to himself.

fourteen

E-mail from Fiona Moore
To: Sean Brophy

Sean, I owe you one. No, scratch that, a hundred
and one. Like I said, you've changed my life.
It's been a lean few years. Getting stuck into
this series is brilliant. I'm back down to Cork
tomorrow to talk to that young installation
artist, God help me and I'll strut my stuff with
Slimer—oops, Smiler—at the same time. Like I
told you, he can't get the bile out fast enough,
so I'd better keep on the right side of him. He
bangs on and on about Spain. Have you managed to
dig up anything on the sainted Evangeline? I'm
on the track of her alleged husband. He was an
art historian with the Courtauld but died years
ago. The bookseller in Oxford is next on my
list. Lunch on me? Same place or would you like
a change? I suppose a late dinner isn't on the
cards?
Fi

ST. BRIDGET'S WAS a fine, modern hospital just outside Clonmel. Cressie and Murray climbed the newly painted staircase to the first floor and then walked down a long corridor to the ward, which was broken into a series of four-bedded rooms. Halcyon was in a small room—hardly more than a cubicle—right in the middle, opposite the nurses' station. One of the beds in it was empty; the other two held elderly women, both either asleep or comatose.

Cressie had last seen Halcyon about five months before, and she was shocked to find her so frail. She, too, was asleep, lying perfectly still. Tendrils of her white-blond hair curled damply on her forehead and over her ears. As Murray approached, her eyes fluttered open but they looked through him and beyond to where Cressie stood at the foot of the bed. "Halcyon?" she whispered. The dull eyes held hers for a moment, then drooped.

Murray took the girl's hand. "Hi, honey," he said. To Cressie's surprise, Halcyon eased her hand away, and she thought she caught a flicker of annoyance on the blank face. Either Murray didn't notice or chose to ignore it. He sat down at the side of the bed and lifted the lifeless hand again. This time Halcyon let him hold it, or else she drifted off to sleep again. Murray turned to Cressie. "She's beautiful, isn't she? She's grown so like Evangeline." Cressie fetched a chair from the corridor and placed it on the opposite side of the bed. She tried to shut out the sound of Murray's whispered endearments.

She couldn't get over the change in Halcyon. Nearly thirty years of age and she looked no more than an anorexic teenager. The scene was reminiscent of a Victorian illustration of a deathbed. But if that was disturbing, Murray's behaviour was more so. He clucked around the cramped space like an old mother hen, tut-tutting over the stale flowers and the empty water jug when anyone with half a brain could see that the poor girl was way past drinking or looking at dreary chrysanthemums.

"Anything I can do?" whispered Cressie, exasperated. But he said no, went to the nurses' station, and came back with a damp cloth and began to wipe the patient's brow. At first she remained passive, then she repeatedly tried and failed to push him away; her arms were too weak to do more than flail about helplessly.

"I don't think she wants you to do that," Cressie said gently. Murray ignored her and continued his ministrations until a nurse came in and asked him to stop. "Let the poor creature be," she said quietly but firmly. "You'll get her all agitated. Don't you know she hates being touched?"

"Busybody," Murray muttered when she'd gone. He sat back and looked at Cressie disconsolately. "She liked having her hair brushed," he said.

"Yes, I remember. Even when she was at her most manic, she liked that."

"Do you think she'd like it now?"

"Yes, Murray, I do. I have a soft brush in my bag. It's the only thing I brought for her. The only thing I could think of that she might like." She unwrapped a child's pink hairbrush and pushed it across the covers to him and was so touched by his gentleness that she could have wept. He started to run the brush gently over the fine hair. At first there was no response, but after a little time, Halcyon's mouth twitched in a faint smile.

"I never did enough for her," Murray said. "She's so adorable. I've been thinking about that home in Whitney, y'know? But I reckon I'd like to have her come live with us. I think she's ready for it."

He's mad, Cressida thought. "Will she recover, Murray? It would be quite a journey for someone so ill, wouldn't it?" *We're both mad,* she thought.

"Oh, she's going to get better. She's much brighter today." He touched Halcyon's forehead with the back of his hand. "Her temperature is way down." He continued stroking her hair for a while longer. "I used to do this for Evangeline. I was wild about her, y'know. Ever since I can remember. She came to live with us when I was about ten. Her parents were divorced, and her mother lit out for Watts County with some folksinger. My mom was her first cousin. Vangie had no one else. For years I wanted to marry her. . . ." He hunched his shoulders. "I remember when this little one was born. Yeah, she'll be OK with us in Oxford. No point in her staying here, is there? I wish I'd thought of it sooner."

He was still talking when Cressie tiptoed out. The nurse caught her halfway down the corridor. "Are you related to Halcyon?" she asked.

Cressie hesitated. "No," she said. "I'm just a friend. She's very ill. Isn't she?"

"Yes, very. But Mr. Magraw doesn't seem to understand, does he? I've tried my best to break it to him. She's not going to last very long, and he keeps telling us he's going to take her home to Oxford. He's very attached to her, isn't he? And God help us, he gets very little in return."

"She can't talk, you know. And she's deaf. She's never been able to communicate—well, not by speech."

"Oh yes, I know all that. But . . ." Something was troubling her. "I was wondering why she was in the . . . I mean him being so fond of her and all. . . ." She brushed the air with her hand. "It doesn't matter. It'll all be over soon enough," she said abruptly and turned away.

_____regression 5

fifteen

Duncreagh Listening Post

(archive discovered by Gil Recaldo)
The body of a Trianach fisherman was recovered
from the Baltiboys Rocks early yesterday by the
Passage South lifeboat. It is believed the man died
while attempting to save the life of an unidentified
yachtsman.

THE SULLIVAN BROTHERS were OK—a bit nosy at first, full
of questions, but I can work the old deaf act pretty well.
They soon got the message and backed off. When we were
out at the mussel beds we worked flat out and didn't have
much time for chat even if you could make yourself heard
above the wind and the waves. The weather just got worse
and worse. You'd have thought the place would lose some of
its appeal, but somehow, without me realising, it was growing on me. The best time of day was the early morning before the rain started. The light was spectacular and the
colours extraordinary. Multicoloured sky at dawn, cotton

wool clouds, and emerald green grass. The constant deluge seemed worth it—at least until it started again.

I was at work at six each morning: on the first day I finished around ten. After that it was more variable, and it was usually noon when I got away. The afternoons were my own. Mick let me have the use of the boat whenever I wanted. "Just leave it as you find it, son, and you're welcome." I never met them except at work, mainly because their hours were much longer than mine. Also, they lived in Passage South, and I went there as seldom as possible. Most of the time I kept myself to myself.

Apart from the occasional wave from passing cars, I hadn't come face to face with any of the neighbours, though that was in part because I only moved outside the cottage when I'd made sure there was no one else about. I convinced myself—laughable really—that if I didn't see the neighbours, they didn't know about me. I was a bit nervous about squatting, because if anyone started asking questions there was no way I could justify myself. I made up imaginary confrontations where I was dead cool and the neighbours welcoming. In reality I'd no idea what the local reaction would be and I wasn't ready to find out.

The nights were turning chilly, although it was only the beginning of September, and the leaves were beginning to lose their colour. On the odd day there were a few hours of brilliant and sometimes even warm sunshine, but the cottage had been lying derelict too long and never warmed up. Still, I was able to manage—more or less. I'd found a small camping stove in Sullivan's boat shed, which I borrowed for minimum cooking and even more minimum heat. Thank goodness I had a warm sleeping bag. On really bad days I spent long hours huddled in the back bedroom. In a way I was behaving like a wounded animal nursing himself to strength—in solitude and silence—for whatever dragons lay in wait. Because there were dragons, I had no doubt at all about that. The urge for action ebbed away; I harvested mussels, made a few little expeditions in the heavy old rowing boat, and that was that. It seemed enough that I was able to get through the days. Getting up at six every morning on a lousy diet was no joke. I was constantly hungry. I felt aimless, weightless, half dead. And completely pissed off.

I'd arrived all hot fired to discover my past history, lay the ghosts. Somehow, away from the estuary, it seemed that just making the journey would, spontaneously, provide solutions without any effort from me. I had this quaint theory that my story would be etched into the landscape for me to read. But the opposite was true; memories hovered just out of reach, impossible to grasp. At some level I recognised that the key to my past was in the hearts and memories of the people around me. Working this out was one thing; confronting the keepers of the information was something else again. Much easier to skulk in my safe little corner.

Because of my childhood deafness, communicating had always required substantial effort, and I'd never lost my mistrust of strangers. Thoughts of going home to prepare for university gradually slipped away. The future became vague. Since I'd got back to Ireland, I'd not been directly in touch with home or spoken to my mother. While I was at Provender, I had kept my mobile charged, and I was able to leave my usual messages, carefully avoiding all mention of my whereabouts. When it went dead, things became trickier. I stuffed it at the bottom of my backpack and made the odd call from the phone box in Passage South. I didn't want to give the game away by sending postcards with Irish stamps, and since I didn't have any other bright ideas, I did nothing. Something would turn up.

It did. I was reading on the bed one night and had just dozed off when something disturbed me. I pulled myself upright and sniffed. And immediately identified the faint smell behind the other smells that had been puzzling me for days. I took off my boots, padded to the door, eased it open, and peeked into the living room. Here, the smell was stronger, though nothing seemed disturbed. The second time my eyes swept the room I saw the girl in the shadows. She was hunched on the old sofa with her legs tucked under her, staring into space. As she would.

I stood pressed against the bedroom door, silently watching her. She had already stubbed out the joint, but its cloy-

ing scent still lingered in the musty air. The faded jeans and
sweater she was wearing blended well with the dingy grey
blanket I'd found in a cupboard and thrown over the exposed springs of the sofa. She appeared so blissfully un-
aware of my presence that I thought she was completely
stoned until she blinked. "Howya," she said nonchalantly,
motionless.

I nearly burst out laughing. "You comfortable, then?"

"Yeah, grand," she said, calm as you like.

"Who are you?"

"I could ask you the same."

"Why don't you?"

She stretched one longish leg out and nonchalantly examined a scruffy white track shoe. "Don't need to," she said
casually. "I know already."

I did my best to keep a poker face. And failed. "What are
you doing here?"

"What are you doing here?" she mimicked, and tittered.
"D'ya always talk like that?"

"Like what?"

"Like you've a plum in your mouth."

"Yeah, I always talk like that. D'you mind?"

She lowered her leg and sat up a bit straighter, but not
much. "Doesn't bother me. One way or the other. Sounds a
bit weird though, but then, I suppose you would."

"Why's that?"

"No why." She shrugged, bored. "By the way, I finished
your beer. It was warm. Disgusting. Made me feel sick."

"Really? Am I supposed to feel sorry for you?"

"You can if you like." Her shoulders began to shake, almost imperceptibly at first but eventually she threw back her
head and laughed outright. I could barely stop myself join-
ing in. And while she was still whooping away, I stayed cool
and edged nearer. Not easy to get a good look at her until my
eyes grew used to the dim light. But then . . . well, she was
all right. My age, or maybe a bit younger. Good-looking. Or
would be if she cleaned herself up a bit. Short black curly
hair with orange or red stripes, kept straight with a phalanx
of hairgrips on either side of her high forehead. She had a

glinting stud in one nostril, and both ears had rows of silver rings, climbing from the neat lobes 'til they disappeared into the hairline. Her skin was amazing; either it was unnaturally white or she was wearing some kind of luminous makeup.

"Bjork, I presume?"

She wrinkled her nose in disgust. "Get off. No way, Sweeney." I almost jumped out of my skin.

"Aha," she crowed and sat up straight. "That got ya."

"That's not my name."

"No? Why did you jump then?"

"Jump? Who jumped? What're you doing here, anyway, besides spliffing and nicking my beer?"

She threw herself back against the armrest, releasing a cloud of dust. "Checking you out, Sweeney," she said defiantly, and when I didn't flinch, she looked uncertain.

"Why Sweeney?"

"Why not? I like the sound of it. Kinda cool, isn't it?" She sat up. "Matter of fact, I was thinkin' of it for myself, but then I had a better idea."

"And you are?" I plonked myself on the arm of the sofa, which groaned ominously.

"*Shay* Donovan."

"Shay? As in Seamus? Bit butch, isn't it? You look like a girl to me. Well, almost." My mind was racing. Donovan. Donovan?

"Feck off," she replied, but I hardly heard. Why had the name some sort of resonance? More to the point, how the hell did she know who I was? I could feel the shivers running up and down my spine. Her hand brushed mine, then immediately withdrew. "I was thinking of Sweeney, but it doesn't go with Donovan, does it? Sweeney Donovan? Nah, you need something short, one syllable. Shay Donovan's got a real ring to it. Better than Noreen anyway." She turned her head, and I saw that she was a lot younger than I thought. About fifteen or sixteen. A kid.

"Noreen? That your name?"

"Yeah. Called after my grandmother. Never even met her," she added in disgust. "I just made up my mind. From now on I'm going to make everyone call me Shay."

"And I'm the first? I'm honoured, but actually I prefer Noreen."

"Actually?" she mimicked. "Hmm, easy for you. Ever heard of anyone famous being called Noreen?" She made a face.

"And you're going to be famous?" I grinned. "Pop idol?" I loved the way she talked. Her clear, light voice lilted up and down, making it easy for me to hear what she said.

"Nah. An actress. A famous actress. Like Fiona Shaw. She's from Cork, you know. Or I might be a film star." She pronounced it fill-um, and star with a long, flat *a*. "Fill-um staar."

I did my best not to laugh. I didn't want her to go. "Bet you will, too."

"Stop laughing at me, you. I'm dead serious."

"Am I laughing? No, I'm not. Tell you what though, lose the hardware, Shay. The ears are OK, but holey noses won't look too good, will they? In close-up, I mean."

Noreen, alias Shay, peered up at me to see if I was having her on. Reassured, she delicately rubbed her nose. "Holey noses. Ha ha. Holy Moses, very funny," she said witheringly, but she couldn't suppress a grin. "You could be right," she said. "Tell you the truth, I'd be glad to get rid of it; it's always getting infected. I only got it to wind the mammy up." She giggled. "God-awful when you get a cold."

"Shouldn't you be in school?"

"When? Now? I don't go to night school, do I?" she drawled. "It's all day school around here—we're that ordinary, God help us." She stood up, pulled open the curtains, and looked out. She was shorter than I expected, about five five. Fantastic shape, with a six-inch expanse of pale flesh between her jeans and sweater. I tried not to stare. The girl was gorgeous. I could almost see the poster: Shay Donovan, Drop Dead Gorgeous. Bit of attitude, too.

"God," she moaned suddenly, "would you look at the feckin' rain. This place'id put years on you. Middle of feckin' nowhere." She sighed. "Are you from London?"

I nearly said yes, but somehow I couldn't lie to her.

"Nope." I should have left it at that but didn't. I don't know why. "I live in Dublin. Oxford sometimes—my mother's English."

"That where you got the accent?"

"What accent?"

She shrugged. "Whatever. So what's the story?"

"About Oxford? None. My grandfather lives there—lived there. He just died. My mum was looking after him. I stayed with my dad in Dublin." I sniffed to make the point that it was a pain. Hoping she'd get off the subject. Did she, hell?

"Pain in the neck, parents. Did you mind your mam being away?"

"Not much," I lied. I didn't want her to think I was a sad bastard.

"Same as me. My folks are away on holiday. Bit of a relief. Are you at college? In Dublin?" she asked. Which put me in a quandary. If I admitted I wasn't yet in college, she'd lose interest. I really wanted her to stay—for a while at least."

"I'm starting in October. I took a year out after school. I've been travelling around Europe."

"I won't do that. I'm going straight to London. To RADA," she said and sniffed as if it were a foregone conclusion and she was already bored. Then I noticed her fingers were crossed. She'd make an actress, all right. "But not 'til next year, worst luck. I can't wait to get the hell out, but I've another year of school."

Seventeen then. Great. I felt like dancing a jig.

"Why? It's lovely here."

"Oh yeah? And you're the expert, I suppose? Right. Easy knowing you haven't your mother on your back the whole time. Nothing ever happens here. I'm bored stiff with it."

"I know what you mean," I said. "But it's not the place, you know. It's the feeling that while you're in school you have to do what other people want all the time, isn't it? I felt like that the last couple of years. I hated—"

She swung around, and I saw her mood had changed. I suppose she thought I was patronising her. "Fat lot you know. It's the place, all right. The only bit of excitement that ever happened here was years ago. But then, you'd know about that, wouldn't you, Sweeney?"

"Stop calling me Sweeney. My name's Hollings."

"Yeah? I bet," she cackled. "Hollings what?" She mimicked me again and rolled her eyes. "Rotten luck then. This isn't your gaff, is it? You're trespassing, same as me."

"What makes you say that?"

"'Cos this place doesn't belong to you, does it? They say the old guy that owned this place left it to a kid called Sweeney—though he's probably not a kid anymore. Spain he was called, the old guy."

This was news to me, and I didn't believe her. I mean she might have believed it herself, but it was probably just local gossip.

"You OK?" Shay asked. "You look a bit peculiar. . . ."

"It's the bad light. I'm fine. What were you saying about the old man?"

"The cove down the way is called after him: Spain's Cove. Some say he was a bit odd, but they're always hedging their bets around here, so that probably means he was a downright old pervert. I mean, why would he leave the place to a *boy?*" she said innocently but she had a sly look in her eye.

God, I nearly exploded. It all seemed so familiar somehow. That awful word and poor old Tar. His face flashed before my eyes. Old man dies, cottage lies abandoned. Of course the locals made up stories about it. But surely if by the remotest chance it was true, then Cressie would have known. And if Cressie knew, then she would have told me, wouldn't she? Well, wouldn't she? As these thoughts were racing through my mind, I was overtaken by something more sinister: *not if it was true.*

I stood up and went over to her. I was a good few inches taller than her, but she stood firm, though she was clearly intimidated. "You don't know what you're talking about," I said angrily. My voice was shaking; so were my hands. I clenched them and stuffed them in my pockets so she wouldn't notice.

"Yes I do, so there. People still talk about it." She sniffed and made a face at me. "OK, OK, I'm making it up. I never knew a thing about it until I asked my Aunt Marilyn about this place when I noticed you coming in and out of it."

"You saw me? Shit. You didn't tell anyone, did you?"

"Keep your hair on. Who would I tell?" She grinned cheekily. "What they don't know won't kill them. I just happened to get talking to the aunt and said something like how sad it was that the place was going to rack and ruin. No mention of yourself, sorry to disappoint. . . ."

"Thank you."

"You're welcome. Wouldn't you do the same for me?" I could see she was teasing, but she waited for an answer all the same. I closed my eyes and tried to breathe evenly. "Yes. Shay, I'd do the same for you." *I never saw the gear.* "Now, tell me."

Shay laughed. "Right so. As I was saying when rudely interrupted, Aunt Marilyn's great. 'Twas her told me about the old man and the boy and how the old man was driven to his death by the gossip," she said in a rush, then waved her hand in the air and made a deep bow. What a drama queen.

"And she said the old man left the cottage to the boy?"

She coloured. "Well, not exactly. She just mentioned that there was some talk about Spain and the little boy." She looked at me mutinously. "Well, it *might* be the reason the place was abandoned, mightn't it? Anyway, I thought it was really romantic and all. I mean, it could be true, couldn't it? It's not impossible."

"So she just made it up?"

"My Aunt Marilyn?" She giggled. "I wouldn't be too sure about that. I bet she knows more than she let on," she said. "Didn't she used to work for the boy's mother? That's how I know they were called Sweeney. Cleaned the house for her—before she got grand and started the B and B below." She rolled her eyes.

"Where's below?"

"Where does she live, you mean? Near the old slipway. Huge barrack of a place, but it's always full in the summer. My mam says they've only ruined the old place putting bal-

conies all over it." She whooped with laughter. 'Key West,'
she calls it, but she's only jealous. Marilyn's worth a fortune
these days."

"Did you tell her I'm here?"

"Ah for God's sake, what do you take me for? I don't
even let on I come here myself, or she'd tell my folks and
then I'd be in for it. So will you, if you're found. Trespassing, it's called, in case you don't know." She raised her eyebrows. "Breaking and entering. They'll have Guard Ryan on
to you, for sure. Unless, of course, you *are* the Sweeney
boy?" she added sweetly.

I didn't answer. Why didn't I remember her aunt Marilyn
if, as she claimed, she worked for us? "Do you live on Trianach as well?"

"Yeah, on the other side." She rolled her eyes. "The remote bit, wouldn't you know? Our nearest neighbours are a
quarter mile away. 'Tranquillity,' the mammy calls it. It's so
embarrassing. She has a B and B as well, but I often stay
with Marilyn. That's how I know this place. I've been coming since I was a kid." She gave a defiant little smile. "I used
to call it my secret den. Sad, eh?"

"Not sad," I said. I wanted to put my arms around her, so
I changed the subject. "Has John Spain been dead long?"

"Years and years. Ten, twelve. Maybe more. I didn't say
his name was John," she added sharply.

"Didn't you? Know what happened to him?"

"He drowned."

"Anything else?"

"How d'you mean?"

"You said there was gossip, scandal."

She shrugged. "I suppose it was something about the auld
fella being one for the boys. . . ."

"Really? You know that for sure, or is it something else
you're making up?"

"What are you? The thought police? I suppose I took it
for granted." She shrugged. "Scandal usually means sex,
doesn't it? Gay sex, even better. You gay, Sweeney?"

"Neither gay nor Sweeney."

"Ooo-ooo," she mocked cheekily. "Don't worry, it's dead cool, being gay."

"Yeah, I can see it turns you on, but sorry, no. How long have you been squatting here?"

"You've a bit a cheek, haven't ya?" Her lilt became more pronounced as she got angrier. "'Tis you that's crashing, not me. I've been coming here forever, and no bother, until you turned up asking questions. Who d'you think you are, anyway?" She grabbed a knapsack from beside the sofa and staggered towards the door. When I put out a hand to stop her, she slapped it away angrily.

"I'm sorry," I said. "Don't go. Until your head clears. You can trust me. I won't tell anyone you were here."

"As long as I don't tell on you, is that it? That's a good one. Who do you know around here, anyway?"

That's when I decided I'd have to trust her. "I don't know."

She cocked her head to one side like an inquisitive bird. "Is that nobody? Or you don't know who you know?"

Sharp as a knife she was. I think I might have fallen for her at that moment.

I thought about it. "The second. I don't know who I know. That's why I'm here. I might need a bit of help. Would you split another warm beer with me?"

It only took a second or two for curiosity to get the better of her anger. "Only if you tell me who you are. Your real name, not some old made up thing." She was priceless.

"Gil."

"*Gil?*" She looked perplexed. "Gil?" She dropped the knapsack on the floor. "Are you having me on or what?"

"No. My name's Gil. It's not all that unusual."

"Gil Hollings?" she asked but fortunately didn't wait for an answer. "Do you know something? That Sweeney kid I was telling you about was called Gil as well. But you know that, don't you?"

We shared the bottle of beer.

sixteen

E-mail from Sean Brophy
To: Fiona Moore

Hi good-looking. I've sent you the stuff I dug
up on the late Mr. Walter and those antiquarian
booksellers you mentioned. You'll find it all in
your pigeonhole. Incidentally, you may find when
you've finished with the Walter case that unless
I'm much mistaken, this new info has thrown up
another little mystery. It seems Magraw's wife
was involved in some curious shenanigans in the
early nineties. All of this makes me realise what
a clever little pussy you are, you are. You've
hit a gold mine, girl, it'll run and run. I had
someone from RTE on the blower just now and I
trailed your cloak, as it were. His reaction
makes me think we could go global. What say you?
Sue is going away to her mother's for a week from
tonight. Holiday time?
Sean

CRESSIDA WAS BACK in Oxford staying with Grace for a couple of days while Murray remained in Ireland with Halcyon. Grace was surprised and not a little upset when he rejected her offer to go over to Clonmel. "I prefer to go it alone, honey, at least for the time being," he said. Then in an entirely uncharacteristically maudlin way, he pleaded for time to get to grips with how he was feeling. "I don't think I ever really mourned Evangeline, y'know. Or my parents either. Hally's dying, honey. I never saw anyone, not even my mom, *dying*. I guess it's the big thing, isn't it? So I'd like to see it through."

"He doesn't want me there," Grace told Cressida. "I feel he's punishing me for not liking Halcyon enough."

"Oh, Grace, no," Cressie said gently. "I'm sure it's not like that. There are some roads you just have to go down alone. I felt that with my father. I always worried that he didn't think much of me, but what I really needed was to try and understand how *I* felt about him—if that makes sense?"

"Hmmm," Grace murmured. "I'm not sure if it applies to Murray. Maybe." She gave a bitter little snort. "I think our problem is more to do with us not having a family. Me not being able to. It doesn't half make you feel useless. Halcyon was never a substitute child for me," she said starkly. Her voice rose. "Murray has got so bloody pious about her all of a sudden. I don't know what's wrong with him. I can't stand all this sentimental getting-in-touch-with-your-feelings twaddle. To tell you the truth, the whole thing has been a bone of contention between us for years. Ever since Halcyon arrived on the scene, now that I come to think of it. I'm sick to death of her." She let out a long, pent-up breath. "Not very charitable, am I? Oh well. How was he, when you saw him?"

"In an odd mood. I didn't stay long in the hospital; felt I was in the way, so I got an earlier train to Dublin. He didn't mean to be unkind, but I could see he didn't want me there. And since we seem to be letting our hair down, I had the weirdest feeling he was playing—this is going to sound awful—happy families?" She wrinkled her nose.

"Tell me about it," Grace said wearily.

Cressie took her literally. "Well, you know how difficult

it is to get Halcyon to keep quiet? Stop her screaming? Tearing around? Fiddling with the blasted television? She's always on the go. You're so frantic trying to calm her down that you never really look at her. Well, I'll tell you something, Grace, she has a lovely face. I don't think I ever really noticed before. She was lying quite still in the hospital bed. Her cheeks all flushed and her hair soft and blonde, as if it had just been washed. Murray was very gentle with her; he held her hand the whole time I was there. He kept talking to her, too, as if she could hear, understand. And the strange thing was that she looked normal. Extraordinary. She's got very thin again and really quite beautiful. Murray said she was the image of her mother at the same age. I never heard Murray talk about Evangeline before." Cressie bit her lip. "I was kind of shocked. I never imagined anyone actually liked her," she whispered. "But I could see Murray did."

"Oh yes, Murray *adored* Evangeline. He just idolised her," Grace said softly. "I couldn't stand her, nor she me, but that didn't change Murray's feeling one little bit. He thought she was the cat's whiskers."

"I see." Cressie nodded her head slowly. "Watching him with Halcyon was a bit surreal, all right. I didn't bring Evangeline into the equation until then. Somehow, I had the feeling that maybe Murray felt guilty because he didn't help her with the child—after . . . after . . . Val . . ." Her lip trembled. "After the sod abandoned them," she said in a rush.

"Maybe," Grace said thoughtfully. "Murray and Evangeline, that whole relationship is . . . well. I never really understood. Not sure I want to. He always said he didn't mind not having children. In fact, he was always quite positive about it. Until recently, he regarded Halcyon as a real nuisance. I don't have to tell you how hopeless he was with her, especially when she first appeared on the scene. He'd never have managed without your help," she said earnestly. "Even visiting her in the convent was a huge production—he'd never have gone at all without you showing him it was possible to make some sort of contact."

"Either that or I made matters worse, gave her expectations none of us could fulfil? Maybe I shouldn't have interfered?"

"Who knows? You did your best. Murray did, too, but I really don't know where all this 'I'm the only one who cares for her' stuff is coming from." She looked up. "I think I've lost him. He's been seeing someone else."

"What? Are you sure?"

"No, not sure. He hasn't said anything, but haven't you noticed how often he goes to the States these days? Between that and these trips to Halcyon, he's hardly at home. It used to be just one lecture tour a year; now it's two, sometimes three."

"But maybe that's all it is, lectures?" Cressie said.

Grace gave a little shrug. "He's hankering after the fruit of his loins. He wants a child, even at this late stage."

"You can't mean it? Aren't you upset?" Cressida asked curiously.

Grace thought about it for a moment. "I don't know what I feel, to tell you the truth. Murray and I have a good life. We have a nice time together. I like his sense of humour, though there's been precious little sign of it for a while." She held her head on one side. "It's all crept up on me very slowly, a hint here, a careless remark there, and then one day you realise your way of life has been decided without you being aware of it. I feel sad, that's all. And that's a pretty lame thing to say after almost twenty years." She wrinkled her brow. "You know, there's always been something missing. Children? I didn't think so, but now I wonder. Maybe marriages need the cement of children? I just feel very, very tired."

"Oh, Grace, I am so sorry."

"Don't look so tragic. It might be nothing. All in my head. Young Jamie stopped by yesterday with Reggie in tow, looking like the dear old lummox he is." Grace laughed. Reggie was her first husband and Jamie one of his two children by his second marriage. "He and Dee have finally divorced. I'm not sure I ever outgrew him, you know." She shrugged. "He treated me like shit, but even now . . . well, I always enjoy his company." She looked at Cressie. "Sorry. This business of Halcyon's really got to me." She drew in her breath. *"Evangeline's Legacy,* I call her. Or, if I'm in a really foul mood, *That Bitch's Legacy."* She smiled wryly. "Always much easier to blame someone else, isn't it?

I just don't know how I'll cope if we have to have her living with us, if the place in Witney doesn't work out."

Cressie bit her lip. "More of my meddling, eh?"

"Not at all. We'd be in one hell of a worse mess if you hadn't found it."

"I don't think it's going to be necessary," Cressie said. "The nurse in the hospital more or less said she wouldn't survive."

"Oh? She's very strong."

"You haven't seen her lately. Not any more; she's a shadow. Emaciated."

Grace took a deep breath. "Cress? I've always wanted to ask why you stopped having Halcyon home with you."

"You must be reading my mind, Grace." Cressida rubbed her eyes. "Strangely enough, I've been thinking of little else since I saw her. She was looking so sweet and innocent, it was hard to remember what a terror she could be." She put her hand to her mouth. "She almost killed Katie May," she said softly. "Sometimes I wonder if I imagined it, but then the whole thing flashes through my mind. Every detail, and I start to shake." She hesitated. "Katie May was only eighteen months old. Halcyon was with us for the weekend. I remember it was a warm, sunny day—late afternoon, Frank was working upstairs. He had a desk at the window of our bedroom, overlooking the back garden, thank goodness. I was in the kitchen with Halcyon, trying to do the washing up. She'd put on a lot of weight. She'd gone from child to woman suddenly and was very unpredictable, if you remember. I was keeping an eye on the children through the window. Gil was about twelve at the time and very nearly my height. He was holding Katie May by the hands, swinging her up and down between his legs.

"I didn't notice Halcyon leave the kitchen until I saw her lumbering down the garden. I had a kind of premonition that something awful was going to happen, but I couldn't move. She stopped a little away from the children and pointed her finger at Gil, jabbing it in the air. She regarded him as her private property and hated him paying attention to anyone else, especially the baby.

"There was a strange expression on her face. She began moving back and forth in time to Katie May who was squealing with delight. Next thing, without any warning, she made a lunge at Gil, knocked him over, and grabbed hold of the baby. When Gil tried to get up, Halcyon gave him a vicious kick in the side. I screamed for Frank and ran into the garden. Gil was on his knees, clutching his stomach. Halcyon didn't notice me—she was twirling Katie May round and round over her head. Faster and faster. At first Katie was laughing, but then she got frightened and began screeching.

"It all happened in a few seconds. Gil got to his feet; Halcyon turned around and saw me. She stopped, with Katie suspended in midair, and looked from one of us to the other. Then she started shaking the baby. The more she shook, the more Katie screamed. The nearer Gil and I got, the more furious the shaking. Then Katie went quiet. It was shocking. More shocking than the noise. Behind me, Frank said, 'Don't move; don't move, Cress.' It was uncanny. Though she couldn't hear, Halcyon turned towards him. She had a strange, terrifying expression on her face. Both her hands were around the baby's middle as she slowly raised her above her head. Katie May was all floppy, like a rag doll, and all of a sudden I knew Halcyon was about to pitch her across the garden.

"'Keep clear! For God's sake move away from her,' Frank yelled and came barrelling past me. Halcyon let go, and Katie made a perfect arc in the air as Frank threw himself forward. She was almost on the ground when he caught her. He lay winded, with Katie spread-eagled on his chest, as if she was asleep. She was blue in the face. My legs went from under me. I crawled over to Frank and tried to breathe into Katie's mouth. Halcyon was doing a lap of honour around the garden, whooping, her arms above her head like a footballer. Gil stood rooted to the spot, white as a sheet.

"Katie May wasn't moving. We carried her into the house, and I ran next door for help. Our neighbour was a nurse, and, thank goodness, she was at home. She drove Katie and me to the hospital and insisted on staying with us.

She knew they'd think I'd harmed my baby. She was right. They did. But Marie explained what happened; I don't know how I'd have convinced them otherwise.

"Poor Frank stayed at home with Halcyon. He was in a terrible state because he couldn't come with us. 'She's going back,' he said as we left for the hospital. 'Now. I'm driving her myself. She's not staying in my house another second.' I knew he couldn't bear to say her name. Gil said he'd go with him to keep her quiet. Poor little fellow. So brave. Terrified, but he went anyway.

"By the time we got to the hospital, Katie May was breathing properly. They kept her in for observation for a few hours. But she was fine, thank goodness. No lasting effects. 'That's it,' Frank said when he and Gil got back that night. 'She's never coming back here again.' And she never did.

"He said a lot more when Gil went to bed—blamed me for being naïve, for thinking that I could manage Halcyon when it was clear I couldn't. It was awful. 'You're not responsible for that girl,' he shouted. 'Feeling guilty doesn't make you a good person. It's a waste of time. Our responsibility is to Katie May and Gil. They're the ones we have to protect. She damn near killed our baby.' When I said she didn't realise what she was doing, he said he didn't understand why I had be so fucking understanding, doing my Mother Teresa act with every waif and stray that turned up, why I put Halcyon above my own children. 'Get your bloody priorities straight, Cress,' he kept saying." She fell silent.

Grace went off to the kitchen and came back with an opened bottle of Meursault.

"That's pushing the boat out a bit," Cressie remarked absently.

"Reggie brought it. We need cheering up," Grace replied. "What about Frank, Cress?"

"What about him?"

"Are you going back to him?"

"Back? I haven't left him, Grace," she said.

"So why are you here?" Grace asked bluntly. Cressida began to list the things still to be done in Oxford, in much the same way she had with Frank.

Grace listened until she ran out of steam. "You know you're very welcome to stay, Cressie. As long as you like, darling, but I think you should be at home with your family. Don't let things slide. Frank is a lovely man. I know that's not what you want to hear at the moment because you're upset with him. All right, he can be a bit selfish, but you two are really good together—most of the time. And you're smashing parents. I'm a lot older than you, so take my advice: you need to be together. Not apart. It's no good bottling things up; they'll just get worse. I know what I'm talking about; I'm in the same boat."

"Oh, I'm going back, Grace. I love Frank, always have. But I bore him. I've become such a wimp."

"That's rubbish," Grace said firmly. "And you know it. For heaven's sake just look what you've gone through in the past four years. No wonder you're feeling low."

"I was really angry with him for not coming over after Gil finished school last year. He could have. We've drifted apart, Frank and me. I just need a bit of time to get my head sorted."

"Like Murray, you mean?" Grace said laconically.

Cressie shrugged. "We were getting on all right in Waterford until Frank coolly admitted that he hadn't done any police work for the last year. I mean, can you credit it? That was the supposed reason for remaining on in Dublin when Gil started his gap year. He lied to me, Grace."

"Economical with the truth, I think it's called, Cress. Be fair. How on earth could you have squeezed Frank into Elsfield? There was no room. Besides, what would have been the point? Your father demanded every second of your time."

Cressida made a brave attempt at a smile. "Four years is a long time. A lot has changed, Grace. I've changed. I'm fed up playing the bloody doormat. I want to start again, but on my own terms—if that makes sense. Frank's been protecting me too long. Kept me in a state of arrested development. Looking after my cantankerous old father taught me that." She laughed at the expression on Grace's face. "Yeah, well. I hadn't worked it out at the funeral." The atmosphere lightened.

"And now you have?" Grace grinned at her.

Cressie suddenly looked like a cat with a bowl of cream. "I didn't come straight here after seeing Halcyon. I stopped over in the Isle of Man for a few hours."

"My goodness, Cress, you're full of surprises."

"Not me, Grace; Daddy. He didn't die penniless, whatever fancy tale he told his in-laws. And Frank and me for that matter. He had a nice little stash in a bank over there. He came out with it about six months ago, when I threatened to go home and leave him to his own devices."

"When he was giving you hell, you mean? Was this a bribe to make you stay?"

"You could put it like that, but of course I would have stayed anyway. Seventy-five thousand. Crafty old sod didn't tell me it was in my name, did he?"

"Told Frank yet?"

"Not yet. Haven't had a chance," she said sheepishly.

"He rang, you know, after you left Clonmel. And the next day, when you must have been in the Isle of Man."

"Oh. What did you say?"

"I told him some porky or other. Said you'd gone to see the lawyer," Grace said drily. "I prefer not to lie, Cress, if I can help it, not to Frank. I think you should talk to him."

"It's OK, Grace. I already did, early this morning. I didn't say anything about the Isle of Man. I prefer to do that when I get home. He's agreed we can move out of Dublin. We talked about it in Waterford and again this morning."

"He mentioned it vaguely at the wake. Any idea where you'll go?"

"The country. Somewhere near water. Other than that, not really," Cressie said evasively. "One thing's for sure, no matter how much Frank is earning right now, my father's wadge is going to make a hell of a difference to what we can afford. Whatever we buy, I'll have a stake in it." She beamed.

Grace doubted Frank would be as pleased. Seventy-five thousand would have paid for nursing care, perhaps for as much as four years' nursing care. It seemed a paltry price to put on a marriage.

_____regression 6

seventeen

Duncreagh Listening Post

(headline from archive discovered by Gil Recaldo)
MAN SOUGHT IN CONNECTION WITH TRIANACH
KILLING DROWNED

AFTER THAT SHAY copped off school. She was in her final
year, so she had her own timetable, which was handy, but
she went to a lot of trouble all the same. The school was in
Duncreagh, and the bus stopped at the causeway every
morning to collect the kids who lived on Trianach. If she
didn't catch it, questions would be asked. So she did, which
meant she had to double back to Spain's Cove, any way she
could. Apart from saying it was a bit of a nuisance, she
didn't complain. The first few days, she was usually waiting
for me when I got back from the mussel beds, around
lunchtime, or as she said, "Dinnertime, Sweeney. Don't be
so feckin' posh." She always called me Sweeney. I thought
at first it was just to annoy me until I realised that underneath the histrionics, she was quite shy. So I let it be. I called

her Shay; she called me Sweeney. Like characters in a play. I didn't have to tell her not to call me Sweeney outside the cottage. Shay was one smart woman—she loved conspiracies, and I was dead popular for providing one.

So there I was, at the beginning of September, with a place to live, a boat, a pal, and enough dosh to keep me going for a few weeks. I was feeling clever but, on the whole, not much wiser about my history. That was soon to change. Shay made all the difference; she was so clued in. "First thing, we have to get you sorted," she said. Bossy but practical. She took home my mobile and recharged the battery. She also came up with a good cover story for me. At first I was to be a new boy in her class, but then she decided I looked too old. "Bet you're dead sporty, Sweeney, with those shoulders," she said and whacked me on the back. When I didn't flinch, she said, "Right on. You're the relief sports person." She put on a posh accent. "The jocks are always leaving. Duncreagh hasn't got a sports centre, so they soon drift off," she said grandly. "The school can't get good staff, these days." I don't know who she was imitating that time, but she made me laugh. "Let's see. You're between school and uni, so you're just taking the job for a few weeks till they get someone permanent." She sniffed. "Which they won't, of course. Whatever. We'll call you . . ." head on one side, "Julian Wray."

"No. That's a wanker's name."

"Shut up. We will."

"You know someone called Julian Wray?"

"Certainly do. He took a job in the school last term. English. Lasted exactly one feckin' week, so if you didn't play tennis you never even got a squint at him."

"And you play tennis?"

She laughed. "Would have, if he'd lasted a bit longer. Hunky, he was. Like yourself, Sweeney."

"I'll take that as a compliment, then?"

"Whatever. Julian."

"OK, Noreen," I said and got another biff on the shoulders. For seventeen, she could be quite childish. Soon, some of the more useful contents of the Donovan house gradually began to appear in Spain's cottage. As well as a steady supply of food, Shay "borrowed" a couple of oilskin jackets, her father's old bike, a small paraffin heater, clean towels, and a duvet. "Won't your mum miss them?" I asked.

"No. She's got loads. Anyway, she's away. None of this stuff will be wanted until next year, if ever. Think you can make that old bike work?"

She slipped in and out of the cottage all the time. Several times I found her studying at the table when I got back from the mussel beds. When I worried that someone would see her, she told me she'd been going in and out of the cottage for years and no one the wiser. "They will eventually, though," she said. "If they haven't already. But you don't have to bother, Sweeney. They'll just think the 'young Donovan one' is up to something. But nobody'll say anything straight out. Ever notice that old people are a bit afraid of young ones? Ever notice that, Sweeney? Let them worry. We're not doing any harm, are we?"

I don't know if the Sullivan brothers knew where my gaff was, but I suspect they did. Like Shay said, Trianach was a funny place that way; information oozed up from the wet grass. Or somewhere.

We began to explore the estuary in the afternoons. "Evenings, Sweeney, evenings. We don't do afternoons around here." But not every afternoon and not always at the same time, though we kept to the same routine. I'd describe the houses and places in my head, and if she recognised what I was looking for, she'd take me there. The one place we avoided like the plague was her aunt's place, because Shay didn't want to be caught copping off school. The first few times, I kept it fairly general, but on the third day when I asked her where the woman was murdered, she nearly fell off the boat.

"What woman?"

"The woman in the garden," I said and stopped. Not because Shay's mouth was open in a great, surprised O, but because of the pictures running haphazardly through my head. Dark, but I could see a woman. Naked. Laughing. I swallowed. "A woman died somewhere around here."

"Murdered? You said murdered." There was excitement in her eyes. "When? Where?"

"I thought you'd know," I said and told her about the article in the *Duncreagh Listener*.

She shook her head slowly. "Is that what this is all about?" She waved her hand at me, at the river. "Murder? Wow."

"No—I told you, I don't know anything. It's something in my head."

"Was she related to you?" she asked curiously.

I shook my head. "I don't think so." Suddenly I was shaking so badly I couldn't pull the oars. Shay grabbed hold of them and elbowed me aside. "Let's go back to the cottage. We need to talk."

When we got back, I lit the paraffin stove and started at the beginning. Told her I was born Gil Sweeney and that I lived on the estuary until something terrible happened to my father and we had to go away. And that the house was somehow part of it.

"Which house?" she asked.

"The house where the woman died, I think." She listened carefully and didn't make a single snippy comment. "How do you know it was here? On Trianach?" she asked. "How can you be sure?"

"I can't—" I started and stopped. I closed my eyes and concentrated hard. "It's near here. It's near this cottage." It was like having the words pulled out of my mouth on a long string. I felt Shay's arms holding me, and I dropped my head on her shoulder. "I was there."

"You were in the house?"

"No. In a car, high off the ground. It was dark." I stopped.

"High off the ground? Do you mean a four by four or something? A jeep?"

Frank had a jeep; we had it for years. "No, not a jeep. Something like an Espace? Maybe a Range Rover? I can't remember."

"Tell me about the house? What was it like?"

"Big. Isolated, with huge rocks around it. A tall building. I've looked all over for it, but I couldn't find anything like it." And then my jaw hit the floor. "God, I forgot. I've got a picture of it."

"You what? God, you're something else, you know that?"

"Hang on." I hauled out my backpack and rifled through the pocket where I kept the newspaper cuttings and the page I'd torn from *Cara* magazine. It must have got wet at some stage because it was stuck together. By the time we'd unravelled it, it was crumpled and torn. Shay looked at it for only a second before she said very quietly, "Get your mobile, Sweeney, and dial this number. If anyone answers, just switch off." I did what I was told, and after the fifth ring, an answering service came on, so I passed it to Shay.

"Right on. I thought she might be out. She goes to the hairdresser in Duncreagh this time every Friday. Come on, Sweeney, I want to show you something."

"What?"

"The house, stupid." She grabbed my hand, and we crept out of the cottage and shot across the lane to a gap in the hedge. We waded through two mucky fields, along a narrow track, then climbed a rocky outcrop and slithered down into dense shrubbery. "Wait here," Shay hissed and disappeared. "Nobody home," she said when she got back. "Let's go."

It was a monster. It looked a bit like one of the buildings at my old school, except that it had wrought-iron balconies on every window, painted white and full of bright red geraniums. It was not the house. Shay waited for my reaction, all excitement, but I shook my head. "No chance."

"Oh for crying out loud, Sweeney, use your imagination." She pushed the magazine page under my nose and dragged me through the terraced garden down to the riverbank. "Now," she said and pulled me down on the wet grass. We sat side by side in the lotus position. Nothing was the same. The house I remembered had huge rockeries at the side of the house and a wide lawn sloping down to the river with fields on either side. A tree by the water's edge where the woman always stood—and as I turned my head, she materialised for an instant. Her head was thrown back, and she was laughing. I read her lips. "Does your Daddy know where you are?" The laughing face repeats and repeats. I faced Shay. "No," I said. "It's nothing like."

"Well, of course it isn't. Marilyn's made it over. She watches too much television. Scrooge up your eyes and look again," she ordered.

She smoothed the magazine cutting on her lap. "Where do you think the rocks for that awful terracing came from? Bulldozed. Marilyn thinks she's a feckin' film star. I told you what my ma said. Lose the balconies, Sweeney. Now what do you see?"

But all I could hear was "Marilyn."

"Your aunt lives here? Your aunt? I don't understand." My head was spinning.

"Yeah, my aunt. That's why we didn't come this way before. Is it the house or what?"

I couldn't answer for fear I'd cry. I felt so confused all of a sudden, disorientated. And afraid. But I still didn't recognise the house. The tide was low, beginning to come in. I took off my shoes, then my jeans, and waded into the icy water. I didn't look back until the water was up to my waist. I made slits of my eyes and tried to make out the shape of the house without Marilyn's fancy balconies. The shrubbery was so dense at either side of the house that it was easy to pretend they were the rockeries I thought I remembered.

"Well?" Shay shouted. I took a while to answer. "Yes." I nodded. "Yes."

"You better get out of there or you'll get your death of cold," she cried.

Cressie used to say that. She'd take me by the hand and put her mouth to my ear. "Come little darling." Her butterfly lips shaping the words that floated into my head with her perfume. "Come on, little darling." I saw her running across the lawn, darting in and out of the reflection from a lighted window. I put my hands to my mouth, then slowly sank into the cold, cold river.

When I surfaced, a woman was walking down through the terraces towards Shay. She called, "Noreen? What are you doing here?"

Shay waved and then ran off along the bank towards

Spain's Cove. "I'll be back in a few minutes, Marilyn," she shouted and disappeared into the hedge. Marilyn lit a cigarette and parked herself on the low stone terrace wall. I don't know if she could see me, but she seemed to be looking in my direction as she blew out the smoke. Her hair was white-blonde, and she was wearing an old-fashioned red dress with a wide belt. I half expected to see the wind catch up her skirts, like that famous photograph of Marilyn Monroe you see all over the place. Except this Marilyn wasn't laughing.

I struck out for the opposite shore.

eighteen

E-mail from Fiona Moore
To: Sean Brophy

You'll never believe who I saw when I registered Lulu at her new school today. Your man Recaldo. Couldn't miss him. Six foot four or five and still drop-dead handsome. OK, OK keep your hair on, I only fancy guys with red hair these days. Sean, his kid's going to be in Lulu's class. He's not in the telephone directory I checked, so I'm going to have to wait until school starts, then follow him, unless you can think of anything else. Thanks for all your info. The dossier is filling up nicely. Sean, a favour. Could you do the Ventry interview? Slimer gave me a couple of leads I want to follow up. Your woman Walter had a kid. Brain-damaged, stashed away somewhere in Tipperary. I'll fill you in tonight. My place?
Fi

FRANK AT LAST admitted he was seriously ill when they got back from Kerry. He felt utterly drained and exhausted after the long, tedious drive. He packed Katie May straight off to bed with a glass of milk, sat down at his piano for a half hour to unwind, and followed her shortly after, without even checking the mail or telephone. He slept reasonably well and was over the immediate panic when he padded downstairs next morning. He listened to the telephone messages while the kettle was boiling. There were ten in all, including three from Gil that hardly varied. He continued to enjoy the sea and the job. He sent love to them all and each time signed off, "Weather's good. Swimming's great. See you soon. Got your puppy yet, Twink?"

"Is this a conspiracy?" Frank asked over breakfast.

"No, I told you, Daddy, you just never listen. Gil wants a puppy, too."

"So do we all," Frank said resignedly. "But why don't we wait until Mammy gets home? I need to do some work, so could you skidaddle for a while? Watch television or something. We'll go into town after lunch, if you like. OK?"

"OK," Katie May said obligingly and went up to her room. Frank sat down at his computer and stared aggresively at the blank screen. Grace Hartfield's chance remark at his father-in-law's dismal wake had lodged in his brain, and he couldn't shift it. He began to type.

EVANGELINE'S LEGACY

The fallout from Evangeline Walter's murder lasted a long time. Every family it touched was marked, though in different ways. Almost as if her languor and venom had leeched into their lives, insidiously poisoning them. It seemed not to matter whether or not they had held her in any regard because Murray Magraw, her cousin as well as her true friend, was not immune, nor was Smiler O'Dowd, who, in his own way, genuinely loved her. Others fared worse. Within a week of Evangeline's death, her ex-lover, V. J. Sweeney, was in flight from the police for her murder. When overwhelming evidence of his guilt was found, he was already dead, drowned when his yacht ran aground. Since he could not be charged, the case was quietly closed. Sweeney's widow and son left the estuary under the protection of Frank Recaldo.

Even for those who got away, happiness proved elusive in the long term. Evangeline Walter's life had been driven by hatred and a furious need for revenge on the family of V. J. Sweeney, who had loved and abandoned her as a young woman, leaving her with the severely brain-damaged daughter he denied. Perhaps if the unfortunately named Halcyon had died in childhood as was expected, Evangeline's unhappiness might not have flourished until it was uncontainable.

Evangeline was not a woman to be trifled with. For almost two decades she stalked Val Sweeney. It was no coincidence that she eventually fetched up on the same remote estuary, their two houses within sight of each other. Inspector Phil McBride, who investigated her murder, remarked more than once that her outlandish name was misapplied; 'Medea' might have been better suited to a woman with such a sublime sense of personal wrong. He didn't say whether or not this observation was prompted by the fact that her particular Jason—Valentine *Jason* Sweeney—was married to a much younger woman and the couple had a beautiful, intelligent little son.

The discovery that V. J. Sweeney's second child was deaf—and for a long time, mute as well—prompted Evangeline Walter to reassess her own child's condition, for which Sweeney had always held her accountable. She began to devise a means of revenge that would destroy not only her ex-lover but also his new family. Evangeline took it as a personal affront that Cressida Sweeney, whom she regarded, as she did most other women, as a silly little fool, didn't give up on her son, as Evangeline had her daughter. She clearly doted on Gil, who was forever at her side. By contrast, Halcyon had been confined to one institution or another since childhood, with only infrequent contact with her mother.

The final straw for Evangeline was her discovery that old John Spain had taken a hand in the boy's education. Worse, it was clear even to the unobservant that Gil flourished under his tutelage. Up to now, she'd regarded Spain as just another of her casual conquests, a randy old man, easy and amusing to seduce and as such, strictly her private property. His defection to the opposition made her see him in a somewhat different light. He'd joined the ranks of her enemies; therefore, his disloyalty had to be punished. It didn't take a woman of her flamboyant imagination long to work out how easily Spain's ambiguous position as a disgraced priest could be used to wreak her revenge on Sweeney.

At that time, in Ireland, there had been a series of child-abuse cases involving priests and religious institutions. Public outrage was running high and, naturally, there had been some local speculation about Spain in this context. Nothing easier than for a mischief-maker to put it about that the old man had an unnatural interest in the eight-year-old boy. Evangeline, much too devious to make a direct accusation, chose her words with care. Her pal Smiler O'Dowd could be counted upon to pass the word—if the word was neatly enough put—and in this case the serpent was highly persuasive. "I worry," Evangeline murmured in his ear, "at that silly Sweeney girl letting her little boy near old *Father* Spain. Alone. On the old guy's boat. Up and down the estuary they are, all the livelong day. My, my, but someone ought to warn the child's father, don't you think? That poor kid is deaf and dumb. I mean . . ." Slim shoulders hunched, hands elegantly outstretched. "I really, really worry about him. There's no way he could call for help or anything."

The plot was laid, but it turned out to be something of an overkill. Literally. Did she guess that within a very short time those few vindictive words would lead to three deaths and ruin many more lives? Hardly. A good-looking woman well past her prime, who was, in any case, dying of cancer, couldn't be expected to value her own, much less anyone else's life. Suffering rarely ennobles the soul. Evangeline regarded her disease as a personal insult; it disgusted and appalled her. Since she was doomed, she became determined to take her enemies with her. The trouble was that her definition of *enemy* blurred. Soon even those who professed to be her friends were sucked into her apocalyptic scheme.

She might not have been so triumphant had she realised how well she served V. J. Sweeney by placing in his hands the means of forcing his wife into selling her beloved house. Sweeney's various business ventures had gone pear-shaped, and he was virtually bankrupt. Coribeen was worth a small fortune, placed as it was in twenty-five acres on the banks of the River Glár, close to the mouth of the estuary with some of the best sailing on the south coast of Ireland. A prime site, ripe for development, as Smiler O'Dowd often remarked avariciously.

Sweeney wasn't too troubled about the fate of either his wife, whom he despised for a fool, or his deaf son, whom he regarded as an imbecile. But he knew for certain that if forced to choose between Gil and Coribeen, there was no question but the child would come first. All he had to do was threaten to report his wife to the social services for allowing the old man unsupervised access to Gil.

The threat was enough. Once the accusation was made, Cressie knew it could not be unsaid. The sluice gates had been opened; they were all going to be swept away: herself, Gil, and John Spain. When she started to protest, her husband attacked the child and knocked her out. When she came around, V. J. had disappeared, and the nightmare had been set in train. . . .

Frank scrolled back to the beginning and read through what he'd written, then tilted back his chair. He thought about it carefully, then decided not to show it to his editor until it was more developed. The names would have to be changed, as would the location. He always agonised over naming his principal characters, though minor ones usually popped into his head complete. Trouble was, the names in this particular story were locked into his brain and would not be easy to dislodge. "Henrietta's Legacy," he scribbled, then crossed out Henrietta and replaced it with Hester, which looked worse. He told himself to forget the names for the time being. He had a rough outline, and if he could disguise the characters enough, he'd think about renaming them later.

He could hear Katie May moving around upstairs. He

raised his eyes to the ceiling and followed the pitter-patter of her feet. After a while, she began to play her clarinet. He listened to her practice scales then switch effortlessly to a little passage from the Field nocturne he'd been trying to play the previous evening. She had real talent, and better still, clearly enjoyed her music. Frank swelled with fatherly pride. He turned off his computer, put his head in his hands, and wept.

That afternoon he registered Katie May at her new school. When they got home, the little girl returned to her "Can we get a dog?" campaign. Finally, in exasperation, Frank handed her a copy of the Yellow Pages and challenged her to find the nearest kennels with Irish setters for sale. Mistake. Within a couple of hours, he was driving down from the Dublin Mountains with a very excited Katie May on the backseat nursing a tiny, yapping puppy for which Frank had just parted with an obscenely large cheque. He gave private thanks for TV windfalls, and he switched on Radio Three for *In Tune* while his little daughter downloaded her brain. Mercifully, most of her prattle didn't demand his attention until: "What'll we call him, Dad?"

"Rafferty," he named the programme's presenter absently, with half an ear on Brahm's "Alte Rhapsodie."

"Sean Rafferty or just Rafferty?" Katie squeaked impishly. Frank laughed. "Rafferty. I don't want to get sued."

"What about Finnegan Two? Or Fudge? Or . . ."

"Whatever you like, Twink, you decide. Quietly."

There was a nanosecond of silence before she piped up. "I think I like Rafferty best after all, Dad. It's kind of smiley."

Frank turned off the radio resignedly. "So it is. You're going to have to train him, Katie, I don't want him peeing all over the house." *Or crapping*, he added under his breath.

When he opened the front door, the phone was ringing.

"Darling?" It was Cressie, and Frank's heart sank. He knew from her strained tone that something was wrong. "It's Halcyon, Frank. She died last night. Passed away in her sleep. Murray's arranged the funeral for the day after tomorrow, at the convent in Twomileboris. Grace and I will drive over in the VW, and then I'll come home directly from there. Is that OK with you? You wouldn't like to come to the mass, would you, Frank?"

"No, Cressie. It would be hypocritical. You know how I feel about her." He felt too full up to continue, too disappointed. "I'll see you on Friday then?" he said and hung up the phone. He leaned back against the wall and closed his eyes, waiting for the angina attack to pass.

regression 7

nineteen

Duncreagh Listening Post

(archive discovered by Gil Recaldo)
BIRTHS, MARRIAGES, AND DEATHS
Spain, Reverend John Andrew, late of the Society of Jesus, deeply mourned by his twin, Sister Mary Philomena of the Reparation Convent, Twomileboris.
Walter, Mrs. Evangeline (of Minneapolis and New York), sadly missed by her companion and friend, Jeremiah O'Dowd. Funeral private, no flowers by request.
American and Swiss papers please copy.

"YOU'RE MAD, YOU know that, Sweeney? Nobody swims across this river. The currents are too strong," Shay said as I dragged myself aboard the boat. She was right; the tide was coming in fast. Another five seconds and I'd have expired. I'd been in the water about twenty minutes, and I was at the refrigerated but exhilarated stage. "I was almost there," I said grandly. "But thanks for coming anyway."

"You were in your hat, Sweeney. You'd at least half a mile to go."

It was hard to steady the boat; it was bobbing about like a cork. I collapsed in a heap at her feet.

"You're full of it, you know that?" She was laughing, her face pink, the wind ruffling her hair. I wondered what she'd say if I dragged her down on top of me and snogged her? Probably push me back overboard. She took off her sweater and threw it over my face. "Get yourself dry and put on your jeans. I don't know where to look."

"Away, while I get off my wet knickers," I said, and she fell backwards with laughing, but she certainly didn't look away. Had we not been wedged in so uncomfortably, I might have jumped on her. She looked like a raspberry ripple ice cream, and there was only one thing to do about that, but the wet underpants were a bit of a turnoff, for me if not for her. We changed places and, as I took over the oars, the boat turned into the wind and faced Aunt Marilyn's house again. She was still there, still smoking, still watching us. Shay paid her absolutely no attention. "So where are we headed?" she asked.

We were not even halfway across the estuary. I pointed to the far bank, which was just emerging from the mist. "Over the other side, if we can. We should soon see a house."

"You mean Coribeen?"

I was just pulling up my zip, and I almost cut my balls off. "You know it?"

"Are you soft or what? Of course I know it. Isn't it only the biggest estate around there?" Shay waved nonchalantly to two people who passed us on a sailing boat heading upstream.

"Does anyone live there?"

She gave me a withering look. I couldn't tell what she was thinking. "Why d'you want to go there?"

I shrugged. "Not sure," I mumbled.

"I thought you trusted me?" She was suddenly angry. "You're full of shit, Sweeney. One minute on the level and then next . . ." She looked close to tears. "I'm trying to help, in case you haven't noticed, and all you do is ration out the information as it suits you. I feel a right eejit bunking off school for you, d'you know that? Well, I'm in for it now."

"You think your aunt's rumbled you?"

"Course. What d'you think she's standing there for? She's waiting for us, that's what. Feck."

"Will she tell your parents?"

"No, that's one good thing. Marilyn's sound that way. But she'll have a go at me herself, and that's just as bad." She gave me a ghost of a grin. "Didn't I tell you a few days ago that my folks went to Florida? Didn't I happen to mention I was supposed to be staying with the aunt? I told her I was sleeping over at my friend's house."

"Me?" I leaned towards her.

"You wish. Don't try anything on, Sweeney, I'm still mad at you. You feckin' lived in Coribeen, didn't you? Marilyn worked there. For a Mrs. Sweeney." She glared at me. "And since she lived in Coribeen then, you must have as well. So stop messing me about. Either we're in this together or we're not."

A sharp breeze had blown up, and she was beginning to look as cold as I felt—more blueberry currant than raspberry. "I'm sorry," I said. I rested the oars in their locks and put my hands out to her. "Forgive me?"

Shay didn't answer; she just stared past me as if I didn't exist. I thought she was sulking, but she wasn't; she was scheming again. "You're over eighteen, aren't you? Have you passed your driving test?"

"Why do you ask?"

"Would you stop answering questions with questions, Sweeney, it drives me spare. Have you?"

"Yes. I haven't had a lot of practice, but I can drive."

"Right so. Look at us in this stupid tug—going nowhere fast. How much headway have we made? Square root of sod all. It takes hours trying to cross this feckin' river, and how many hours have you got?"

"Not all that many. But it would take longer to cycle."

"Who's saying anything about cycling? Look, it's six

miles to Duncreagh and another six or eight by road to the Coribeen place." She raised her eyebrows at me.

"We need a car," I said, "obviously. But who'd rent a car to an eighteen-year-old? Even if I could afford it. No one, that's who."

"I wasn't thinking of renting. I was thinking more of, like, *borrowing*. The mammy's Fiat Punto is sitting in the garage, and no one to use it." She threw back her head and laughed. "The keys are on the dresser at home. So what d'you think?"

I looked at her dubiously. "I don't know. I don't want to get you into more trouble. I mean, if it was you borrowing it, that would be one thing, but me? Your mother would have your guts for garters."

"God, you're full of yourself. I wasn't thinking of you. I was thinking of me," she said gleefully. "I'm seventeen and a half, you know. I *have* a provisional license. But I need a full licence holder with me. I'm always driving Mammy around. So? Are you up for it?"

I looked at her for ages. Her cheeks got redder and redder until I thought her face would burst into flames. I licked my lips and tasted the salt. "Shay? Why are you doing all this for me?"

She wouldn't look at me. "Why not?" she mumbled. She seemed fascinated with her feet. "I suppose I, er, must like you."

"Like?"

"Fancy. I fancy you rotten, cretin," she said and covered her face with her hands.

I stretched out fingers and touched her damp hair. "Oh, Shay." I said and beamed at her. "You are one fantastic girl. I think about you all the time. You're lovely." I leaned over and kissed the back of her hand. I was heading north when she pushed me off, though I could tell she didn't really want to. We looked back at the house, and Marilyn waved. "You want to call it a day?" I asked.

She nodded. "Yeah. D'you mind? I better go and sort her out. Gil?" She looked at me shyly. "I don't want to . . . you know?"

"Make out?" I asked. Shay nodded. She was such a funny mixture. All that "I'm hard" stuff, and underneath she was gentle and sweet and probably a bit afraid. Same as me, really. "It would have to be the right time, and it would have to matter. For the two of us," I said.

Shay looked relieved. "That's how I feel," she said and grinned. "As my dad would say, 'game ball.' So, start sculling, Gil." I liked the way she suddenly switched to my name; it felt friendlier somehow, more intimate. A shared secret, same as "Shay." I knew without her saying so that I was the only one who used her alias and she wouldn't want me to start calling her Noreen unless other people were around.

We headed straight for Aunt Marilyn's dock, or at least tried to. It couldn't have been more than a couple of hundred feet away, but it took another half hour. Even then, the dock was very rickety, and we couldn't tie up. But in any case I had to get the Sullivans' boat back to its mooring, which was a couple of hundred yards further downstream at the old slipway. I didn't mind; I was happy to be with her, and she didn't seem to mind either. We didn't talk much. The breeze was strong, the tide was pouring in, and we kept being pulled off course by a ferocious undertow; it took all my strength to keep control of the boat. When we'd tied it up and stowed the oars, she led me down an overgrown track, through a couple of private gardens to her aunt's house. "It's called The Old Corn Store, by the way," she said as we walked up the garden. There wasn't time to ask her why, because Marilyn was waiting for us by the kitchen door.

She put her hand on Shay's shoulder. "Who's this?" she asked, looking at me. "A friend," Shay mumbled, wriggling free.

"Haven't I eyes in my head? What friend?" I must have looked a sight; my wet hair was plastered to my head, and I was blue in the face with the cold. Close-up, Marilyn looked older than my mother. Dark eyes, black eyebrows, heavy makeup, and very red lips. Just like the geraniums. I could tell by looking at her that the "feck the rain balconies," as Shay called them, were her idea. *Miami on Glár.* She looked like she might be fun, but I somehow didn't feel like cross-

ing her. And when she said, "Well, Noreen, I'm waiting," I
knew why. Tough bloody woman, no mistake.

"Julian," Shay started.

Marilyn was eyeing me up and down. "You're the boy
that was working for Mary Cronin? Aren't you?"

' I was flabbergasted. I mean, she was hard to miss. If
she'd been in the restaurant. I'd have noticed. "Yes," I said.

"How do you know that?" Shay squeaked.

Marilyn looked at us pityingly. "Yirrah, for God's sake,
Noreen Donovan, I'm not as green as I'm cabbage looking.
Doesn't the band play there every weekend?"

The jazz trio? I looked at Shay.

"Yeah, well, she's talking about my dad and Uncle Steve.
And Johnny Moran. They've been jamming together for
years."

"You didn't say."

"You didn't ask." She blushed. "Anyway, what does it
matter?"

I don't suppose it did.

"You staying here tonight, Noreen?" Marilyn asked in a
way that didn't offer any choices.

"Yeah. And just in case you want to know, I wasn't at
school today, but I'll be there tomorrow, so don't start giving me a hard time. OK?" They were easy with each other;
as if they were the same age, but I could see Shay wanted to
impress her, keep in her good books.

"Would I?" Marilyn laughed. "You're fine so. Now upstairs with you for a hot bath. Use one of the guest rooms.
You're frozen, girl." She turned to me. "You can use the
downstairs shower room. I bet you haven't had a good wash
for a while, have you? I'll shove your wet clothes in the
washing machine, if you like?" In other words, *I know all
about your comings and goings, young sir.* Subtle, or what?
"We might be able to find something for you to change
into," she said. "While your kit is drying. Would you like
something to eat? Julian?" She arched her eyebrows at me
and then casually touched the side of her right eye. "Now off
with ye. Pair of drowned rats." She hooted with laughter.
"The shower's over there."

One thing for sure, I'd never been in that house before. Even ignoring the black leather furniture spread all over it, the room was so huge and oddly shaped it would be impossible to forget. There was a boy of about twelve slumped in one of the sofas watching television. He looked so much like Shay that I thought he might be her brother. "Meet my cousin, Liam," she said as we went past. "Otherwise known as The Howler." She ruffled his black wiry hair playfully.

"Aw get off," he grunted and gave her a shove.

"Homework, Liam," Marilyn shouted from the stairs. "Turn it off. Now." She handed me a pair of worn jeans that were too big around the waist and a sweater that was a bit on the small side. I had a scalding shower and shampooed the river out of my hair. There wasn't a brush or comb, so I just ran my fingers through it. I needed a haircut. Shay was still upstairs when I took my wet clothes into the kitchen. Marilyn loaded them straight into the machine and switched it on, then she turned and looked at me full in the face. There was a moment's silence. "Gil? You're Gil Sweeney, aren't you?"

What could I say but yes? Subterfuge suddenly seemed pointless. I was in it up to my neck now. *Gil Sweeney, murderer's son.* I half expected Marilyn to throw me out.

"Gil Sweeney? Well, I'll be . . ." This time she spoke much louder.

"Gil Recaldo," I said.

"Ah, yes. Frank," she said, looking a bit misty eyed. I've noticed he has that effect on women, being the strong silent type. "Frank and your mother got married then? I'd heard that all right. They were always mad about each other. This the first time you came back?"

"Why are you shouting?" Shay asked from the doorway. "He's not deaf." Marilyn looked at Shay and then, pointedly, at me. I began to feel afraid of her. In the same instant I remembered her—not as a person, but as a presence, in my childhood. The look on her face was one I was used to, when people discovered I was deaf. The "is-he-also-thick?" expression, too easy to read. Marilyn was a bit nervous of me.

I went to Shay and took hold of her hand. "Yes, I am," I

said. "But only a little. I couldn't hear at all when I was younger." She stared at me. "God, but you're stingy with the info," she said in disgust and plonked herself down at the table.

I think it must have been the most uncomfortable meal of my life. I kept losing concentration, and when that happens, my hearing goes to pot. I was tempted to throw myself at Marilyn's feet and beg her to keep my secrets but there were also things I wanted her to explain. I didn't much like her, though, but maybe that was because I suspected she'd turn Shay against me, if she could. Shay kept looking from one of us to the other, and I was sure the minute I left, her aunt would fill her in.

But what did she know? What did anyone know for certain? The article from the *Duncreagh Post* was ambiguous; you could read it any way you liked. "Man sought in connection with Trianach killing drowned." It could have meant either of them. Spain or my father. "Man sought for killing." But I knew which of them it was. Or thought I did. *Gil Sweeney, murderer's son.* The one important thing I hadn't told Shay, my friend, my champion.

Sitting at that table with the light outside fading fast, things began to crowd in on me. Images kept flitting past, but I was unable to grasp their meaning. I was too concerned with keeping the conversation at the table from me and my family. Not a chance. "How is your mother?" Marilyn asked blithely. "You know I worked for her? Do you remember me?" That at least I could answer truthfully. "No." But I remembered the feel of her in the room, and when she brushed past me to make the tea, I knew why. She still wore the same perfume.

I pushed back my chair. "I should go," I said.

Shay looked up. *Ask me to show you the way,* she mouthed.

Awesome. She'd worked out that if I was deaf, there was a good chance I could lip read.

"Could you show me the way back, Noreen?" I asked.

Marilyn turned around. "Your stuff should be dry," she said, and I was afraid of her again.

"Thank you for everything, Mrs. Donovan. The tea was wonderful."

She smiled and put out her hand as if she was saying good-bye forever. "Give my love to your mother and Frank." Then she surprised me. "Tell them they are welcome here any time. We've plenty of room." She looked as though she was about to add something else, but she changed her mind. "Hurry back, Noreen. It'll soon be dark."

twenty

E-mail from Sean Brophy
To: Fiona Moore

Fi, I read the book and fixed up the interview
with Ventry for next week. You're right, he's
good. The TV company has apparently optioned all
his stuff, so he must be pretty hot. There seems
to be very little info on him and no interviews.
I'm in awe at the way you go straight for the
up-and-comings. Precious little info on the
jacket, but the name makes me wonder if he's
Irish. I'll leave the sleuthing to the expert.
Did you notice the death notices this morning?
The one at the bottom—Walter, Halcyon. In Tipp.
Could this be the daughter? Sorry about the hiatus. Family probs. In spades. I'll tell you all
when we meet.
Luv, Sean

NEMESIS CAUGHT UP with Frank stealthily, unrecognised.

Early next morning, his editor rang to discuss publication dates. "We want to get the timing right, Frank. Are you with me? This is what I'd like to do: A TV tie-in of the second book, to coincide with its screening in October. They sent us some smashing stills. Then, hot on the heels of that, we do the hardback of your third in November and go all out with it for the Christmas market. Brass bands, banners, the whole razzmatazz. What do you say?"

"Sounds good," he said, uncertain. Rebecca refused to be discouraged. "The really great news is that we've also got interest in radio serialisation. The sales are going to be phenomenal. Did I tell you the initial hardback print run is going to be twenty-five thousand? Maybe more. I'm so excited. You're going places, Frank Ventry."

The author and scriptwriter gave silent thanks that he'd had the foresight to use a pseudonym when he wrote his first novel. Ever since, he had been punctilious in maintaining the fiction that it was his real name. Only his family, his few close friends, and his bank knew different. He had written his travel books under his own name, because he'd contracted the series before the Walter murder, when anonymity wasn't such an issue. Even though Recaldo was a highly unusual name, very few of the people he met associated the policeman or the ex-policeman with the author of the travel series. Not that it mattered; his readership was modest and the publicity minimal.

Happily he'd realised the same might not be true when he turned to crime writing. It was not that he expected his novels to hit the high spot so quickly, but the same instinct that had kept his family private and safe for over a decade prompted him to use a pen name when he submitted his first manuscript. He chose Frank Ventry simply because Ventry, County Kerry, was his birthplace, and it had the right punchy sound for crime.

"I'll say this for you, Troilus, you've a powerful imagination I don't think," Phil McBride had snorted. "Why didn't you go the whole hog and use a different Christian name while you were at it?"

Frank had replied that his own was common enough. He'd grown quite fond of it and would find it hard to get used to another. Much easier to cope with a change of a surname. You didn't use it nearly so often.

"Did you hear what I said, Frank?" Rebecca cut in on his thoughts.

"I did. Will they sell? Seems a hell of a lot."

"I'll say. But that's the power of television for you. When are you moving to the Bahamas?" she joked.

"Soon." He laughed. "After the screening. You'll be there?"

"Wild horses wouldn't keep me away. I got the invitation this morning. I hope you realise I just cancelled a week's holiday? Have you seen the rushes yet?" she asked.

"Only the first episode."

"And?"

"And yes." He laughed. "Michael Gambon is very good indeed. I think it's all right. But maybe I'm not the best judge."

"Well, if you say it's OK," she chortled, "then I say it must be bloody marvellous. Congratulations. We're all delighted. Did I tell you, we're putting on a dinner for you at the Criterion. Let us know who you'd like to invite," she gushed. "I'm really looking forward to meeting your wife— Cressida, isn't it? Will the children come?"

"Yes," Frank said, crossing his fingers. His own invitation had been waiting for him when he got back from Kerry, but he hadn't mentioned it to Cressida. "If my son Gil gets home from France in time. There might be one or two others I'll want to invite. I'll send you the addresses."

"We'll book a hotel and the airline tickets for the family, Frank. I'll get Ruth to phone you for the details. Two nights OK?"

"No thanks; we'll just stay the one. Cressie won't want Katie May to miss school. Now, tell me, have you had time to look at the outline I faxed?"

She hesitated just a fraction of a second. "It's not a real-life case by any chance?"

Frank's heart skipped a beat. "Why do you ask?"

"Because it's something of a change for you. The story's all there in the outline, isn't it? And that's a first—you usually leave me guessing. Or are there other twists you haven't mentioned?"

"Something like that," he said uncomfortably.

"Mystery man. Not giving anything away, huh? All I'm asking is how you're going to tackle it?"

"God knows." He chuckled. "I'll try inspiration—if you think it'll work."

"It's extremely visual; just wait till the film people see it. Geoff's been on the phone almost every day. He thinks you're the best thing since sliced bread."

Frank suddenly panicked. "I'd prefer you not to show it to anyone," his voice rose, "for the time being." He kicked himself for sending it off. He hadn't meant to do so at all, but he'd been feeling sore with Cressie for haring off to the funeral, and when he rang Phil McBride to sound him out, his partner, Mark, said he was in the States and wasn't expected back for a week. For reasons that he now found completely spurious, Frank sat down in a white-hot fury and changed the location and the names. With startling unoriginality he'd set the story in the very north of Donegal and retyped the outline. As he listened to Rebecca, he hoped he could make it unrecognisable to Cressie, but he knew in his heart that he was underestimating her. Still, it would all change in the writing. Or would it? "I've been having second thoughts, Rebecca," he said slowly.

His editor said nothing for so long that he thought she'd hung up. "Whatever you say, Frank." She spoke carefully. "Are you telling me it's 'true crime'?" she asked shrewdly. "If so, then I've two things to say. I need to know every detail, chapter by chapter. I'll need to get a legal on it. Frank? Take care. Being sued is hideously expensive. You do still work for the Irish police force, don't you?"

"Not anymore. I jacked it in last year," Frank said coldly. "And don't worry, I won't embarrass either of us. I think the plot needs more work, that's all. And I came up with a better idea last night," he added mendaciously. "I'd like to run with it, see how it works out. Maybe it's time to get away from the strict detective form? It's beginning to bore me."

"What?" Rebecca spluttered. "Don't be absurd. How many crime writers do you know with your police experience? For heaven's sake, Frank." She went on with the usual flattery—his writing skills, his unique ability to open a window into the real world of police investigation, etc., etc., etc.

"I was only pulling your leg."

"Oh? I'm a bit confused," she said after a pause. "Let me get this straight? You're not withdrawing *Henrietta's Legacy*?" She giggled. "I'll say one thing: the title will have to go. Not you at all. Sounds like an Aga saga."

"Working title. I'll have a bash at the new idea first." He heard his voice grow tense with anxiety and he touched the wood of his desk superstitiously. He asked himself what exactly he thought he was doing—saying. There was no new idea. How could there be when he was totally preoccupied with his failing health and his marriage going to pieces? Apart from her call about the funeral, he hadn't really talked to Cressie properly for three days. *Fuck Evangeline and her bloody legacy,* he thought savagely, then edited it to: *Fucked by Evangeline's bloody legacy.*

"Fine. As long as you don't change direction, Frank, take your time." Rebecca's mellow voice penetrated his train of thought. "You've been working like a dog. End of October, we'll need something for the spring catalogue. Just the usual little blurb—about a hundred and fifty words. Tell you what." She became all businesslike. "Why don't I just return *Legacy*?" One of the things he most liked about his editor was that she let him make his mistakes in decent obscurity. She was giving him a chance to withdraw the outline, and if he did, then she wouldn't refer to the wretched thing again. But if he chose to revise it and send it back, she would accept it as new and make no more cracks about the title. Which he'd change, in any event.

"Do," he said courteously. "Thank you, Rebecca."

"Anyone ever tell you, you have beautiful manners, Frank? I'll put it in the post right away. I haven't made any

copies, in case you're wondering. I'll data post it, shall I?"
she asked.

That was the moment Nemesis tapped his shoulder. "Oh,
one other thing, Frank," she said casually. "We'll want you
to do some publicity. That OK with you?"

"We?"

"Me. The sales and publicity departments."

"No, Rebecca. You know that's not part of the deal."

"Ah, don't be like that, Frank. Things have changed. You
knew when you sold the film rights that it would be expected—if not from us, from the TV people."

"I told you—and them—from the start what I will and
won't do. No publicity stunts," he said tightly. "You know
that."

"But darling, it's out of my hands."

She got no further.

"Don't darling me, Rebecca. You only do it when you've
already committed yourself to something you know I'll hate.
So, what is it? Spit it out."

"Heavens, Frank, you sound exactly like a policeman.
Not me, guv. Our publicity people got together with theirs. I
promise you, it's nothing very heavy, just a couple of radio
interviews, newspapers, etc."

"What does that mean?" he asked harshly.

Rebecca sounded annoyed. "What I've said. A few miserable interviews. No telly—they're using a trailer for the
telly, so you'll probably be on the blower telling me they're
not giving you enough credit. Radio. Any objection?"

"Radio OK, just no photographers. They can use the one
from the book jacket." Mystery man himself. A side view,
sitting down, which disguised his height, a hat to obscure his
features.

"What is it with you? You're a great-looking guy."

"My privacy is more important to me than my looks, as
you know," he said primly, then stifled a hoot of derision at
his own pomposity. "Your words, Rebecca: 'If you want to
keep your identity private, do so from the beginning,' " he
quoted. "Good advice. I'm very grateful." He knew as well
as she that on the publishers' part as well as his, playing hard

to get had been a deliberate publicity ploy, which had paid dividends. There was, it seemed, nothing more desirable than a camera-shy author.

"What else?" he asked in a more conciliatory tone.

"Couple of the heavies want interviews. *Times*, *Telegraph*. Hang on, hang on. We agreed on condition you have approval on the interviewer. *You* have the right of veto. OK? And we'll limit it to say, six, altogether."

"A few minutes ago you said two." He felt too tired to argue.

Rebecca went all quiet. "OK then," she agreed after a long, pregnant pause. "Two in London, two in Dublin. And the radio, of course."

"Of course. Have I any choice?"

"Only on who interviews you, which took some doing, I can tell you. You want your books to sell, don't you?" *Otherwise why would you be writing them?* hung in the air.

Frank thought of the money he'd earned and was going to earn if he bent his self-imposed rules just this once. "I suppose it could be worse," he conceded. "Just don't give out my address, OK?"

"As if," she said briskly. "You better buy a new hat. They insist on a photographer."

Oh help. In the instant, he decided to grow a beard, get spectacles. "Well," he said, caving in, "I'll have to work something out, won't I?"

"Yes," she said sweetly, "I'm sure that won't be the least bother. You're quite a guy, Frank. I can't see a couple of photographers getting the better of you."

And Frank, flattered, allowed himself to be persuaded. Which was naïve of both of them.

_____regression 8

twenty-one

Duncreagh Listening Post

(archive discovered by Gil Recaldo)
Daingean Council have refused planning permission for Coribeen House to be knocked down and a hotel and marina built on the site. A council spokesman says that "it would be sheer vandalism to raze such an important landmark."

SHAY WALKED WITH me back to the cottage. There didn't seem to be much point in creeping about anymore, so we just went straight for it.

An elderly man passed us on the lane. "Grand evening, thank God," he said and touched his cap as though he knew us, though I'd never seen him before.

I glanced over my shoulder and found he was doing the same. "Who's that?" I asked Shay.

"Who?"

"The old bloke who just passed."

"I didn't really notice who it was." She looked around, but he was gone.

"He seemed to know you," I said.

"Well, it's a small feckin' island, so I suppose he would. What does it matter?"

After that, we didn't talk much. My stomach was a bit upset. It could have been the huge fry-up we'd just sunk, but it felt more like a premonition of disaster.

"Will you come in?" I asked at the back door.

"No, I better get back, or she'll come looking for me." She giggled. "Marilyn thinks the worst."

"A minute?"

We were all over each other before we got inside. "I have to go," she kept saying every time we came up for air. I really wanted her, but all sorts of fears grabbed my gut. She would go away and never come near me again once she heard what Marilyn had to say. Or, if she did come back, I wouldn't be able to make it. And if I could, she wouldn't enjoy it. The place was so grotty and smelly. Not a bit romantic. I wanted a bit more than a quick shag, but I was afraid she'd think I was soppy, stupid, clumsy. Uncool. I wanted her to hold me tight and love me, and most of all, I wanted to tell her everything about myself that I'd held back. But I knew I'd left it too late; everything was scrambled in my head. I hadn't a clue where to start. I wanted to die. I didn't know what Marilyn would tell her or what Shay guessed beyond the bare essentials I'd already told her.

There wasn't time to prepare her, step by step, so I didn't even try. "Will you come tomorrow?" I asked. She pulled away, laughing. "Seeing as there isn't time tonight, you mean?" she said, all hard. But she looked like a rosebud.

I grabbed her and held her close.

"Listen, Shay. There are things I didn't tell you. Not things I know but what I've guessed, worked out."

"You're afraid of my aunt, aren't you?" she whispered. "You shouldn't be; Marilyn's sound."

"Is she? I found her a bit scary. She doesn't like me much, does she?"

Shay giggled. "It's not *who* you are, you sap, it's *what*: a big, hairy ape, out for my virtue."

"Well, she's right about that, anyway." I kissed the tip of her nose. "Promise me you'll come back?"

She stood up and brushed herself down. "Promise."

"No matter what?"

"No matter what?" Shay tittered. "Don't push your luck, Sweeney." She opened the door and peeped out. "Coast's clear," she whispered and looked over her shoulder at me. "You didn't like her knowing who you are, did you, Gil? You didn't like her calling you Sweeney," she said before she darted away.

I sat in the dark for a long time going back over what had happened that day. I thought about the aunt's house, the garden. In that moment when I'd stood in the river looking back, something clicked in my brain, but as usual I couldn't find the right connections. That might have been because I'd got into the habit of shutting down whenever the past threatened to break through. Now I steeled myself to open up and invite the ghosts in. Solitary confinement in that dingy cottage was the ideal place for it. I lay down on the bed, emptied my mind of everything else—especially Shay—and allowed the memories to seep back.

A couple of hours later I got up again. It was dark, and I couldn't stop shivering. It wasn't just external cold; it was more like I was chilled inside as well as out. A thing apart, nothing could actually touch me. I dressed warmly and went out into the night. This time, I followed the open road to the old slipway. It was the long way around, but that is what I felt compelled to do. I was on autopilot.

At first the night was pitch black, but after I'd walked a mile or so, the clouds parted and a weak half-moon showed through. The rustling in the hedgerows was deafening and spooky. The closer I got to the slipway, the more I felt I was retracing old steps, yet I couldn't remember walking along those narrow roads as a child. In the car, maybe, but never at night. Except that once. I was half dead with fear.

It was a clear night, and the wind had died down. I sat on an upturned boat watching the water softly lapping the shore, while I worked up my courage. It was all different; too many hedges, the lights of too many bungalows. Yet that afternoon, when Shay and I got into to The Old Corn Store garden, I knew I'd been there before. At night. But I couldn't remember how I got there, or why. The moon had gone in when I stood up and looked around.

Suddenly, Gil, aged eight, materializes. He is sitting up on the backseat of a Range Rover, his little white face pressed against the window. The car door is open, and the driver's seat is empty. He crawls over it, climbs out of the car, and looks around. He is clutching one arm to his side. His face is bleeding. The image fades.

I walked slowly down the shingle to the riverbank and keeping to the waterline, crept across the two gardens until I came to the boundary of The Old Corn Store. I slunk through the hedge and crouched in its shadow. The high roof was outlined against the sky, and I let my eyes travel slowly downwards. The flickering light of the television danced around the edges of the curtains on the huge French windows.

Silence. Now little Gil is back. The light from the house runs nearly the whole way down the garden, over the sloping lawn. There's a table by the open French windows, a bench. A bottle on the table. My eyes travel up and down, searching, searching, and I catch a glimpse of dark figures hidden in the bushes at either side of the house. I cannot see them properly, but I sense they're there. A tiny glint catches my eye, further up from where I'm standing. Something big and black rustles the leaves—not at ground level but higher up, much higher than my head. I see the thin branches stir, then stop.

A woman comes floating through the window. She is wearing a long, light dress, and it's fluttering in the breeze. Is she dancing? She stretches out her arms and twirls and twirls around like a ballerina. I see her white breasts and the dark hair at her crotch, and I feel hot and excited because I know who she is: the woman who always points at me when I'm in the boat with Tar. She's pointing now. I turn my head to follow her long white arm. Tar is walking up the garden, holding a fish in his outstretched hands. The silver skin glistens in the light. As the woman goes towards him, she faces my way and, for an instant, I see her lips move, but before I can read what she's saying, she turns back to Tar. She laughs, grabs the fish, and tosses it on the ground. They stand facing each other. I freeze. She holds her breasts in her hands, moving them up and down, up and down. Tar is coming towards her, nearer and nearer. He stumbles, and she pulls his head to her bare breasts. I want to wee.

They are walking backwards now, up the garden, clinging together. Up, up the slope they go, towards the paving by the window. Someone is standing there, behind them; they cannot see. I notice the movement for a split second, but I'm distracted—I prefer to watch Tar and the woman. I am mesmerized by what they are doing. She's pulling down his yellow oilskin dungarees. The straps are holding his arms to his sides; he struggles to free them. Now she throws off her dress. Naked. His overalls are around his ankles, and she's on her knees with his thing in her mouth. Oh God. Suddenly he pitches forward on top of her. Pushing, pumping up and down, up and down. Up and down. I can't see Tar's face, but the woman is happy, because she's smiling, maybe laughing. Tar falls on his face and rolls off her and away. He rises to his knees and holds his head in his hands, as if he's crying. Then, suddenly, the shadow behind the woman moves, grabs her hair, and yanks her to her feet. The woman swings around, but the figure in black pushes her away. Hard. She falls against one of the boulders by the house and lies still.

The other person stands looking down at her; then slowly turns towards where I'm standing. For a split second the light from the window catches her face. I see my mother.

I don't know what to do. The pee is running down my legs and all over my shoes. Tar has his overalls on now; he's pulling the straps over his shoulders. Mama runs to him. I can't look.

The woman sits up. She looks around and sees Tar holding my mother's arm. Now she's laughing. She keeps doubling over, then throwing her head back. Why? I don't understand. They must be talking, shouting, but I can't hear

them. The silence is thick and furry. Tar is pulling Mama
away, down the garden to the water.

My legs won't work, and I can't remember the way back,
so I crawl up the garden, keeping close to the hedge. A large
brown muddy shoe steps on my ankle, and a hand grabs at
my shoulder. I wriggle free and escape through the hedge. I
dash across the field without looking back and keep running
'til I get to the car. Something or someone is following me.
I scramble into the car and lie facedown on the backseat and
cover my head. With one arm. I can't move the other.

Something hits the car. I wait for the vibration to die, then
I slowly raise my head and look out. Tar sees me. He has his
hand on Mama's arm. There are tears pouring down his face.
Mama looks at me, and she's crying, too. There is a huge cut
over her eye and blood all down her face. And I suddenly
remember why we're there.

twenty-two

GRACE AND CRESSIDA were delayed by heavy traffic leaving
Oxford and barely caught the overnight ferry from Fishguard to Rosslare. All the cabins were taken, and they were
forced to spend the night huddled under coats in the bar.
Both were in sombre mood, preoccupied with the uncer-
tainty of their individual futures. The crossing was mercifully calm, if uncomfortable, but it was pouring with rain
when the ship docked at quarter to seven. They headed
straight for the Talbot Hotel in Wexford for a shower and
breakfast before pressing on. A few miles from Clonmel,
Cressie, who had been quiet since leaving the ship, suddenly

put her foot on the brake and pulled into the side of the road. She was sobbing.

"Cressie? What's wrong?" Grace was alarmed.

"Funerals," Cressie sniffed. "Too many funerals." She pulled a crumpled letter from her pocket. "I found this yesterday when I stripped the bed in Elsfield."

Grace read the note from Frank's GP confirming an appointment with a cardiologist. "Oh my goodness, poor Frank's having trouble with his heart again?" Though Grace sounded surprised, she wasn't entirely so, since she'd noticed how washed-out Frank had looked at the funeral. "Lousy timing, isn't it? Didn't he say anything to you?"

Cressie shook her head and wiped her eyes. "Oh, Grace, I feel terrible. I told him I was fed up nursing. He must have thought I meant him."

"But that's irrational. How could he, if he hadn't told you about this?" She reread the letter.

"You know, I keep thinking things come in threes. I'm so frightened. He's going to die. I know he is."

"No he's not, Cress. It's probably for a routine checkup, but even if he has to have treatment, he'll get through. You both will."

"What if it's another bypass?"

"Oh, Cress, you're jumping to conclusions, but even if it is, it's a marvellous operation. I know several people—"

"How many do you know who've had it twice?"

"Two," Grace lied. "And both of them are hale and hearty and a good deal older than Frank. Cressie? Shouldn't you go home? Abandon this, and just drive straight to Dublin?"

Cressie bit her lip. "No," she said after a while. "No." She was curiously emphatic. "I know you think I'm heartless, but I'm not. I just don't feel I can face it yet. My head is all over the place; I can't think straight. I feel so bloody drained. I just can't seem to get a night's sleep."

"I'm not surprised. You were up three or four times a night with your father for months. But, darling, wouldn't you both be better off together? Wouldn't it be easier?"

Cressie considered this. "I'll ring Joe—our GP—as soon as I get to Clonmel; he'll give me the lowdown. I'll make him give it to me straight out. I want to know just what we're in for." She rubbed her cheek, then dried her eyes. "I'm sick to death of being treated like a child," she burst out. "I want to be an equal partner. I'm not playing Frank's games anymore."

"Come again?"

"Frank thinks that if he tells me he's ill, I'll only come home out of duty, and then he won't know if I really want to. Get it?"

"Oh, Cressie, come on." Grace brushed her hair off her face wearily. Cressida could have been describing her own situation. It was too damn familiar. Did all couples have to go through these gut-wrenching convolutions? Pussyfooting around, afraid to be straight with each other and thereby making something fragile even more likely to break. "What do *you* feel?" she asked.

"I wish he'd trust my love for him, but I don't know if *he* loves *me* enough for that. Or trusts me."

Grace bit her lip. "I really don't think you're thinking straight, Cress."

Cressida stared mutinously out of the windscreen. "Oh yes, I am. That night Halcyon attacked Katie May, Frank and I had a terrible row, and that's when the rot started. He accused me of putting our baby at risk, and I knew he was remembering how it had been for Gil. He didn't say it, of course, but he wouldn't let Katie May out of his sight. It went on for months. Awful, awful. I hadn't realised he could be so angry." She closed her eyes. "It just seemed to fill the house, his fury. Like Val's. Gil was practically catatonic with shock. His face, as he watched Halcyon almost kill the baby, will haunt me forever. That's when he began to go in on himself. He became terribly introverted. I couldn't talk to Frank about Gil, or any of it. I was too afraid of losing Katie May."

"Oh my dear, I had no idea. No idea." Grace put her arm around Cressida's shoulder and held her head to hers. *Evangeline's poison,* she thought furiously, *touched us all.*

"So why did you go on seeing Halcyon?" Grace asked quietly. "It wasn't as if she ever noticed or communicated."

"I couldn't abandon her, could I?" Cressida replied slowly, "I suppose I thought of it as a sort of penance. Atonement?"

"How very Catholic. For what?"

"For Gil. For Gil being OK, when she was not. For my beautiful, perfect, little daughter. It was my way of touching wood, all tied up with guilt about Val, I suppose." She put her hand on Grace's arm. "I hoped that if I did something good, something I found very, very difficult, then bad things wouldn't keep happening. It's hard to put into words, but I had this superstition that Halcyon held the secret of what went wrong—with her and her mother and me and Gil. I had to get her on my side because I felt that somehow if I loved her enough she would . . . she would . . . disclose it, help me understand. Help me to stop feeling that the whole thing was my fault. Then Frank and I would be all right."

"But Cressie, love. Halcyon has no intelligence. She's mute. How could—?"

"Oh but she did. That day in the garden, I saw it on her face," Cressie said intensely. She looked at Grace. "You see, I always believed something in me made Val violent. But that day I realised he must have hurt Halcyon as well. That it was his nature. It was almost as if she was reenacting something that happened to her."

"That's what Murray's always thought," Grace said thoughtfully.

"What?" Cressie swivelled around. "Why didn't he ever tell me? Why didn't you?"

"Oh, Cress, how could we? None of us ever talk about any of it, do we? Not properly."

"That's true. There's something I never told anyone except John Spain. Something Frank and Gil don't know." Cressie spoke dreamily. Grace tightened hold of her hands.

"I lied about Gil's deafness. I knew about it, long before it was diagnosed."

"Yes?" Grace kept her voice neutral. Cressie had never before discussed Gil's hearing disability, which had steadily improved since Grace had first met him when he was about eight years old.

"People always said I never left him, that he was always at my side. But that wasn't entirely true, I did leave him once. He was about eighteen months, beginning to talk. The same age Katie May was that awful day. I'd put him down for his afternoon nap. Val had just come in from sailing and was having a bath. I asked him to keep and eye on Gil while I went to the supermarket. I left them alone in the house."

"But what was wrong with that?" Grace cried. She looked at her friend closely. "Had Val started abusing you? Even then? So early on?"

"No. Honestly. Not then. But he didn't have much to do with Gil. Or me, for that matter. He was away a lot of the time. He never got involved with bathing the baby or feeding him or anything like that. Gil had to be clean, changed, all dressed up, before Val would even pick him up. He claimed he was too old for 'all that new man stuff.' " Cressie made quotation marks with her fingers. "Val couldn't stand mess."

"Charming," Grace said succinctly.

Cressida shrugged away the interruption. "I took a bit longer at the supermarket than I intended. When I got back, Gil was screaming. His nappy needed changing. I thought that was why he was crying, but when I picked him up, there was blood on the side of his head, running out of his ear. Val was fast asleep on our bed, and when I faced him with it, he said he hadn't touched him, that Gil had been screaming since I left, banging his head on the side of the cot. I asked him why he hadn't changed Gil's nappy. I don't know why I bothered, Val never changed him, couldn't stand the smell. He couldn't stand the baby crying, either. He told me off and went out."

"What do you think really happened?" Grace asked quietly.

"I don't know. I can't be sure. Gil *did* sometimes bang his head on the side of his cot. He was quite a strong baby. He used to grab hold of the cot rails and shake and shake. I'd tied a little bell on one of the bars and he liked to hear it tin-kle."

"Hear?"

"Yes." Cressie admitted in a strangled voice. "Oh yes. Gil could hear."

"But not after that?"

"I can't be sure," she repeated. "His nature seemed to change; he cried a lot and became very clingy. It took me a while to realise his hearing was gone or partially gone. Weeks, months even. I colluded with Val, didn't I?" she burst out. "I should have followed my instinct and had Gil's hearing properly investigated immediately. Maybe they could have done something if I'd gone to the doctor at once, but I was afraid, you see. Afraid they'd think I abused him. It was ages before I took him to the clinic for a test. Five or six months. The nurse asked me a lot of questions. Then the doctor grilled me, because they'd done the early hearing tests. They asked me if I ever lost my temper with him, shook him, things like that. I didn't have Marie with me that time, like I had with Katie May, but somehow I must have convinced them. I never again left him on his own with Val."

"And Gil doesn't know?" Grace asked.

Cressida shook her head.

"Frank?"

"No, but . . ."

"What?"

"Gil asked me about it after Halcyon attacked Katie May. Not directly. In a roundabout way. I knew what he was get-ting at. That strange expression on her face when she was holding Katie May in the air haunted him. He asked about her, not himself, but it must have been in his mind. But how could I tell him? He doesn't know anything about his father. I could never bring it up. I wanted him to forget. Even now, I couldn't tell him."

"Oh?" Grace was skeptical. "What about Halcyon? Does he know she was his sister?"

"Half sister, if anything. It's only hearsay. No, he doesn't."

"Surely he's guessed?" Grace suggested. "Gil's extremely bright."

"How could he? We've been very careful."

"But don't you remember? *You* made that connection, Cress, the very first time you saw her," Grace said mildly. "You told me so yourself. So isn't it possible that Gil did, too?" She was afraid to say more.

Cressida looked at her fearfully. "He couldn't. He was so little. . . . Oh, Grace. I've been so frightened all my life. I have this feeling someday a hand will grab my shoulder and . . . and . . . I'll be clobbered with all these awful, awful questions. . . ."

As she covered her eyes with her hands, like a child, Grace wondered how she had ever found the strength to make any sort of life. Yet in spite, maybe because of, her uncertainties and fears, she was a thoughtful and devoted mother. And then the saddest thought of all occurred to Grace: she realised how much more relaxed Cressida was with young Katie May than with Gil. And yet when Gil was the same age, she was marvellous with him. *Questions. Cressie had just admitted that she was terrified of questions. What questions?* Pity welled up in her. "Is that when Val started abusing you, Cress?"

"I kept asking what had happened to Gil. He slapped me about, said I was hysterical."

"And it went on from there?"

"No, not for a while." Cressie bowed her head like a penitent, casting Grace as confessor.

"Are you saying that your husband abused you and your child, and *you* feel *you're* the guilty one?" She shook her head in disbelief. "Oh, Cress, your God is vengeful."

She might not have spoken for all the attention Cressida paid her.

"Val was really ashamed. He kept telling me how sorry he was, didn't know what came over him, promised he'd never do it again. He was very sweet for a long time afterwards."

"Because you covered up for him?" Grace said.

Cressie blushed deeply. "Maybe, but I didn't know for sure."

"Oh, Cressie."

"You sound just like Frank," Cressie said, and restarted the engine.

_____regression 9

twenty-three

Duncreagh Listening Post

(archive discovered by Gil Recaldo)
Art experts from around the world yesterday gathered in Cork for a memorial service for the late Mrs. Evangeline Walter. The ceremony was arranged by the late woman's friend and colleague, gallery owner Mrs. Rose O'Faolain.

I DON'T KNOW what time it was when I got back to the cottage, and I didn't care. How the hell could I have got it so wrong? I was rigid with the fear and misery I knew I must share with my mother. All these years it must have been eating away at her. Why had she attacked the woman? Why? Why was Tar screwing her? She'd wanted him to, I saw that; she'd forced herself on him, I remembered that as well. She was disgusting; she'd made him look like a fool. She'd pulled his trousers down around his ankles, trapped him, gone down on him like an animal. I hated it. I hated it. Who was she, this woman who laughed?

I couldn't stop shaking. My eyes felt like sandpits, wide open, staring into the dark. Shay would never come back. How could she? Until I held her, the thought of sex always disgusted me. Now I knew why. I had seen the reality at its most brutal. But even so, I couldn't understand the forces at play. How could I have forgotten so much? The more I thought about it, the more furious I became. Why didn't my mother trust me? Frank? Cowards both of them. I should have been told. They had no right to keep it from me. How dare they? Did they think I was a complete moron? They must have known that one day I would go back. I banged my fists against my head and ranted and railed in the empty cottage until I my anger began to die and reason crept back. I had baulked at telling Shay more than the minimum. My mother had to confront it all, and there was much more at stake for her. What could she possibly say to make it all right—for either of us? *Gil Sweeney, murderer's son.*

Had she known there was someone else in the garden? As I asked myself that question, I was certain she had not. I had the advantage of her: because I was deaf, my eyes had not been distracted. And my sense of smell has always been acute. What about Tar? I could hardly bear to think of him. I pictured instead the shoe coming down on my foot, the hand grabbing my injured arm, sending shooting pains through my shoulder up into my head. For a moment I saw me, the little boy, sobbing and terrified, wriggling free, the dead arm—the broken arm—hanging limp by my side. Eyes tight shut, I conjured up the muddy shoe. A brown shoe with stitching on the front. A brown brogue, like my father wore, and cords with caked mud on the cuff. And now I smelt his aftershave, and I was even more terrified. What was my father doing in that bloody garden? He had been after me. He was going to hurt me again.

The broken arm worried me. It had some significance I couldn't fathom. I'd always known my wrist had been broken when I was a child because it was weak even now. But, I'd been told, the accident happened after we left the estuary, sometime before Katie May was born. Accident? What accident? I remember being in hospital with the doctor standing at the end of the bed with his stethoscope around his neck. He let me listen to my heart and told me my arm hadn't mended properly; it would have to be reset. He was a fat man with a huge, beaming face. I watched his big, purple lips. "Count backwards from ten," he said. "Can you do that?"

When I opened my eyes, the first thing I saw was Cressie sitting on the side of the bed, smiling at Frank. He had his arm around her shoulder. Later on it became family lore that I'd broken my arm when I fell out of an apple tree at the cottage. "Reset" meant nothing to me then. It did now. I went back over it very slowly. My arm was broken for the first time that night. Which was why I couldn't move it.

My childhood was like a silent film: unless people were looking directly at me, I couldn't read what they said. But I was always quick to sense when things were wrong or about to go wrong. I still have that knack. Whenever my father went to hit me, I'd duck, just a second before he struck. My mother wasn't so quick off the mark, or was it that she took the brunt for me? The night in question we both got it, but I have a feeling that particular attack was meant for me. What provoked it?

I put myself back in the Range Rover and slowly wound back the film as I tried to recall what happened in the hours before we ended up at the slipway.

I am on the boat with Tar. My mother is away somewhere, and he is minding me. We have our lessons, and then I ask him to take me to watch the seals. He doesn't want to at first, but I know if I keep on nagging he'll give in. And he does, because I distinctly remember being on the boat with him.

The sun is shining on the purple mountain. Frank passes by in his funny little sailing boat, folded up like a big black stork. I laugh and wave, and he waves back. A speedboat goes past and nearly capsizes our boat. We row along by the garden where the woman is standing. She has a basket in her hand. She waves and laughs. Tar looks sad and upset. The woman points at me and laughs again. There is another woman—a girl—running down the garden. She's wearing a long white dress and her hair is white, too. But not as white as the dress.

We only stay a little while at the Crags, watching the seals. On the way back, my father's yacht, *Azzurra*, passes by, on the way out to sea. The motor creates a great wake that opens out in a giant V, and sets us rocking like mad. I am following the wake when something catches my eye. The woman and her friend in the long white dress are on the yacht with my father and another man. Tar touches my shoulder and points to where Frank is trying to right his sail. Distracting my attention, I suppose, but I sense he is afraid of something. Someone?

It's much later, the sun is setting, and now I'm in the car with my mother, bowling along the main road to Duncreagh. She always drives fast. She is pointing to a petrol station. She turns in too quickly and nearly crashes into a big black car waiting at the pumps. The driver jumps out, and I see it's Mr. O'Dowd, who is sometimes on the yacht with my father. He is furious. My mother gets out of the car and goes to talk to him. I climb out after her. They bend over the back bumper, their heads close together.

Suddenly, my heart was pumping. I knew what was coming. I sat upright and crossed my arms on my chest, rocking back and forth as I recalled the first time I saw Halcyon.

The girl in the white dress gets out of Mr. O'Dowd's car and runs over to me. She starts to paw my face. I am afraid of her and back away. Mr. O'Dowd straightens up, says something to my mother. I only make out one word he says: "lady." He looks first at me then at the lady. I think it's her name: Lady. We are all standing very still. Each time he turns his head it seems to take hours. First at me, then at her. Once, twice, then he looks straight at my mother, and he is smiling like always. I am by her side so I can see his face clearly, but though I watch his lips, I cannot understand what he says. Something about the lady, I think.

When we get home my father is on the phone. My mother takes me upstairs and puts me to bed, but I don't go to sleep. I keep thinking of the lady in white. I get out of bed and go downstairs.

I am in the kitchen, in my pyjamas, holding my teddy. My parents are at the table opposite each other. My father is drinking a glass of red wine. He is wearing a navy blue jersey and light brown cords. One of his feet is resting on a chair, and the brown brogues have left mud stains on the seat. He is smiling at my mother. I've been practicing all the way downstairs; *Laaaaady, laaady, lady. Paaaapa.* I want him to smile at me. Tell me I'm a clever boy to be able to say the words. *Papa, I saw Lady.* It comes out right. Now he will smile at me. I say it again. He shoves back his chair, but he's not smiling. His face is all twisted. He flings the glass down the table at my mother. She gets to her feet; her mouth is open wide. "Run, Gil." She stretches out her hands, palms upright, pushing the air. "Run. Run." Suddenly I'm flying across the room, and my face is pushed against the skirting board. My mother is on the floor near me. I peep through my eyelashes and see my father raise his big brown shoe and bring it down on her head. He keeps kicking her.

Now I'm under the bed curled up in a ball, holding my aching arm. My mother is lying on the floor, trying to coax me out. One of her eyes is closed. Her face is covered with blood, and she looks terrified.

Halcyon/Lady. Lady/Halcyon? They were the same. I'd always known her name, but until now I never associated her with the girl I'd seen that day in the woman's garden, on my father's yacht, and later on the forecourt of the filling station. The oddest thing of all was that while I tossed and turned, I kept seeing my father's yacht, *Azzurra,* skimming along the water in slow motion, with me in Tar's little boat riding the wake. When at last I fell asleep, the same image became part of my dream, repeating over and over, and all the time I was riding the wake, I kept getting closer and closer to the stern until I could stretch out my hand and touch it. Thinking about it when I woke up, all at once I remembered something very strange indeed. The name on the transom was not *Azzurra* but *Halcyon.* The letters were dark blue picked out in gold. I told myself it was a dream, that I unconsciously associated one peculiar detail with another. But deep in my heart, I knew it was important.

twenty-four

E-mail from Fiona Moore
To: Sean Brophy

Sean, Bingo! I followed Recaldo from the school. He was walking so it was easy. He kept stopping, and at first I thought he'd sussed me out, but then I realised he was short of breath. Not a well man, I think. He lives about a half mile from the school in a rather miserable looking semi. I didn't even have to nudge Lulu in his kid's direction, since she's already fixated. They are the only new girls in their class, so they naturally cling together. That's the good news, now the bad. That guy O'Dowd turned up yesterday. God, he really fancies himself and thinks I do, too. Yuk. But he has a story all right. It's been festering for years. Just caught him at the moment of explosion. Well done for spotting that house for sale. A mausoleum, but a perfect intro. Sad and gay—is that a contradiction or what? He's the type that likes a bit of arm

candy, and guess what? I've got the job. I re-
mind him of Vangie, it seems. Must be the accent.
Have I got a story? See ya.
Fi

THE DUBLIN NEWSPAPERS were first off the mark, and it was
clear that the TV company had already made contact with
them, if not his publisher. The journalist who rang his mobile was a pleasant, youngish-sounding man called Sean
Brophy. "I'm going on holiday in a couple of weeks," he
opened. "I just wanted to fix a date before you get too busy.
You're going to be in great demand. I really enjoy your
books," he said. "I sometimes review crime, under a different byline," he added, identifying himself as the author of
Frank's best notice. This, of course, immediately broke the
ice. The interview was set up for the following week. When
asked what venue he'd prefer, Frank suggested the National
Gallery—in London—the day after the TV screening.

"In London? Oh. I understood from your publisher that
you'd be doing some publicity in Dublin," Brophy said, and
Frank gave private thanks that the journalist hadn't been
told where he lived, when he should have recognised that
Brophy was pumping him for information.

"That's true," he said evasively. "I can make it Dublin if
you like."

"Great stuff. What about the coffee shop of the *Irish* National Gallery then?" he returned with a laugh.

Frank agreed.

If a week wasn't long enough to grow a beard, he'd have
to manage with designer stubble. Or perhaps it didn't rank
as designer stubble if it was grey? He slipped the phone in
his pocket with the sinking feeling that fate was catching up
on him.

For years he had pushed all memory of those five fateful
days out of his head, but now he was back living in it. It
haunted him, day and night. He began to sweat as he recalled how carefully he had edited John Spain's story. How
he suppressed the vital clue of Cressida's presence in the

dead woman's garden that night. When the two officers from the city, Inspectors McBride and Coffey, arrived on the scene, they rumbled him straightaway and promptly placed him in the frame, if not for the murder, then for leading the witness. Two uncomfortable days and the tide, for no discernible reason, turned, and Phil McBride swung to his side. How would things have panned out, had he not? After that false start, the two men worked well together and very quickly unearthed damming proof of Sweeney's guilt. They'd been close friends ever since.

Recaldo reopened the *Legacy* folder. He thought for a moment, then changed his own name to Hanrahan in an effort to stop picturing the dramatis personae as he knew them. That one change of name had a surprising effect; it changed his perspective, and as he reread the outline, the policeman took over from the writer.

Early one morning a woman is seen standing by a tree in her garden, by the water's edge. An old fisherman approaches her to pass the time of day and discovers she is dead, covered in blood, but still standing. He lays her on the grass and calls the local policeman, who in turn calls his superiors at headquarters. By the time they arrive, the fisherman's story is well rehearsed. In the new version Jack Hanrahan begins to sift through the evidence as presented: the fisherman is an ex-priest with a steamy past. He left the Jesuit order for the wife of the Spanish ambassador to Italy, who later committed suicide.

He is friendly with a young Englishwoman and teaches her deaf son.

The dead woman has been spreading salacious gossip about them and also accuses the old man of paedophilia.

She has a seventeen-year-old brain-damaged daughter whom she keeps secret, locked away in a remote convent. The father denies the child. The woman has been stalking him for years.

She has terminal cancer.

Putative murderer X is practically bankrupt. Victim Y buys his beloved yacht through a friend, under an arrangement, which promises X use of it, but then she reneges on the deal and sells the yacht.

X crucially discovers this the day before Y is killed. At the same time, he meets his daughter for the first time since she was three.

Recaldo read back what he'd written and impatiently abandoned the Xs and Ys before going on.

Later that day, Cressida sees the girl and realises who she is.

Gil tells his father he's "seen the lady."

Gil spends the afternoon with Spain. Sweeney sees them together and threatens to report Spain for pederasty unless Cressida agrees to the sale of the house. When she refuses, Sweeny attacks her and his son. Later, he is seen going across the river towards Evangeline's house.

Cressida goes to warn Spain and finds him being sexually taunted by Evangeline in her garden.

Cressida sees red, grabs Evangeline, and knocks her out. In the struggle Cressida loses her comb.

Spain drags her off and dispatches her and Gil to the city, where she hides out.

What happens then is unclear. The version Spain gives the police is that he stumbles upon the dead body. But eventually he admits revisiting the garden during the night, though he's evasive about how many times. He insists she is still alive around midnight, standing at the lighted window.

The dead woman's neighbour and friend, O'Dowd, claims to have heard Ella Fitzgerald's voice coming from Evangeline's house at around one o'clock that morning and believes her to be alive at that time. He, too, is suspected of knowing more than he lets on.

Apart from Spain's later visits to the garden, Cressida eventually corroborates his testimony. There were other details, but that was the drift. Reading it through, Hanrahan believes that Spain fudged the timing to give himself time to search the garden and tidy up a bit before calling the scene-of-crime officers.

The autopsy shows that the woman has had violent sex more than once and with more than one person before she was fatally punched in the stomach where she'd recently had surgery. The *modus operandi* inevitably points to the wife-batterer Sweeney, who is missing, though there is the small matter of getting the stories straight and producing concrete evidence. Which they do, but not before Sweeney and Spain are drowned.

Frank sat back and thought it through for the umpteenth time. Several things leapt out. The time lag between Cressida's attack on Evangeline to the discovery of her body was a good eight hours. What else was Spain doing during this time, besides, as he claimed, sleeping?

Cressida? It was too damn neat. A woman who was almost universally feared, dispatched by a man everyone seemed to loathe? Who then conveniently drowns? Or is drowned? After a decade, the loose ends were on the escape.

The whole thing stank. If Hanrahan were to carry out the investigation, then he would look more closely at Spain and Cressida's evidence, for a start, and he'd have had Recaldo off the case in double quick time.

"Bah," said Recaldo and unceremoniously deleted his invented policeman. Remorse almost choked him. He rubbed his hand over his chin, lost in thought. There was no way he could write this book. If he did, he would have to relive that terrible time and cast a cold spotlight on people he loved, not least the darling of his heart. Without further ado he consigned the entire file to the dump bin.

Troubles never come singly. The phone rang. Frank snatched up the receiver.

"Mr. Recaldo?" It was his GP's secretary to say his hospital admission had been fixed for the week after next. "Dr. Boylan would like to talk to you."

"Now? You want me to come to the surgery?"

"No, the doctor's on the line," she said.

"Frank? How have you been?" the GP asked, and the sweat broke out on Frank's forehead.

"I've been fine, Joe," he said. "No problems at all, in the last few weeks. The new regime seems to have done the trick."

"What are you saying to me, Frank? You're not trying to

postpone surgery again? Do you know how much trouble I've had trying to rearrange it? Man, you're pushing yourself beyond the limit, not to mention myself. Is your wife home yet?"

"No," Frank was forced to admit. "She'll be here in a day or so." He crossed his fingers.

Cressie had to come of her own volition, choose to be with him again. Telling her he was ill would be tantamount to coercion, and he couldn't bear that. It was not his style to be an object of pity.

"You haven't told her, have you, Frank?"

"No. How could I? She's been nursing her father for the last four years. How the hell can I tell her she's in for another marathon?" he asked plaintively.

Joe Boylan was made of sterner stuff.

"I'm afraid you're going to have to, because you can't postpone this operation any longer. I'm sorry, Frank, it's very hard luck, but, you know, you've had a good few years since the last one. How long is it?"

"Fourteen," Frank mumbled, "next November." He'd been thirty-eight then, unreasonably young to have a quadruple bypass. Now he was to have another. Doctor Boylan had first suggested that it might be necessary seven or eight months earlier, but Frank refused to hear. Over the following months, however, it became more difficult to ignore the increased ferocity of the angina attacks and the attendant changes to his lifestyle. His libido waned. He stopped his long-distance walking, then couldn't manage even short distances. He restricted all activity, drank less, ate less, slept less. Lifted nothing, didn't fly unless he had to. But he still put off confiding in Cressie. How could he when he couldn't admit to himself how bad things had become? But in the past three or four weeks, when he started having attacks at rest, the alarm signals reached him at last.

"You have two remaining unblocked arteries. And one of those is iffy."

"So I've been told," Frank said drily. How had the cardiologist put it? "You need a spot of replumbing."

"Well then?"

"I've been down this road before, Joe. Would it surprise you to hear I'm just a little apprehensive?"

"No, it would not then. It's a grim prospect, but you know the technology's moved on hugely. You'll find it much less traumatic this time. And once it's done, you won't know yourself."

*Ah, but will my love know me? Grá mo croi.**

"They'll keep you in for four or five days after surgery," Dr. Boylan said briskly. "So, in on Tuesday, operation Thursday morning. You'll be home the middle of the following week. If your wife wants to have an . . . a chat, tell her to ring me. Any time."

Frank thanked him and hung up.

*my heart's beloved.

twenty-five

E-mail from Fiona Moore
To: Sean Brophy

Sean, You must be psychic. Ventry is Irish, though not the garrulous type. Bit of a recluse by all accounts. I was down in Waterford talking to that young film producer Ian Whyte. And what do you think? Not only has he optioned the entire Ventry oeuvre but has the first one in the can. He doesn't let the grass grow, that's for sure. It'll be screened in the UK in October and here a month later. He may also have sold it on— to France and to the States. Starts shooting the second in the spring. That's the good news. The bad is that Ventry lives somewhere in Oxfordshire and absolutely refuses to give interviews. The J. D. Salinger *de nos jours*. Any ideas? Friday night as arranged, then?
Fi

E-mail from Sean Brophy
To: Fiona Moore

Fi, Not Oxford, Dublin. I rang Ventry to confirm
the interview. He tried to pretend he lived in
London. Wanted to postpone yet again. But I managed to pin him down. Tell you all tonight.
Sean.
PS: S has lowered the boom, given me till next
week. I've a headache even thinking about it. Any
thoughts?
S

EVANGELINE'S TROUBLESOME PRESENCE rampaged through
his dreams. Frank tossed and turned all night worrying about
his health, Cressida, the children, the past, the future—in
short, everything. Most of all he was weighed down by his
failure to help Gil come to terms with his origins. When he
had adopted the little boy, he had voluntarily taken on that
responsibility. He loved the child as if he were his own, but
yet he'd never even begun to address the issue. Worse, he
hadn't allowed the slightest room for manoeuvre. What he
and Cressida intended, what they wanted, was to create an
environment of trust and affectionate acceptance in which
Gil could approach and then deal with the horrifying brutal-
ity of his early childhood. No use blaming Cressie; she had
so much more to lose—at the very least the possibility of
total alienation from her boy. It wasn't that they hadn't an-
guished about the problem for years; they had. But in her
confusion and terror, Cressida had allowed herself to be
guided absolutely by Frank and he, poor man, was floun-
dering around in the dark. He had messed up.

Hidden in the universal pain, the murder was the most
troublesome specific. He was in a highly anxious state when
he got up next morning and completely freaked when he
saw the messes Rafferty had made on the kitchen floor,
which poor little Katie May was inexpertly trying to clear
up. He took the mop out of her hands. "You take that yoke

outside. Now. And don't let him in until I tell you." He
sluiced the kitchen out, which proved therapeutic, and made
the breakfast. Afterwards he dictated a shopping list, which
Katie May laboriously wrote out with Rafferty curled up on
her knee.

When she'd finished, the pair of them looked up at Frank
with exactly the same pathetic expression and watering
eyes.

"You're not still mad at us, are you Dad?" she asked.

Us? Frank looked down at her fondly and smiled. "No,
sweetheart, you were doing your best. Sorry I was such a
grouch. I didn't sleep that well, but I'm fine now. Why don't
you entertain his nibs while I do a bit of work? Then we'll
change the beds and clean the place up for Mammy. What
do you say?"

Katie May tied a length of twine to Rafferty's collar. "I'm
going to train him to walk on a lead," she declared confidently and was not noticeably abashed when the reluctant
puppy staged a sit-down strike and had to be dragged across
the damp floor on his bottom. She picked him up at the door
and carried him out to the garden for his first lesson.

Frank watched her through the kitchen window for a few
minutes, and then, because he couldn't leave it alone, he sat
down at the computer and resurrected the *Legacy* folder
from the dump bin.

He tried hard to persuade himself that after more than a
decade hardly anyone would remember the crime beyond a
few individuals in Passage South or Trianach, but he'd lived
in cloud-cuckoo-land so long that his thinking was askew.
His alias was a well-kept secret, and he'd always been ul-
tracareful about publicity. Now he regretted having ignored
Phil McBride's advice to go the whole hog and drop Frank
along with Recaldo. But who on earth would link the in-
creasingly popular Frank Ventry with the lowly Garda
Sergeant Frank Recaldo, as he then was, or with the murder?
The hullabaloo had died down quickly; interest in the estuary shifted by a spate of terrorist-linked bank robberies in
Dublin the week after the murder. It had been easy to assume the general amnesia would last, though hardly wise.

So, who would recognise the story? he asked himself.
Apart from Phil McBride, devoted reader as well as friend.
Like everything about Phil, his reaction wouldn't be easy to
predict. Cressie? Ah, Cressie was another matter. She would
be devastated. She might even believe he was trying to get
at her, punish her—for what? Her reluctance to come
home? Frank pushed away the thought guiltily.

The oddest thing about all Frank's introversion was that,
until he abandoned, definitively, the *Legacy* plot, it didn't
enter his mind that *he* might be a focus of interest. For years
his considerable intelligence was concentrated on protecting
his wife and family, not himself. For a man who could and
did devise the most complex and chilling plots, he proved
extraordinarily obtuse when it came to his own life; he
couldn't see the woods for the trees.

And Gil? What about Gil? Through all Frank Recaldo's in-
tellectualising, the small, silent figure of the child Gil in-
truded, stealthily, intermittently. But now he was at Frank's
elbow the whole time. Gil the unconsidered, stifled witness.
Even now Frank barely acknowledged that at no time did he
or either of his colleagues try to discover what part, if any, the
little boy played. Or what he might have seen. Gil, who was
never allowed out of his mother's sight. But, critically, the day
of the murder Gil had been with Spain while his mother drove
a friend to hospital in Cork. Images of Evangeline's garden
floated in front of Frank's eyes, the dead woman on the grass
at his feet. John Spain also kept materialising in the most un-
settling way, mulishly sticking to his well-prepared story.
"When did you last see her alive?" he heard himself ask.

"Before I found her dead, you mean? Standing by that
tree when I came in from fishing last night."

"You were alone?"

"Why wouldn't I be?" No mention of Gil being with him
all afternoon.

Whenever he thought of Evangeline Walter, the same
questions and the same dread came bubbling to the surface;
Recaldo had not seen Cressie for a couple of days before the
murder. In all, she was missing for four days: two before,
two after the murder. In his mind's eye he saw his fingers

curling around her little tortoiseshell comb. She loathed the American woman, whom she suspected of having an affair with her husband, and feared her vicious tongue for other reasons.

Frank put his head in his hands and closed his eyes. When Cressie at last showed her face, it was badly cut and bruised. Gil had his arm in a sling. It took longer for her to confess she'd bashed Evangeline over the head.

Spain reluctantly confirmed this but claimed Evangeline hadn't been badly hurt. "She was lying there laughing at us when I dragged Cressie away. I saw her later on that night by the open window of her house. There was music playing. Ella Fitzgerald."

"Where were you?"

"Out on the river, in the boat, of course."

"You said you were in bed. Mind telling me what you were doing back there?"

"I wanted to make sure she was all right."

The story had to be dragged out of him almost word by word. What emerged was terrible. The night of the murder, Spain went to implore Evangeline to stop traducing him, but she laughed in his face and compounded the insult by goading him into a brutal sexual encounter that Cressie, who witnessed it, later described as rape, with Evangeline as the aggressor.

Cressida's account, too, came in tiny, painful instalments: Earlier that day, by chance, she encountered Halcyon for the first time. One glance was enough for her to guess her paternity, because the girl was the image of Val Sweeney. And this confirmed what she'd always believed: that Val was sexually involved with Evangeline. And further, that it must have been going on well before and throughout her marriage. When she confronted Sweeney, he turned the tables by threatening to report Cressida to the authorities for leaving their eight-year-old son in the care of "the pervert priest." The scene for violence was set. When Spain and Cressida made their separate ways to Evangeline Walter's garden, they were in despair and furiously angry.

When Frank had asked where Gil was at the time, Spain

said he was in the car or in the cottage, catatonic after witnessing his mother beaten to a pulp by her husband. And so the detectives thought he was protecting Cressida. Had Gil been the main focus of his concern? And Evangeline Walter's sick interpretation of his affection for the little boy? Frank moved on and considered the evidence against V. J. Sweeney that had been found in the boot of his abandoned car: the dead woman's blood-soaked clothes, Sweeney's similarly stained sweater and cords, and a wooden chest crammed with her personal papers. But most damning of all, wrapped in that day's newspaper was a tiny dictating machine, which, by luck or design, was left switched on during a conversation between Evangeline and Sweeney. Phil, rocked to his unshockable foundations, described it as a verbal snuff movie, and it left no doubt of Sweeney's guilt. Convenient, to say the least.

One thing had always secretly bothered Frank. Because of Sweeney's timely death, the tape recorder never had to be produced in court, and so it had not been subjected to the rigorous forensic examination that would have demanded. Neither was the conjunction of newspaper and recorder ever thoroughly explored—at least not to Frank's knowledge. It was not something he cared to query, and between himself and Phil McBride the subject was, by unspoken agreement, taboo. Yet here it was, after ten years, still niggling away. Frank had never doubted Sweeney killed Evangeline Walter; it was more that he wondered if Sweeney had had a little help. The question was, from whom? And why?

Little Gil was tugging at his elbow again. In praising Cressida for her devotion to her deaf son, every single witness had used almost the same phrase: "He was always at her side, never out of her sight." *Jesus,* Frank thought, *supposing that was quite literally true? What then? That's enough,* he thought, *no more of this. No more!*

Frank deleted the wretched file and switched off his computer. Gil was once more pushed into the background. He had enough on his plate. His wife was on her way home, and he hadn't mentioned hearts or hospital to her, and he knew she would regard it as yet another example of him living in his head when in fact he was completely unable to confront his own terror. He registered guiltily that he hadn't warned his publisher about the forthcoming surgery either. When Rebecca had said she'd cancelled her holiday in honour of his forthcoming visit, he hadn't reacted. It hadn't been intentional, more a wish that, by ignoring it, he could will the operation away. He smiled wryly and ran his fingers through his hair, thankful that he was off two tiresome hooks; no previews and definitely no celebratory dinner, and there was also the possibility that if he played it cannily, he might also manage to avoid the rest of the publicity as well.

It occurred to him that some sort of diversion might help them over the crisis—speed his recovery? Had he started the search for a new house instead of haring off to Kerry, they would, by now, have some options to consider. He looked around the dingy dining room and realised how dismal it was going to be for Cressie to come back to. She'd always hated the house, the suburb, the proximity of the city. If he hadn't spoiled things that day by the river in Waterford, they might have found their ideal home, but the moment he realised they were avoiding all mention of Coribeen, he knew no other house would ever live up to it, and his courage had faltered. There was no going back. How could they? How could they ever expose the children to what had happened, face their judgment?

He shook himself out of his lethargy. There were thousands of lovely places they might go. And could probably afford. The production company had paid a substantial sum. The only worry was, how long would the bonanza continue? Like every writer, he worried how long his inspiration and luck would last. Frank crossed his fingers, pushed back his chair impatiently, and called Katie May.

"Want to come into Dublin?" he asked the little girl. "I need to do a few things, but we'll have time for a hamburger. What do you say?"

"We should get some flowers for Mummy," Katie May suggested.

"Sound thinking." He put his arm around her shoulders and laid his parched cheek on hers.

Three hours later they arrived home with a huge bunch of red roses, a leather collar and lead for Rafferty, as well as a bundle of house listings from five separate estate agents. Father and daughter sat at the kitchen table and trawled through them.

To his astonishment, halfway through the pile he came to a lavish description and full-colour photograph of Coribeen. He stared at it before pushing it across the table to his daughter.

"What do you think of that one?" he asked.

"I like this one better," Katie May said in a nice, uncomplicated way, after a cursory glance. She held out a single sheet with a badly produced black-and-white photo of a beautifully proportioned house near Avoca in County Wicklow. "Look, Dad, there's a kennel in the garden. Rafferty would love it."

"The question is, little one, would you?" he asked.

She nodded her head so hard it looked in danger of dropping off, and her enthusiasm woke Frank to the realization that somehow, somewhere, in his and Cressie's calculations, not just Gil but Katie May, too, had been sidelined.

"Did you hate it in Oxford?" he asked gently.

Katie May looked up in surprise. "Sometimes," she said slowly. "I didn't like the school much. Other children laughed at me. They said I sounded funny." Her lip curled. "Not half as funny as they did," she pronounced robustly, then gave him a wistful little smile. "I didn't have friends. Not a best friend, 'cos I couldn't have them home for tea or anything. On account of Grandfather." She shrugged. "I'm really, really glad to be home, Dad."

"What about Grandfather? Did you like him?" Grandfather. Such a grown-up word for a little girl. It spoke volumes that she never reduced it to the diminutive.

"Well, he was a bit cross, 'specially when I was little." She looked at her father cheerfully. "He wanted me to be quiet all the time, because he didn't like noise. But not always. Sometimes he told me stories. About the war." Her eyes widened. "Did you know, Dad? Grandfather was a soldier in Greece. All his comrades got killed," she said. "Dad, what are comrades?"

"Friends," Frank told her. "They were his friends."

Katie May considered this for a moment. "He used to cry for them and their immortal souls," she parroted. "Isn't that so sad? I didn't know old people cried." She sniffed. "Then he'd get angry and shout at me to go away. He was a bit funny like that. You could never tell if he was going to be nice or not. Mammy said he didn't feel well because he was so very, very old."

"But you liked him?"

Katie May considered this carefully and wrinkled her nose. "Not *like* exactly. He wasn't always kind, not like you and Mammy. I prefer being here with you, but it'll be nicer to have Mammy here as well," she said matter-of-factly.

Her father realised he had never put himself in the little girl's place, pictured what it must be like to live at the whim of a capricious, curmudgeonly old man. He and Cressie hadn't meant to, but they'd made a mess, and he was the more culpable.

He'd shut Cressie out. He'd used his work and Gil to give him space to pursue his new career. He convinced himself that he did so because he wanted to make a success for his family, but this was only partly true. He loved writing and wanted to continue because he knew he was good at it. Having come to it late, he cherished its freedoms all the more. But the inevitable fallout from publicity terrified him. As it did Cressie. Knowing this, was writing sheer self-indulgence?

The night before Piers Hollingsworth's funeral, Cressie accused him of always pushing her to the limit, perpetually setting impossible tests of her love for him—hurdles over which she had to jump. She had been right. And even if she didn't say it all again when she heard about the operation, she would see it as another failure. Of his love or hers? Why did he do these stupid things? Guilt. And humbug. She knew as well as he that the real reason he refused to live in Oxford was not just because he didn't get on with his father-in-law but also because he couldn't bear to start from scratch in a

place where he had no history. It had not crossed his mind
'til now that his little daughter might feel the same.

He got to his feet heavily. "Come on, little one, let's go
down to the pizza joint and get something for tea."
He looked dubiously at the puppy, who was taking an old
T-shirt apart.

"He's coming, too," said Katie May firmly. She picked
up the puppy and cradled him in her arms and followed her
father to the car.

When they got back, half an hour later, the VW beetle
was parked outside the house, and Cressida was standing on
the doorstep, looking anxious.

Katie May tumbled out of the car. "Mammy, Mammy,
Mammy," she yelled, and ran into her mother's open arms
with Rafferty yapping at her heels.

"Who's this?" Cressie bent down, picked the little dog
up, and held him to her face.

"That's Rafferty." Katie May danced up and down with
joy.

Cressie looked at Frank over her head. She blushed.

"I'm home," she said quietly. "Oh my darling, I'm home.
I can't believe it."

Frank put his hands on her shoulders. "You've cut your
hair," he said and turned her around. Freshly highlighted,
short and stylish, it made her look boyish and young. "It's
lovely," he said. "You're lovely. Oh welcome back *a
stoír*.*" Frank took her in his arms and buried his face in her
hair. It smelt of peaches.

*darling

_____regression 10

twenty-six

Duncreagh Listening Post

(archive discovered by Gil Recaldo)
CLOSURE OF ATLANTIS HOTEL
Well-known Passage South landmark, originally
designed and built by Swiss hotelier Otto Bleiberg
and opened by the then Taoiseach Charles
Haughey, is to be closed and a new holding company formed. Planning permission has been
granted for its conversion to super-luxury flats.
Woman murdered on Trianach last autumn had
shares in original company.

WHEN I WOKE up it was broad daylight. Someone was banging on the back door. I knew it wasn't Shay because she
never knocked. I was stiff, cold, and starving, and I didn't
want to see anyone, but it continued getting more and more
impatient. Then a voice called, "Open up. I know you're in
there." A woman's voice: Marilyn Donovan. Blast.

I staggered to the door and let her in. She looked around

and sniffed the foul air. "Jesus," she said fervently. "I won't ask you what you've been up to." I felt like thumping her. If there's anything I hate, it's middle-aged parents trying to be all understanding and cool. In fact, I was right off adults, period. I gave Mrs. Donovan my most challenging don't-mess-with-me stare, but she just laughed.

"Well," she said, "I can see you're a ferocious bastard and all that, but I was wondering if you'd like a bit of breakfast? We need to talk. *I* need to talk to you, Gil Sweeney."

"If it's about Shay—"

"Shay? Who the hell's Shay?"

"I meant Noreen. We weren't up to anything, as you put it."

She sniffed. Pointedly. And it got right up my nose. "So, you call her Shay?" she laughed. "Shay Donovan, star of stage, screen, and the latest pop idol, I suppose?" She cocked her head on one side. "The star is at school, for once. I drove her there myself. So if you're thinking of hanging around waiting for her, I shouldn't bother. Now, what about breakfast?"

"Have I a choice, Mrs. Donovan?" I asked.

"Yes, Gil. You have. You can come. Or not. Whichever you like." She paused. "Why are you so hostile?"

Without warning and to my complete disgust, my eyes filled with tears, and I heard this awful sobbing, which seemed to be coming from someone else. She didn't move, or put out her hand, to offer easy words. She stood quietly waiting until I pulled myself together and then said simply, "I can only imagine what coming back here has done to you, boy. But you've nothing to fear from me, I promise you. The car's outside." She turned away and went to the door, and after a moment's hesitation, I followed her.

For once it wasn't raining, but it was overcast and the air was damp and chilly. We were driving along in glum silence when a black Mercedes saloon, as big as a hearse, came tearing around a corner and nearly ran into us. I got a quick glimpse of the driver and recognised him as the old bloke who'd passed Shay and me on our way back to Spain's cottage the night before. "That fella will kill someone before he's finished," Marilyn said sourly. "He's got very erratic lately."

"Who is he?" I asked, and she looked at me curiously, her head to one side.

"Don't you know? That's Jer O'Dowd—otherwise known as Smiler." My heart missed a beat but I was too busy trying to keep calm to say anything, and Marilyn didn't say another word until we were sitting at her kitchen table with a big pot of tea and a heaped plate of thickly buttered, homemade brown bread between us. To my relief, she made small talk, giving me time to get myself together. She chatted about Noreen first, told me how clever she was; her parents had high hopes for her and wouldn't tolerate any messing. Noreen was funny and kindhearted and great with young Liam. Then she said she had a daughter called Aisling who was studying to be a solicitor in Dublin. She talked about the jazz trio and told me Frank used to play with "the lads" when he was stationed in Passage South and how he sometimes played the grand piano at the hotel to make a bit of extra money. "He's a brilliant musician," she said. "And he was the most respected guard we ever had around here." That was how she moved from the present to the past, effortlessly and kindly. In spite of my earlier suspicions, I could see why Shay was so fond of her.

"I worked for your mother, you know? In those days I was the charwoman supremo of the county," she tittered. "Full of myself. Do you remember me at all?"

I shook my head. I didn't want to say I remembered her avoiding me, but she must have read it on my face.

"You were a lovely-looking child, about two or so when I first went to Coribeen, but you threw temper tantrums all the time, cried, screamed, banged your feet on the floor. Sometimes your head. I was a bit afraid of you. To tell you the God's honest truth, I couldn't really handle it. I was never much good with little kids, even my own. I suppose that's one of the reasons I worked all hours. Aisling practically brought up Liam, I'm ashamed to say. But I enjoy them more as they get older." She smiled at me. "You used to go mad if Cressie wasn't in the room. I thought that was why she always looked tired and stretched." She paused. "It took me a long time to figure things out. What's she like these days?"

I shrugged. "Much the same. Quiet, a bit vague. She's been in Oxford looking after my grandfather for the past four years."

Our eyes met.

"She allows people to take advantage of her," I added.

Then she surprised me. "Don't you believe it. The Cressida I knew had a mountain of strength as well as a kind heart. Don't look so surprised. Your mother may be quiet, but she's strong—'specially where her family is concerned."

I didn't want her to go on. I didn't want her to tell me my father was a savage. "Why did you leave?".

"I didn't leave," she said bluntly. "I was sacked. I made the mistake of commiserating with Cressie, and she wouldn't have it." She shrugged. "I understood that; I'd have been the same myself."

"Did you tell Noreen all this?"

"Some of it. We talked for a long time last night. She knows how it was for you at Coribeen. She was talking about taking you there, so I thought she had the right. She's mad about you, in case you haven't noticed. As well as concerned. I don't want her hurt, d'you hear me?"

"What else did you tell her?"

"As little as possible. I was really trying to find out how much *you* told her. She asked me about John Spain."

"And?"

"What could I say but what I know? Which isn't all that much, mostly hearsay and gossip. You'd be better off asking Frank. I bet he knows the full story."

I climbed down from my high horse. "Will you tell me anyway?"

She poured herself another cup of tea. "John Spain was here maybe eighteen—twenty years. He was a great fisherman. Indeed, when he first came, he tried to pass himself off as one. He was humoured, but he couldn't disguise that he was a well-educated man. I've no notion how his past was known, but it was. That's Passage South for you—the bush telegraph can be deafening. Spain was a Jesuit priest once, a university professor in Rome and after that in Harvard, so he must have been pretty hot stuff at the teaching."

"What brought him to Trianach?" I asked.

"He was born not far from here I believe, somewhere near Daingean. One day he just appeared, settled into the derelict schoolhouse, and started trying to do it up. And a right mess he made of it; the poor man was hopeless with his hands. My father-in-law, Des, God rest his soul, took pity on him and did a lot of the work, and got a few pals to help out. It was when Spain volunteered to teach the kids, my Steve and Noreen's dad, that Des got the wind up. That time the newspapers were all the time full of scandal involving the clergy—mostly to do with the kids in their care. Some of it was true, of course, and lot of it was way over the top, in my opinion, but it had an effect all right, and not always on the guilty parties. Once it was known he was a spoiled priest, the rumours started and spread, until a couple of years after, when Steve's Aunt Molly came over from Boston and gave us the whole story. She was full of it. Spain may have been a randy old goat, but he was never interested in kids. It was women were his downfall. Didn't he only run off with some ambassador's wife, and she committed suicide—something like that."

"Consuela." It just popped out.

"What?"

"Consuela was her name. It was written in gold letters inside the boat."

Marilyn stared at me, open-mouthed.

"He used to talk to her."

"And you remember all that? God help us, isn't that the saddest thing?" She gave me a piercing look, her head to one side. "It's the first time you've talked about it, isn't it?"

I didn't answer that. "What happened then?"

"Molly said the woman left her husband and children for him. As well as her glitzy life. But they hadn't any luck, the unfortunates, nor a minute's peace. They were hounded down by the press so much, the poor woman jumped to her death. Aren't those journalists the self-righteous hypocrites altogether?" She sat back in her chair and looked at me as if she was trying to work out how to go on.

I waited.

"There's something you should know, Gil." She spoke slowly, choosing her words with care. "Shortly before John Spain was drowned, all sorts of desperate stories started flying around about him and how he liked . . . how he was a paedo . . . paedophile." She stumbled over the word. Her face was scarlet. "You told Noreen a woman was killed in this house, didn't you?"

"Yes. I'm sorry if that upset you. I mean, I can see . . ."

Marilyn waved me aside. "That's not important. 'Tis well enough known. Anyone could have told her before now; it just happened they didn't. I don't allow myself to dwell on it, to tell you the God's honest truth, otherwise I'd never be able to live here, though I like it well enough. Me and Steve never discuss it. Never. I suppose we're both trying to forget it. It was a sorry business, all round. A lot of people were badly affected." She fell silent again for a moment, and then became all businesslike. "Anyway, what I'm trying to say is: the woman who lived in this house, the woman that was murdered? It was said that she was responsible for the rumours about John Spain. This is hard, Gil. She specifically accused him of molesting you."

Why was I not surprised? Had I known about those rumours? Had Tar said something to warn me? Or my mother? I thought not, because some other hardly-there association told me it was neither of them. I closed my eyes, but it wouldn't come. I could feel my face flush, but I looked her straight in the eye. "He did not. Nor did my father. I would not have forgotten if either of them had. That is one thing I am absolutely certain of. My father beat the living daylights out of me; that is the only abuse I ever suffered, and I remember it clearly. John Spain never laid a finger on me."

Marilyn gave a sad little sigh and slowly shook her head. "Sure, didn't we all know that, Gil. The only reason I mentioned it was because I just didn't want you to get hold of those old stories and think otherwise. John Spain, God rest him, lived in these parts for years and years, and being who he was, people watched him, so if he'd ever done anything like that, I can assure you, it would have been known. That woman was a twisted poor creature who had it in for him. Why, God alone knows, because I don't, though I've pondered it for years."

"Thank you." Shay had been right. Marilyn was sound. "Did you know her?"

"Yes, I worked for her, too. Sure, didn't I work for practically all the blow-ins? I wonder now where I got the energy. She was American, some sort of art expert. She used to write the catalogues for the O'Faolain gallery in Daingean. Your ma worked for Mrs. O'Faolain as well; they were great friends. I suppose Mrs. Walter lived here about twelve years."

The chill crept upwards from my toes. "Mrs. *Walter?*"

"Yes. Evangeline Walter." She giggled and put on an American accent. 'You just call me Vangie, honey.' Whenever she said it, I couldn't help thinking vagina." She chuckled. "I should be ashamed of myself." She sobered up. "God rest her poor, tormented soul," she added piously.

"Tormented?"

"Yeah, I thought so, anyway, and I saw her every week. She was very solitary, completely self-absorbed, and never had a good word to say for anyone, even those who thought she was their friend. Very neurotic."

"Had she many friends?"

Marilyn seemed surprised at the question. "Not locally. She travelled quite a bit. I suppose Smiler O'Dowd—Jer O'Dowd, that is—was closest to her. Thick as thieves they were. The sleeveen," she added, half to herself.

"He was friendly with my father, wasn't he?" I asked tentatively.

Marilyn looked at me oddly. "Well, now, I'm not sure friendly is the word I'd use, though they certainly did business sometimes," she said uncomfortably. "They were on the board of the Atlantis Hotel in Passage South. It's closed down now, turned into flats."

I could tell she was holding something back, but I felt too nervous to press her.

"Was Mrs. Walter a close friend of my mother?"

"Your mother?" Marilyn was astonished. "No, I wouldn't say so. Mrs. Walter wasn't what you'd call a woman's woman. Not by any means."

I couldn't get my head around what she'd just said. The woman who laughed at us, that woman was Halcyon's mother? Why then did my mother look after her loony daughter all these years? But I couldn't ask because I didn't want Marilyn to comment on that or, more to the point, I didn't want her to confirm my other fear. I looked across the table at her. She was staring out the window, biting her lip, mulling something over. I poured another cup of the tepid tea and sipped it while I waited. Strange how inward-looking you can get when what is going on in your head is a lot more interesting than what's being said. I wasn't really taking everything in, at the time. I kept thinking about the yacht, the name painted on the transom, and the people who were on the boat that day. I could identify them at last: my father, Mr. O'Dowd, his friend Mrs. Walter, and the lady in white, Halcyon Walter.

"Had she a daughter?" I wanted it confirmed.

Marilyn swallowed.

"Yes," she mumbled. "I never met her, myself, though I was told she was here the day before Mrs. Walter was killed. Strange that, because as far as I know, she'd never before visited her mother. I believe she was backward. Mentally handicapped. When Mrs. Walter moved here from New York, the girl was put in a convent in Tipperary. With the nuns. They kept her there all the time."

"Why did Mrs. . . . Why did the woman move here?"

"Well, now, there you have me. It was a queer move, all right, for someone so interested in art, wasn't it? You'd think she'd have been more likely to live in a big city. I mean apart from O'Faolain's, the nearest art gallery must be Cork City."

"Why was the girl locked up?"

"I don't know, except there's few enough able to look after someone like that, and I wouldn't say Mrs. Walter was the type. They say you'd never know to look at the girl, that she was . . . well, backward." Marilyn's wide, smiling mouth was all pursed up. We sat in silence while I tried to figure out why my mother visited Halcyon all these years. Up to now, if I thought about it at all, I assumed it was because our friend Murray Magraw was her guardian, and since he and his wife Grace lived in Oxford and we lived in Ireland. . . . Now several other scenarios were buzzing around my head, and one troublesome detail I'd conveniently shoved aside was now haunting me: Halcyon and I had the same colouring, same eyes, even if hers were completely vacant. It doesn't take a rocket scientist to work that one out. *Gil Sweeney, murderer's son.* Had Halcyon something to do with the murder?

"Was there a big investigation?" I asked and caught her on the hop.

"What? For Mrs. Walter's murder? Yeah, it went on for a while, all right."

"Who investigated it?" I asked.

Marilyn seemed puzzled by the question, but that didn't stop her answering. "Well, Frank, of course, since he was on the scene—the local garda in Passage South. There were a couple of other detectives from Cork. One called Coffey; I never met him myself. The guy that interviewed me was from Dublin. McBride his name was. A real Dub bit of a smart-ass." She warmed to the subject. "Meeting him, you'd be inclined to think he was all mouth, full of wisecracks, but he was as sharp as anything for all his old guff. He didn't miss a damn thing. Not polished, like Frank, not educated."

Oh really? Three or four languages—"only to read, old son, read and write. I'd never be able to disguise the old accent would I now, Magillacuddy?"

"Bit of a flirt, he was," Marilyn said innocently. "But not my type."

His partner Mark would be pleased, I thought.

Marilyn stood up. "Would you like go over to Coribeen, Gil? It's for sale, you know. I went in to the auctioneer's this morning and borrowed the keys—in case you wanted to see it. I can take you, if you like."

I shook my head. "No," I said. "No, thank you, not now." *Not ever.*

She raised her eyebrows. "You're not thinking of haring off there with Noreen, are you?" She was trying too hard to be all matey.

"How could we?" I asked innocently. "It's too far to row." I shrugged.

"It wouldn't be that Madam Noreen offered to borrow her mammy's car, would it? If it is, forget it. I had it out with her last night. But if you prefer, we can go over when she gets home from school?"

"No thanks, Mrs. Donovan, I don't want to go there at all. I don't feel ready."

twenty-seven

Sean, O'Dowd keeps coming up with more and more stuff. Dynamite. Calls for a bit of creative editing, I think. I'm afraid he's still a bit keen, which puzzles me. Does he think I'm thick or what? I could tell the second I met him he was gay. Still in the closet but definitely gay, yet everyone around here describes him as "a great lad for the girls," would you believe? Quite possibly they're having me on. If he puts his hand on me one more time, I'll howl.
Fi

FRANK COULDN'T BRING himself to ask Cressie about Halcyon's funeral, certainly not while Katie May was hanging on to their every word. They had supper together in reasonable if strained harmony, both of them concentrating most of their efforts on the little girl and Rafferty, who earned his keep by keeping them entertained. After Katie May had gone to bed, her parents stolidly unloaded the car, spinning time out by doing it slowly, more so than even Frank's heart warranted. It was almost as if they were afraid to be alone together with nothing to do and without the diversion of child or puppy.

When at last the car was empty and everything was piled neatly in the hallway, Frank suggested a nightcap, but Cressie said she'd prefer to get things tidied away. "Otherwise we won't be able to move. It shouldn't take long." When she added, "You go and sit down for a bit," Frank realised she knew about the forthcoming operation. He went into the kitchen and sat staring at the wall, listening to her running up and down the stairs, his thoughts in turmoil, wondering how they were ever going to get back on the same wavelength.

"I'd love a cup of tea, if you're making one." Cressie put her head around the door after a fifth trip upstairs. "I'm very nearly finished." Frank switched on the kettle and made a small pot of tea, then impatiently put two glasses and a half-empty bottle of Hennessy on the table.

A few minutes later she slipped shyly into the kitchen. She'd brushed her hair and changed into an old pair of jeans and a scruffy green sweater he hadn't seen her wearing for four years. It emphasised how much weight she'd lost.

"You look nice," he said.

Cressie laughed. "We're like a pair of greyhounds," she lilted. "There isn't an ounce of flesh between us."

She sounded like her old self as well. The clipped English voice was softened by a return of the hint of Cork he loved.

She took his hand in hers. "I'm here for you, darling. I know about the bypass. Everything'll be all right."

"How long have you known?" He couldn't look her in the eye, in case he saw pity.

"Day of Halcyon's funeral. I rang the surgery from Tipp—nothing to do with you." She didn't mention finding the hospital letter he left under the pillow in Oxford. "I needed a prescription. The usual. I just happened to get Joe—his secretary was away," she fibbed. "He told me."

She laid his hand against her cheek. In fact, Cressie waited until after the funeral before ringing Dr. Boylan to get the score.

"Don't crowd him," Joe advised. "He's in denial at the moment. Keeps telling me he's fine. But with your help, he'll come around. Cressida? You're going to have to be real strong for him, my dear. It's not an easy time for either of you." He promised not to mention to Frank that she'd been in touch.

"You've had four years of sickness," he said stiffly. "I didn't think you'd want any more of it. . . ."

Cressie lifted his head. "Aw, Frank, what are you on about? You didn't think at all. I'm your wife, for God's sake. I'm with you all the way." She drew in a long breath. "Frank? Isn't it about time we talked?"

"Yes, it is."

"Forget the tea then," she said decisively. "Pour a couple of those." She pushed a glass towards him with the tip of her finger and waited until he poured in a stiff shot. She took a sip, then cradled the glass in her hands.

"Why didn't you talk to me?"

"I was afraid."

"Of what? That I'd throw a wobbly? Or run away?"

"Well, you said yourself that you were sick and tired of nursing."

"True. But that was duty. Daddy wasn't the easiest."

"He should have sold those damn pictures and employed a live-in nurse," he said harshly and was surprised when Cressie giggled.

"He had a live-in nurse. He was much too mean to actually pay for one." She looked at him seriously. "The fact is he was terrified of being alone. Afraid to die."

"It wasn't good for us. He didn't think of that."

"No. But it might have been good for me, Frank. I learnt a lot about him and about myself in the last four years." She leaned closer. "I'm stronger. I can forgive. I get furious, but I get over it. I'm not the poor, forlorn creature I was, you know. Living with my father toughened me up."

"At a price."

"Yes. A big price. I realise that." She leaned closer to him. "He was frightened of institutions, and women, too. I didn't count, being his daughter. He used women all his life; my mother, me, and then Marjorie. As long as you were compliant he was as sweet as pie, but I soon saw that he never really liked women. I think he had a weird idea that if he didn't control them, they'd control him. Like Val. That was what amazed me: he was very like Val in his attitudes, but Frank, I wasn't afraid of him." She sounded amazed. "That was one of the things I found out about myself. At first I was always trying to please him, the same as I did with Val. That's not your way, Frank love, but maybe I had to go away to appreciate that. Learn to accept it. You're so grown-up, love, you give people room to make decisions. And mistakes. That can be very challenging—frightening for someone more used to dictators. It's hard to be grown-up all the time, isn't it?"

"Why didn't you tell me all this before?"

"Why didn't you tell me how ill you are?"

"I'm not."

"Stop it, Frank. If you're trying to protect me, just stop it. I've learnt to take control; you have to learn to let up a bit. Listen to me. I'm here because I want to be with you, but I'd really have liked you to ask—to have offered me the choice."

"Maybe I was afraid you'd say no?"

They looked at each other in horror at how close to the precipice they'd got before drawing back.

Cressida put her arms around him. "Oh, my dearest love," she said, "we can get through anything together. Can't we?"

They went to bed, hand in hand, and for the first time in months, made love. Quiet, tender love. Afterwards, they lay awake for hours, chatting quietly about Frank's operation and where they would go from there.

"I want to tell you something, Frank," she said when he was almost asleep. "After that, I want to put it all away and concentrate on getting us back on the road. Together." She snuggled into him. "I've been down a very big hole, not just for the past few years, but forever. You've been very patient."

"I've been a selfish pig."

To his amazement, Cressie giggled. "Indeed you have, but maybe you earned the right? Anyway, there's a pair of us in it."

Frank sat up, switched on the bedside light, and traced the contours of her face with his finger. He kissed her on the nose.

"You've changed. Everything. You've changed."

"Is it OK?"

"More than." He held her close. "Tell me?"

"It's about Halcyon. Something happened at the funeral. I was afraid Smiler O'Dowd might show up, but he didn't. There were only a few people at the mass. Murray, Grace, me, and an old friend of mine, Rose O'Faolain."

"Rose?"

"You know her?"

"I, er, met her. Nice woman." Evangeline Walter had worked for her. He had interviewed her after the murder. "What was she doing there?"

"Bear with me—I'll tell you about Rose later. The mass was in a little chapel at the convent, with the two remaining nuns, both very ancient. It was very touching how they seemed to regard Halcyon as their child. Such kind women. They must be so lonely rattling around that old house with the life they knew all gone. They looked so tiny getting into the taxi to go home. The rest of us went back to the hotel afterwards, and Murray got absolutely legless. And so maudlin, it was awful for poor Grace. When he started on about Evangeline, she went to bed. I stayed."

"Why?"

"Because there were things I wanted to ask him. Things he wouldn't tell me if he was sober. I wanted to know exactly what was wrong with Halcyon and how Val Sweeney came into it."

"And do you know now?" Frank asked gently.

"Yes. Once he started, he couldn't stop. It was like it was all bottled up inside him waiting to pop. Frank, Murray was there the day Halcyon was hurt. Val and Evangeline were living in New York; he was a young graduate at Harvard. He was staying with them. Halcyon was about two, walking, talking, and a real handful. Always having tantrums. They never intended having children, he said, neither of them was very good with her. They were too impatient, giving in to her one minute, then ignoring her, so she was running wild around the apartment.

"It was a Sunday. They joined some friends in Central Park for a picnic. Three or four other couples. Halcyon was the only child there. They drank a lot and were all lying about in the sunshine when Halcyon started to yell. Her parents ignored her. Murray changed her diaper and went off to dump the soiled one in a trash can. It was a good way off, but all the way he could hear Halcyon getting more and more hysterical, so he dawdled. Next thing, he saw Val dragging her along by the hand, still shrieking. Murray stood back behind a tree. He knew if Val spotted him, he'd dump the child on him." She closed her eyes and sighed.

"What happened?"

"Val was jerking the child up and down by the hand—bouncing her—the way you do, to distract them. First couple of times she stopped crying, but he kept on raising her higher and higher until she started to scream again. He was a big, strong man, and she was tiny, so he could raise her almost to his shoulder. And then he just seemed to let go and the child went flying through the air. Murray started running. She came down on the edge of a kerbstone. Val just stood looking down on her. A woman came over to help, but the little girl seemed OK. She was lying quite still, but her eyes were open. Murray picked her up, and they went back to Evangeline, who lay her down and gave her a bottle, and she went to sleep. But when they got home, she started whimpering. Evangeline noticed a lump and bruising on her forehead and wanted to take her to the hospital to be checked over, but Val told her there wasn't time because she had to drive him to the airport at once, otherwise he'd miss his flight.

"He'd arranged to fly to London that night. That was one

of the reasons Murray was staying—to help Evangeline while Val was away. Evangeline thought the flight was at eight, but Val insisted that it was 'eighteen hundred hours, honey, not eight o'clock.' The upshot of it was that Evangeline and Val set out for the airport, and Murray was left holding the baby.

"She wouldn't eat anything, so he put her to bed with another bottle. She was still whimpering, but she fell asleep. When Evangeline wasn't back after a couple of hours, Murray checked on the baby and realised something was very wrong. She was snoring loudly, and her face was flushed. When he turned her over on her side, she vomited. Murray didn't know what to do. It was before mobile phones so there was no way of contacting Evangeline, and he knew from experience that she was quite likely to have gone off to visit friends or see a movie. He left a note for her and wrapped the baby up and ran out in the street and hailed a cab. She was deeply unconscious when they got to the hospital with a lump the size of an egg and bruising on her forehead.

"The staff didn't believe his story, of course. They assumed he was the father, the *abusive* father. An hour went past, and no sign of Evangeline. They kept accusing him of shaking the baby, or dropping her on the ground. They threatened him with the police." Cressie began to cry quietly.

Frank tightened his hold. "Shush, flower," he whispered. "You don't have to go on with this." But he knew she must. Both of them were thinking about Halcyon's attack on Katie May.

"All hell broke loose when it was discovered the child's skull was fractured. Murray was held for questioning until Evangeline turned up four hours later. Then they were both grilled. Day after day for almost a week, until finally the woman who came to help in the park was located. Halcyon remained unconscious for a couple of weeks, and all that time Val stayed in London. In fact, that was the last Evangeline saw of him. Murray got the hell out as well. He didn't see her for years—seven or eight years—by which time she was on Val's trail." Cressie shook her head in disbelief. "She knew everything about him. Even before I met him, she was stalking him."

"He was some shit."

"Yes. And I always thought it was something in me that made him like that." There was wonder in her voice. "But hc'd always been violent."

"She punished him. She punished us all." Frank spoke almost to himself.

Cressie seemed not to hear. "I did the same as she did. I protected Val. I . . . I . . . If only she'd gone after him earlier . . . She should have . . ."

"What?" Frank asked gently. "Had him charged?" He knew from his own experience how much easier it was to blame the parent on hand. How reluctant the police—in any country—were to get involved with domestic issues, how blurred the edges were. At the same time he wondered how Evangeline Walter had managed to wriggle free herself. By claiming it was an accident, probably. He noted that Cressie didn't for one moment believe it was. She had known Sweeney's unpredictable temper too well.

She held him tight. "I've so much more to tell you," she said.

"And so have I," he replied. "But let's sleep on it. You've been on a long, long journey." He held her out from him and smiled. "You are so brave, and so wise." He smiled. "Next time I start pontificating, shut me up. Oh my darlin' Cressie, welcome home, my love."

_____regression 11

twenty-eight

Duncreagh Listening Post

(archive discovered by Gil Recaldo)
Trianach businessman heads up board of the At-
lantis Apartments PLC in Passage South and puts
Coribeen House on the market.

I HALF EXPECTED Marilyn to come back, and indeed she returned to the cottage at about two-thirty, looking flushed and
upset. "When are you going home?" she asked abruptly.

I bristled. "I don't know. Sometime." Meaning, *Get off
my case; it's none of your business.*

The message must have come across loud and clear. She
glared at me. "God, you're a touchy son-of-a-bitch, aren't
you? I don't think I deserve that." She looked as if she was
going to storm out, but when I apologised, she changed her
mind. "Right so. I'll make it snappy. I presume you're in
touch with your parents? And before you get all uptight, I'm
not asking for their phone number. I just want you to give
them a message from me. Will you do that?"

"Yes," I said humbly. "And I'm sorry for being so rude. I—"

"It's all right, boy. You're overwrought. Forget it." She gnawed her lip. No lipstick, I noticed absently. "I was over in Coribeen. The auction is next week. Now listen to me carefully, because I think this may be important. Does Frank write those detective books everyone's talking about? Is he Frank Ventry, by any chance?"

I didn't know what to say—that's one thing Frank forbids us to discuss, and I was beginning to understand why.

Marilyn watched me closely, reading my face. "I see I'm right," she said. "Tell him that there was a woman—a journalist—over there with the auctioneer. She had a bit of an American accent, but she's Irish, all right. He showed us around together. Mind you, he ignored me. Well, he would, wouldn't he? Seeing I'm not a serious contender. I just trailed after them, but she didn't seem to be interested in the house either—this is what really spooked me; she kept bringing the conversation around to your family, Gil. *And* Mrs. Walter's murder," she added pointedly. "I nearly dropped down dead when she started talking about being here at the time and meeting 'that drop-dead handsome Garda Recaldo.' How he was hard to forget with that exotic name, and did we realise that he was writing detective stories these days, as well as the travel books? She had it all down pat, the nosy bitch. Now, this is the important bit. This is what you have to tell him. She said she was writing a series about unsolved crimes for the magazine section of the *Daily News*. Well, working for that rag, I could see where she was headed, right enough. Gil? She's trouble. I took the auctioneer to one side and asked him who she was. Tell Frank Fiona Moore was in Coribeen today. I couldn't place her, but I dropped in on Aoife Hussey below in Passage South on my way back. Aoife reminded me she was here at the time of the murder, asking a lot of questions about John Spain. At the time, she seemed to be more interested in him than in the murder. Remember the name: *Fiona Moore.* Aoife said that someone once told her it was Fiona Moore wrote about him for the American papers after he left the priesthood." She looked at me as if she was about to tell me all about it but I didn't want to hear. I wanted her to stop gossiping about Tar.

"Did you meet her when she was reporting the murder?"

"No, I was sick. I lived next door to the pub then, and Aoife Hussey kept me up to date, but she never let on that I worked for Mrs. Walter. Neither did her husband Michael. Nor Frank, of course. Otherwise I'd have been destroyed; I could never keep my mouth shut. They'd have made mincemeat of me."

That seemed pretty unlikely to me. I started to ask a question but she brushed me aside. "That isn't all. Just wait till I tell you what happened next. I thought I might make a few enquiries of my own, so like the know-all I am, I offered her a lift, but she said she had one. Next thing, Jer O'Dowd comes purring up the drive. Now we know where he was off to when he nearly ran us down this morning."

"Is he interested in buying Coribeen?"

"Buying? Of course he's not, boy. He's selling. Wasn't it him bought the place from your mother? Didn't you know that?" I shook my head, and she was off. "Oh indeed. Isn't Smiler our very own property tycoon? And sharp with it, as I know to my cost. We thought we were getting a nice secluded property, but didn't that greedy bastard chop away the two fields on either side of The Old Corn Store before we completed, and next thing he built four houses, eight if you count the ones built on the site of his own house. Feckin' shark. Instant neighbours are all very well, but it wasn't quite what we had in mind." She snorted. "But Smiler O'Dowd was never one to pass up a bargain. He got stung on Coribeen, though." She chuckled gleefully. "He had all sorts of great plans for it—marina, hotel, golf course. But the laugh of it was, shortly after your mother sold up, the county boundaries were changed, and instead of the Duncreagh planning authority, which was in his pocket, he had to deal with Daingean, and that was a different kettle of fish entirely. Coribeen bested him, and I have a horrible feeling he blames it all on your mother. I'm not sure Smiler's the kind I'd like to cross; there's a spiteful side to him. Of course, the cute hoor is only selling about half an acre with the house, so God knows what he intends doing with the rest."

"Are you going to buy it?"

"Indeed and I'm not then. It's in an awful state, completely neglected," she said impatiently. "And I can tell you something else: that Fiona one hasn't the slightest notion of buying it either. So I ask myself what the hell was Smiler up to, chauffeuring her around? All pally-like. 'Hiya Fiona,' he said when he got out. 'I see you've met Marilyn. She'll tell you all about the Sweeneys.' The cheek. 'Wasn't she their cleaning lady?' I turned on my heel, but he wasn't finished. 'And didn't she work for poor Evangeline Walter as well?' She started saying something, but I ignored her and got in my car. I'll only kill that fella when I see him." Marilyn swept her hair off her flushed face. "The whole caper was weird. D'you know something, Gil? I had an awful feeling I'd stumbled into some sort of setup. I swear O'Dowd knew I was at Coribeen. The auctioneer must have tipped him off. Is that paranoia? God, I don't know, but whatever it is, I could only kick myself for going there at all. That Fiona one was all over him like a rash. Jer this, Jer that. All touchy-feelie. For a minute I was reminded of Mrs. Walter. Made my flesh crawl, it did. He's always been a terror for the women. Never local girls, mind you; Smiler likes something more exotic. A man for Sundays only, not a weekday bloke at all. The lord of the feckin' dance, he thinks he is."

Marilyn was really getting up a head of steam. "That reporter will be down on top of me any minute now, with her feckin' questions. Why the hell does she want to go dragging it all up again?" she burst out. "O'Dowd won't have any qualms about giving her my address, either. I'm going to make myself very scarce, up sticks and stay in Noreen's house for a few days, and the family with me. So my advice to you, Gil, is to do the same and get the hell out of here." She gave me an awkward little hug. "I don't know why I feel so upset. There was something very peculiar going on. D'you know what he shouted after me? 'Didn't I see you this morning with the young fella that's squatting in Spain's old cottage? I've a feeling I know him from somewhere.' He grinned at your one when he said it. With a what-did-I-tell-you look on his self-satisfied mug. Then he burst out laughing. Sounded a bit demented, to tell you the God's honest truth. Thinks he's so feckin' clever. But I hope he knows what he's doing, because that is one woman I would not like to cross. So go home, there's a good boy. Please. I've always been wary of that fellow, and maybe you should be, too."

"Why? He doesn't know me or where I've been staying, whatever he says, I've been really careful."

"Hmm. Not careful enough, I'd say. Same as young Noreen. Ye're not invisible. Several people have remarked on your presence to me. So I'd say Smiler has you pegged, all right."

"What does he look like, Mrs. Donovan?" I asked quietly. She looked at me oddly.

"Didn't you see him this morning when he almost ran into us?"

"Not really, just a quick glimpse."

"That'd be enough for most of us. He's always got a big bloody grin on his face, all the time wandering around in that great big car of his, with his feckin' sunglasses and the cap to hide his baldy head.

So, I *had* seen him. Twice. The first day in Hussey's and the night I met the Sullivan brothers in the pub. Damm.

"Where does he live?"

"He used to live next door to The Old Corn Store; now he's over the other side of the river, but he still has property on Trianach." She fell silent for so long I thought she'd forgotten I was there. "I didn't intend to pass this on," she said reluctantly, "because I'm not sure I understand what that creep was getting at. So I'll just repeat what he said after he claimed to know you from somewhere. 'Mrs. Walter's daughter Halcyon died last week, did you know that, Marilyn? Now there's an unfortunate could tell a story if she hadn't been so dumb. I hear Mrs. Sweeney that was, Mrs. Recaldo that is, showed up at the funeral in Clonmel. Isn't that the strange thing altogether? *Maybe poor Evangeline is going to get justice at last?*' And he took Ms. Moore by the

arm and led her to the car." Marilyn gnawed her bottom lip.
"Mark my words, that journalist is going to rake over the
whole mess again." She nodded slowly. "You'd better get
away from here fast, Gil. Today. I'm sorry things haven't
turned out for you, boy, but maybe you'll come back someday?" She smiled faintly. "Otherwise Noreen will never talk
to me again."

She left me in a complete spin, and I couldn't begin to
sort out my feelings. Up to then, I'd stowed my mother away
for the duration. She was supposed to be in Oxford or
Dublin. News of Halcyon's death didn't really affect me; I
hadn't seen her for ages, and anyway I never liked her, but
the thought of Cressie on the loose, and not far away, made
me realise just how out of touch and out of control I was.

After Marilyn left, I tried to ring home several times, but
nobody was there. I didn't leave a message. I went back over
Marilyn's story, and I worked out a plan. I got out my mobile again and rang Chief Inspector Phil McBride at Garda
headquarters in Dublin.

I was put through immediately, and he must have sensed
that something was up, because he was unusually serious.
No jokes, no nicknames. "Gil? What can I do for you?"

"I need to talk something over with you."

"Shoot."

"No, not on the phone. Could we meet?"

"When?"

"Tomorrow." I had worked out how long the journey to
Dublin would take if I got a lift to the railway station in
Cork."

"You still in France?"

"No, I'm back."

"But not at home?" He sounded more guarded. "I can't
see you tomorrow, Gil, I've something on. I could make it
later in the week or the weekend."

I took a deep breath. "I'm in West Cork. Trianach."

There was a long silence. "And your folks don't know."
It wasn't a question, so I didn't answer. "Is that what you
want to see me about? You'd be better off talking things
over with your parents."

What could I say? That they had their chance, ten years of chance, and blown it? That I had questions they might not want to answer? "Phil, please. I need to know what happened."

"Need? You talk to anyone down there?"

I hesitated. "Yeah. Marilyn Donovan."

"What about?"

"The American woman's murder." I didn't want to admit I knew her name.

"Oh. Right. Make contact with anyone else?"

"No."

"No? So what's troubling you, exactly?"

"Being here brought things back. I went to The Old Corn Store. Phil? I remember what happened in the garden that night. My mother was there, John Spain . . . Cressie . . ." My voice wobbled. Shit, I was turning into a right crybaby.

"I know all that. Listen to me, Gil. Whatever you remember or think you remember, your mother didn't do it." He spoke firmly and calmly but didn't give me a chance to butt in. "Gil? Think carefully. Can you recall seeing anyone else in the garden?" His voice seemed to come from miles off.

"Yes."

"Yes? Yes? Do you know who it was?"

"I only saw his feet."

"Oh."

"Brown brogues, same as my father's." I said it aloud for the first time and felt like Judas. "I smelt his aftershave."

"Jaysus," he let out a low whistle. "I'll meet you in the back room of Boswell's Hotel in Molesworth Street. Two o'clock. If you get to Dublin sooner, give me a ring. Here or at home. Gil? Go straight there. Don't talk to anyone else. Not anyone. Do you hear me?" He put down the phone before I could ask if that included my parents. I packed my things and sat down to wait. Shay came to the cottage at about six, just when I'd given up hope of seeing her. She saw the backpack the minute she came in.

"You're going?"

"Yeah, I have to. I can't hack it. I have to sort my head out. I'm sorry, Shay." I felt numb.

"There's nothing I can do, is there? To change your mind? Will I see you again?" she mumbled.

I put my arms around her. "I hope so. I'll write. E-mail. Phone. I've decided to travel for another year. Far away—Australia, the States. Maybe we could start college at the same time?" Fantasy, fantasy.

She snorted. "And I suppose you expect me to . . . Ah, feck it, Sweeney . . ."

"Please don't call me Sweeney," I said quietly. "Please."

"It was just . . . it was just . . . Oh Gil, I didn't mean anything by it."

"I know you didn't, but it makes me very uncomfortable," I said as calmly as I could, then immediately lost it. "Ask your aunt about the Sweeneys," I shouted. "Ask her. She knows more about us than anyone. Ask her."

"Shush." She put her head against my chest and rocked back and forth. "Come and lie down for a bit? It's too late to go tonight. I'll get the aunt to give you a lift to Duncreagh or Cork tomorrow morning." She giggled. "She doesn't trust me to get to school on my own."

_____regression 12

twenty-nine

Duncreagh Listening Post

(archive discovered by Gil Recaldo)
EXTRAORDINARY SCENES AT PASSAGE SOUTH AS
FISHERMAN HERO IS BURIED AT SEA

SHAY STAYED SO late I was surprised Marilyn didn't come
after me with a shotgun. After she left, I allowed myself to
doze for an hour or so until it was too late for her to come
back or for any of my invisible neighbours to be out and
about. I felt odd, as if I was travelling outside my own body,
as I slipped out into the velvety dark night just as I had on
the night of the murder.

My mother is still sleeping curled up on the bed, still
wearing her black sweater and jeans, when I follow Tar out
onto the lane. He has gone ahead and doesn't seem aware
that I am after him. For once he isn't wearing his overalls,
so he is harder to see in his old navy Guernsey and cords
with his tattered sailor cap on his head. I hide behind a rock

until he gets into the boat and rows away. Then I climb the spit.

When I get to the top he's coming around the other side, a little way out and pulling hard against the current. That's when my father's launch glides away from the bank, further on, and cuts across towards Coribeen. Tar has his back to it, but I suppose he must hear it. He turns his head.

I sit watching him struggle with the tide for a long time, and when he's far enough ahead, I slither down the slippery side of the spit and run after him along the shore. At first I can't find him in the dark, but then the moon shines through the clouds, and I see he's already left the boat, which is bobbing between the oars he'd somehow wedged upright into the mud, between me and the woman's garden. There's a full moon, but it's cloudy, so that one minute the garden is all lit up, the next it's plunged into darkness, like lights going on and off, and I see what happens in minuscule, disjointed episodes.

Tar is running, crouched, up the hill to the house. The huge French windows are wide open, but the lights are out. The woman is lying on the terrace close to the window, exactly where my mother left her. There is something around her head—a scarf?—but otherwise she is naked. She is lying on her stomach with her bottom in the air like I do when I've a pain in my belly. There is something white, maybe her dress, lying a little to one side. Tar bends over her for a long time. I cannot see what he's doing. He straightens up and disappears into the house, leaving the woman where she is. He doesn't help her or anything, so she must be dead. *Cressie killed her! No, no, no.* I start shaking and crying. *No! Please God, let her not be dead.* The moon goes in. Nothing happens for a long, long time. The tide is beginning to run in, and soon I won't be able to get back to the cottage on foot. I wade out to the rowing boat and climb aboard. There's a folded tarpaulin under one of the seats. I pull it out and try to wrap it around myself, but it's stiff and cold. I lie on my stomach with my good arm on the side and wait for Tar. I can't keep my eyes open.

I don't know how long I remain under the tarpaulin. I

keep expecting Tar to come back, but he doesn't. When I peep out again, moonlight floods the garden. Now the woman is covered with a blanket or something. A big square thing standing on the terrace by the open side gate catches my eye. It's too far to make out clearly, but I think it's a big box or a trunk with brass handles. It glints as the light catches it. Next thing, I see Tar coming up—up?—the garden, and he must see the box as well, because he goes up to it. He doesn't touch it but stands looking down at it until the headlights of a car light up the drive outside the open gate.

Tar scarpers sharpish, although I can't see where, because I'm busy watching the headlights get nearer and nearer. The car turns; I see the rear brake lights and then the white reverse lights come closer and closer to the opening. I gasp when I see my father come around the back of his silver Lexus. He goes over to the box and picks it up. It must be heavy, because he staggers and almost falls down. He puts it into the boot and goes back for something else still lying on the grass, which he tosses in beside the box. As he stands at the open boot, I notice he's changed into something dark—a suit maybe. He walks across to where the woman is lying and stops dead. He looks around, then bends down and lifts what's covering her and holds it in the air. It's a white dress or something, but she's not under it. She's gone. I sit bolt upright. She isn't dead. The woman isn't dead. My mother didn't kill her. I want to shout it out, I am so relieved.

But what is my father up to? He tosses the cloth on the table and goes into the house. The lights come on, lots of lights. I can see right inside. He walks around and around as if he's looking for something. Or someone. My heart is in my mouth for fear he'll find Tar and there'll be a big fight. But it doesn't happen. The light from the open window reaches well down the lawn, and just where the steep incline flattens out, Tar is lying facedown on the grass, with his arms covering his head, trying not to be seen. I don't know how long my father stays inside the house—a few minutes, no more. When he comes out, he stands on the terrace. My

heart begins to thump. Now he'll see Tar for sure, but he
doesn't seem to. Yet he's looking in the right direction, facing the river. He raises his arm and waves. Waves? I turn
around to see who he's waving to, and there is the woman
leaning against the tree with a long scarf trailing in the
breeze. When I look up to the house, my father is gone.

I watch the headlights go off into the distance before Tar
moves. He is stiff when he gets up, and it takes a moment
for him to straighten. He goes over to the woman. The scarf
seems to be tangled in the low branches of the tree. I can't
make out what's happening, what he's doing by the tree, but
he must be talking to her, because when the moon comes out
again, I see she is standing beside him and his arms are still
around her. That makes me angry, because we don't like her;
she's bad. They fall backwards on the grass. Oh no, oh no, I
don't want him to start all that kissing stuff again. I shut my
eyes tight, tight. When I look again, Tar is going into the
house, but the woman is lying on the grass near the tree,
stretched out, like she's asleep.

Tar is inside for a few minutes, and when he come out,
he's holding a bucket and sweeping brush. He throws some
water on the terrace and brushes it down just as it starts to
rain. He goes back in. I keep expecting the woman to run in
out of the wet, but she doesn't. And suddenly I know it's because she's dead. Really dead. But how come I didn't see it
happen? Did I fall asleep when she and Tar were rolling on
the grass? He killed her, he killed her. I don't know how, but
I'm relieved it wasn't my mother. But what was my father
doing? Why was he there? I held my swollen arm close. He
could hurt a person without even trying. Why did he wave
at Tar? Because he knew the woman was dead? Oh God,
he's going to come after us again. He saw me in the garden.
Now he'll kill me for sure.

What's that? There's a shadow at the top of the garden.
The house lights go out. A shadow? I peer into the half light
and for a split second, I see someone all in black running
across the window. Not Tar; he is still in the house. Smaller.
Mama. What is she doing? She's gone. Maybe I imagined it?
I could have. Now I am so frightened I wriggle down well

into the boat and keep very still. After a little time, a small bundle is shoved in under the tarpaulin beside me and the boat sinks down into the water and begins to move. The tide is roaring in, and the rain is lashing down.

I touch the bundle with my free hand, cloth with paper wrapped loosely around two small, hard things. I feel them all over but I can't figure out what they are. The boat stops. I feel Tar climb out. I wait. His hand feels under the tarpaulin and pulls out the bundle. I stay very, very still. Maybe I dropped off to sleep? When I next peep out, it's pitch dark. The rain has stopped, and Tar is nowhere in sight. I pull the cover back and climb out. The ground underfoot is slippery. I'm halfway to the cottage when I remember I didn't fold away the tarpaulin. I run back and trip over a rock. Next thing I know, I'm being carried into the house by my mother. Tar is walking beside us, holding on to her. My arm is throbbing.

I LEFT THE spit for the last time and walked like a zombie up to John Spain's cottage. It was three o'clock in the morning. I closed the door and shot the bolt. Then I lay on the sofa and ran back over everything that had happened to me since my return to the estuary. I knew I had missed something, perhaps many things. And I knew that I couldn't leave the cottage until I'd worked it out. But I was completely bushed. I dozed and woke and slept again. I got so cold I crept back into the musty old bedroom and wrapped myself in my sleeping bag. It smelt of Shay. I snuggled down into it, and at last I fell asleep.

I had the weirdest dreams, all featuring Tar, and he was desperate to tell me something. We were together on the boat, watching the seals slither off the crags. We were hauling a fish basket up to the cottage door. We were in his car delivering lobsters to a restaurant. We were in the cottage at the table doing our work. I was writing in my copybook, and he was at the sink. At first he was standing with his back to it, pointing out something. Next he had his back to me. He bent down under the old Belfast sink and after a minute or

two straightened up with something in his hands. Something
for me. Now I am hunkered down beside him, and he is
pointing at the wall under the sink. He pulls out a Mars bar
and laughs. "Magic," he says, and gives it to me.

I was shaking when I woke up, from cold and from fear.
It took me a little time to work up the energy to get up and
brew some coffee over the paraffin stove. I was frozen, hungry, and filthy. I needed a bath and something big and fatty
to eat. But not yet.

We had this game. He would say a word—Beano, tof-
fee, biscuit—and when I worked it out, I'd find whatever
he'd named in the secret hiding place. Magic. I knelt down
beside the sink. It was smelly and mouldy underneath, and
first off I plunged my hand into a nest of mice. I nearly
threw up at the sight of the naked little wriggling bodies;
there seemed to be hundreds of them. I gritted my teeth and
felt along the wall behind the U-bend where I could feel the
edges of one brick standing proud of its neighbours. It came
away easily because the mortar was damp and crumbly. I
put my hand into Tar's secret hiding place and felt around
it gingerly, afraid of finding more mice. I drew out a small
package: a plastic sandwich bag with a bunch of keys and
an old mobile phone wrapped in a bit of newspaper. With
my heart in my boots, I opened the scrap of the *Irish Times*
and looked at the mobile. It was about three times the size
of mine with what looked like a rechargeable battery attached to the back. Quite a weight in your pocket. I'd no
idea why it was there. I examined the keys. The leather tab
with the makers' mark had almost completely perished, but
the metal Lexus tag was intact. I searched the back of the
cavity again and found a second bit of plastic, stuck fast to
the floor. I eased up one corner and gradually worked my
fingers underneath until I could wrench it free. This bag
was folded over and sealed with perished cello tape. Inside
was a small yellowing envelope with faded writing on the
front; I brought it over to the window. My name was on the
envelope, faded but still readable. Inside was a letter from
Tar. Three or four pages written in pencil so that it survived
the damp. Clever Tar.

My Dearest Gil,

I write in the event that you return, as I believe you will one day. For the past three days I have been in my boat writing, writing. It is hard to say good-bye, not to see you and your mother again. You have been the most precious joy of my last years.

My boy, I have lately been accused of corrupting you, and your dear mother has been accused of colluding with me. I can hardly bring myself to speak these things or defend myself. For what defence is there if the poison has already gained ground? I pray you know with the same certainty as I that abusing your mother's or your trust in me would be the very last thing on earth I would do. I swear you were always safe with me. But protestations are useless, useless.

The architect of this calumny is dead, and very soon so shall I be. Would that the rumours die so easily. I killed her. Oh yes, it was I. I may not have given her the coup de grâce, but I struck the first blow. I didn't intend it, but that is what happened. What troubles me more than what I've done, or am about to do, is that you may have witnessed more than any of us realised. I write to set the record straight.

The girl with the strange name, Halcyon Walter, was the catalyst. Your father's first, unacknowledged child. Poor innocent creature was in the care of an order of nuns in Tipperary, of which my own sister is a member. On the day Evangeline Walter realised this, she knew she could keep the girl secret no longer and turned on me. It was suspected that Halcyon's condition was caused by neglect or abuse and, in your father's absence, the blame fell on Evangeline. She'd been after him for years. When you lost your hearing and speech, and it became known around the township that your father was abusing you and your mother, something seems to have snapped in Mrs. Walter; her resolve to destroy Sweeney hardened.

She attacked him every way she knew, financially and personally. Others may be able to explain how, since I don't know the details. What I do know is that the more she goaded him, the more he went to pieces. When his business failed, his attacks on your mother grew more and more ferocious.

When he was forced to sell his beloved yacht, Mrs. Walter bought it, using Smiler O'Dowd as her go-between. Sweeney must have realised who was behind the scheme when she changed the name to Halcyon. She did it as soon as she came out of hospital, terminally ill with cancer. It was then she arranged a sailing party to introduce her deaf-mute, brain-damaged daughter to her father and incidentally to the neighbours. Anyone looking at the two together would know exactly who she was. I did, O'Dowd did, Cressie did. And so, my dear Gil, did you.

If a murder has a beginning, that was it. You mentioned seeing her to your father. He threatened to have me charged and you taken into care. He beat the living daylights out of you both, then lit out for Trianach in the launch. Despite her and your injuries, Cressie came to warn me, but unfortunately I had already gone to plead with Mrs. Walter myself. Cressie followed me, with you in the car and the whole thing spiraled out of control.

I'm filling in this background because over the past few days, I'm worried that if indeed you saw what happened in that accursed garden, you may misinterpret it. If so, you will surely read this. I killed Evangeline Walter by forcing myself on her two weeks after she had a major stomach operation. She was high on medication and drugs, and I was beside myself with anger. I lost control and violated her savagely. Cressie tried to save me and inadvertently knocked Mrs. Walter to the ground. I believe your father was also concealed in the garden and saw what happened; his launch was tied up at the old slipway.

After I got you and Cressie safely back to this house, I went back—again, as I think you know. Between the two visits, Sweeney must also have used her. This I learned from Frank Recaldo, who is frantic about Cressie. I went back to the garden to check that she was all right. I never for a moment thought that Cressie's blow had done more than momentarily stun her. I've told Frank and the other detectives that it was I that killed her, but they won't believe me. I can't work it out. My head aches.

I heard the launch roaring across the estuary as I came close to the garden. I found her dead on the terrace, blood all over the place. I held myself responsible. I was responsible. I became so frantic I didn't know what I was doing. I carried her down to the cold river to try to revive her or clean her, but of course it was hopeless. Then Sweeney came back. I threw myself down on the grass and watched him put a pile of stuff into the boot of his car. When he saw the body was gone, he stood searching the garden. I thought he was looking at the body, which had accidentally got caught in the branches and was still leaning against the tree at the water's edge, but I believe now it was me he was seeking out. He couldn't have missed me lying on the grass near her. He gave a loud laugh and waved. Then he went into the house, switched on all the lights, and turned on the CD player. Ella Fitzgerald in top cry. It was obscene. He must have known she often played music late at night. I often heard it.

I began to panic—not for myself alone but for your mother. The woman had been left on the terrace when Cressida felled her. I was sure he was trying to set her up for the killing—wife catches husband in flagrante and attacks his lover—or her and me both, even better. I set about cleaning things up, obfuscating the evidence. I went inside the house and saw at once that the floor was damp as if it had been mopped. The place looked undisturbed, neat and clean, but I wiped all the surfaces anyway. I found a small tape recorder under a folded newspaper on the coffee table, which he somehow overlooked, and her mobile phone, which had dropped behind the sofa. I listened to the tape until I could bear no more. Dear God, she was sick in mind as well as body. She goaded him into doing what I started. We are all damned. I never intended to evade justice, Gil, but I didn't want your mother dragged down in the mire.

We found you lying unconscious in the cove at three that morning. As soon as we strapped up your arm, I sent you and your mother off to the hospital in Cork. She was in a dreadful state; she kept telling me she'd lost the comb she used to hold back her hair. I promised to go back and look for it, but instead I drove my old banger to Coribeen. The house was in darkness but the Lexus was outside. I let myself in the back door, which was never locked. Sweeney was snoring on the sofa, a half-empty bottle of *whisky on the floor beside him. He didn't wake up when I fished the car keys from his jacket pocket. I drove the Lexus away and hid it on an abandoned farm where it wouldn't be found. I threw mud at the car until it was well covered and went back on foot for my own.*

It was nearly five o'clock when I got home. I changed into my overalls and rowed back to the garden to do a final check before I called Recaldo. I used her mobile phone, which I'd taken from the house. In my panic, I completely forgot to look for Cressie's comb. I let her down.

I am afraid, and afraid of what this might do to you. And that is why I have to make sure there is no trial. For if any of the three of us stands accused, then the stories about me will be taken for fact and Cressie will surely lose you. I am damned anyway. If I can die a hero's death it will staunch the flow, and both Sweeney and I will get what we deserve. It will be justice of a kind. Justice without charity. Forgive me.

It is now five-thirty on Saturday morning. I have been watching Coribeen for days. Sweeney's been hiding in the attic and on one of the boats moored on the estuary whose owner is away. The loss of the car has unnerved him, as I intended. Now he'll be forced to flee by the yacht, leaving the car and evidence behind, and that's what I gambled on. Earlier, when there were few people about, I drove the Lexus to the supermarket car park in Duncreagh, which is always packed on a Saturday. I want it to be found, but not for a few hours. Another gamble. It's unrecognisable, caked all over with mud and dung. I am so tired.

I have the keys of the motor launch, and three spare cans of fuel. I hope it's enough. Sweeney went out to the yacht last night and is still there, so he is about to make his move. . . . I will go to Consuela for the last time and wait. Good-bye my boy. My house is yours should you want it, otherwise let it go back to the earth.

Tar

I rolled up Tar's things in one of my T-shirts and put it in my backpack. I took one last look around and let myself out.

thirty

Sean, Saw the charwoman as well, but she's keeping mum. There is a gallery owner I might tap
into. The daughter died. According to Slimer she
was the image of the sibling—except she was
brain-damaged. But from what I heard elsewhere,
it seems the blessed Evangeline hadn't much time
for her, kept her locked away. Out of sight, etc.
And while I'm on the subject—have I got news for
you! Shy Mrs. Recaldo showed up at Lulu's school
this morning. You'll never guess who she turns
out to be. This is good, this is great. The copper married the murderer's wife! My, my, isn't
he the dark one? Talk about the long arm of the
law. No wonder he left the force. Peach-eee! More
anon.
Fi

THE RECALDOS WERE having a strange and wonderful inter-
lude. Something miraculous had happened between them
since Cressida's return home; the tension had lightened. Su-
perstitious about enquiring too closely into the causes of this
blissful hiatus, or discussing it, they put all their previous problems and disagreements down to their prolonged separation.
Now they were together at last, things would work out fine.

The evening following her return, Frank opened a bottle
of Brouilly, and he and Cressie sat on either side of the
kitchen table going through the estate agents' bumph.

"Thanks for giving me space, Frank," she said. "And for
getting this stuff." She put her hand on top of the pile and sat
back in her chair. "But I'm not sure this is the best time for
a move. I know I've been banging on about it, but Katie
May seems to like the school, and now that Gil is away, this
place doesn't seem so small, does it?"

"He'll be back." Frank put his hand on hers. "You're
thinking of me, aren't you? The operation?"

"Well, yes, of course I am. It helps to be near a decent
hospital and good GP. We have both here. I think we should
at least bear it in mind, don't you?"

"I think the same, but I don't like this place any more
than you do. I've always seen it as a transition stage. I never
thought we'd be here this long." He took a long draught.
"This is good. I could get used to decent wine, couldn't you?
Look love, moving Katie, if we do it quickly enough, won't
be a problem; she's very enthusiastic about living in the
country. We talked about it a lot while you were away. As
long as there's a kennel for your man Rafferty, she'll be
fine." He rubbed the back of Cressie's hand. "Oh, Cress, my
darlin', I'm that pleased to have you back. When I think—"

"Of how we were both feeling and behaving a week ago?
Yeah, me, too." She leaned across the table and kissed him.
"I love you, Frank Recaldo, you know that? Everything's
going to work out, isn't it?" She leafed through the particu-
lars until she came to a glossy folder marked "Coribeen"
that Frank had placed in the middle of the pile, without
comment. She looked up. "Where did this come from?" she
asked. She seemed neither surprised nor upset.

Frank watched with interest as she read through it and studied the picture.

"I didn't realise it was there 'til we got home. We picked up so many, I binned most of them. Can we talk about it, Cress?"

There was a moment's hesitation before Cressie got up and, without a word, went into the hall.

That's torn it, he thought.

But no, she came back almost at once, carrying her voluminous shoulder bag. She gave him a rueful little smile as she plunged her hand into it and brought out an identical prospectus. "Yes," she said. "We do need to talk about Coribeen. Or at least I do. You've always wanted to, but I've been so, so repressive." She smiled wanly. "Still am. But the time has come." She took his hands in hers. "I've been on a pilgrimage to the holy shrine. That's what it became, you know. I could never get it out of my head. I resented leaving it so much that I lost sight of what it did to me, what it represented. Frank? I went back. I've seen it."

"When?" he asked though he'd already guessed.

"After Halcyon's funeral. Rose O'Faolain showed up. I was so surprised to see her, but apparently Murray asked her to help. I hadn't realised she'd arranged a memorial service for Evangeline Walter a few months after we left." Cressie's voice wobbled on the hated name, but after a moment, she continued. "I'm not sure Murray realised Grace kept in touch with Rose. I certainly hadn't, but I was glad to see her. She had the details with her. She thought we'd be interested because it was so cheap. And of course I was. I couldn't wait to see it. So we drove down after the funeral. She borrowed the key from her pal the auctioneer that evening after hours, and we viewed it early next morning." She paused. "The whole thing was a terrible mistake—though maybe it wasn't. But it certainly was a shock. Nobody's lived in the house since we left, and it's had no maintenance either. It's almost back to how I first found it. Not quite, but pretty bad. O'Dowd was never able to get any of the planning permissions he wanted. He's hived off the land and restored the old path to the main road. Otherwise it's as it was. I only got as far as the front hall, Frank." Cressie began to tremble. "Rose waited outside. I stood in the hall, and all I could remember was standing holding Gil's little hand and the two of us shaking like leaves. The smell of fear is still there. I'm not imagining it. I thought of how desperately unhappy I was. Not about how much I loved it. I thought about Gil, too, and I couldn't get out fast enough."

Cressie's head was down, her hands clasped. "Frank? Oh, Frank, I realised something terrible. I kept saying I loved Coribeen. I used that as an excuse not to leave Val. I told myself it was my anchor, my security. Frank, I sacrificed Gil to a pile of bricks."

"And yourself, too, *mo craoi.** You were afraid of losing Gil. Don't forget that. You did what you thought best at the time." *Ponderous platitudes,* he thought and tried again. "Cress, you were absolutely paralysed with fear. Don't underestimate what that did to you. The man was evil. Cressie, he was a bully; he controlled you. That's what abuse does."

"But how could I have exposed Gil? Look what Val did to Halcyon."

"You didn't know that at the time," Frank said reasonably.

"I knew Gil was in danger. I should have taken him away. How could I have put all that out of my mind? I mourned that house for years and years, looking over my shoulder for so long I couldn't see what was in front of my eyes. This is the hard bit, Frank. I blamed you for taking me away. I can't believe it now. You did everything for us, provided us with love, shelter, a home." She waved her hands around the room. "And our beautiful daughter. All I could do was whinge on and on about how dismal this place was."

Frank burst out laughing. "Oh, come on, don't be tragic about it. It *is* dismal. And I don't remember all that much whinging. You think I like it? Of course I don't. But darlin', we've been happy here, haven't we? In our fashion," he sang. "In our way."

But Cressie didn't laugh. "Oh yes," she said fervently. "I

*my heart

didn't appreciate how happy until I went back to Coribeen and remembered what my life was like before I met you." She brightened. "It broke the spell. Even the view is different. There are new houses everywhere. There isn't a square inch of space on the Passage South side. That beautiful view? Gone. I was glad of that, too. I think her house must have been knocked down, you know. There seems to be a hotel or something in its place, covered with balconies." She shivered. "I wouldn't stay there. Not for anything."

"Cressie love, one of these days soon we have to talk to Gil about it all."

"I suppose so," she agreed reluctantly. "But darling, Gil doesn't remember any of it. He's never once asked, in all these years."

"That doesn't mean he hasn't any memories, Cress. Haven't you noticed how withdrawn he's become in the past couple of years?"

"Adolescence?"

"Oh, Cress, he's eighteen; he should be way past that. We're going to have to find a way. Together."

"He hasn't said anything to you, has he?" she asked anxiously. "God, how could we begin?"

"I suppose we could just make it easy for him to talk, ask questions?"

"But we've never stopped him, have we?" she asked.

Frank didn't want to spoil the mood by saying that the bond between her and her son was so intense that Gil would do anything to spare her anxiety. So he let it lie. "You didn't see O'Dowd?"

"No, thank God, I didn't see anyone. Didn't want to. And I don't want to go back. Ever."

"What about John Spain's cottage?" he asked, treading on eggs. "Gil will have to be told about that sometime soon."

"I couldn't bear to go near it. It would bring it all back."

"But he left it to Gil. The boy should at least be told, Cress—he's eighteen."

"How can we? Oh, Frank, that gossip about poor John Spain has never really died away. Rose told me."

"But you know there's no foundation in it. You know

that. I know that, and I bet if you asked Gil, he'd say the same. John Spain was a good man; Gil adored him. That kind of trust doesn't come through fear."

"I know. When he comes back for university, I promise, Frank, I'll talk to him. I'll sort it all out. But whether Gil wants to or not, I'm never again going back."

"Right then," Frank said and poured more wine. "So that's Cork out, is it?"

Instead of answering, Cressie dug in her bag again and passed him a one-page estate agent's listing. "Would you consider Wexford?" she asked shyly.

"You went to Wexford as well? You *have* been buzzing around."

"Rose again. She suggested it. I had the watercolours from Elsfield in the car, and I showed them to her. They aren't her sort of stuff, but she has a nephew who deals in watercolours and small works of art. He has a gallery in Wexford town. So I took a huge detour on the way home and dropped in on him. Rose came, too." She was bursting with excitement. "He's looking for a partner. They suggested I use the collection to start me off. There are fifty good paintings and about as many prints, so enough to start buying and selling. I'd like to give it a go. What do you think?"

"Good. Seems so obvious when you think about it. Everything you've done—your years working for Rose and then Grace—all seem to lead the one way." He got up and took her in his arms, and they waltzed languidly around the kitchen.

"Wexford, eh? I'd really like that. It's a great idea. The opera festival. Good sailing," Frank was excited. "Estuaries galore. Let's ring Gil and tell him." But Gil's mobile was switched off.

"He's probably out crewing," Cressie said. It never occurred to either of them that their son had taken matters into his own hands. But that was about to change.

thirty-one

ON THE FRIDAY after Cressie got home, Katie May's class
was taken on an outing to Dublin zoo. That afternoon, while
Cressida waited with a group of parents outside the school
gate, the headmistress came out and told them that the bus
was delayed in traffic and wouldn't be at the school for at
least a half hour. Cressie set off to a nearby park for a short
stroll and returned about twenty minutes later.

On the way back, she passed Gil's old school and had a

sense of *déjà vu* as she thought about her early years in Dublin, when Gil was little and the fear of being hounded by the press was intense. The brouhaha about the TV and Frank's forthcoming book brought it all back, especially when he told her just how much publicity he was expected to do. And although his illness had given him an excuse to back out gracefully, she worried that someone would rake up the murder and make the connections they'd gone to such pains to hide.

"My love, it's a long, long time. I've been very careful, always."

"We've got Daddy's money, Frank. You don't . . ." She was afraid to ask him to retire, but as usual, he knew what she was thinking and did a skilful little detour. "Ah, Cressie love, how long do you think that will last after we pay off Gil's school loan? It'll hardly cover the rest of Katie May's fees; they're going up all the time. And then there's Gil's university and the move."

Listening to this middle-class *angst,* so unexpected coming from Frank, made them both laugh.

"Oh Frank? What's happening to us?"

"Pathetic, isn't it? But all this won't last. It might, but the chances are it won't—at least not at this level."

"We don't need to move, not yet anyway."

"But you said—"

"Yes. A load of old guff. We'll manage, as long as we're together."

After the turmoil of the previous months, she was slightly amazed at how glad she was to be home. She still didn't like the house, but somehow the realisation that it wasn't going to be forever made it much more acceptable. Katie loved the new school and was quickly making friends. Hardly an ideal moment to up sticks, but Frank had taken the Wexford proposal on board and seemed determined to make it happen. Cressida suspected that it was his way of clinging to the future while he tried to come to terms with the forthcoming operation, so she played along.

That Frank had been so fearful of telling her, afraid she couldn't handle looking after him, appalled her and made her wake up to how dismally she'd treated him for the past few years. When she realised just how terrified he was, her previous resentments turned to remorse. He had a phobia about hospitals, which wasn't surprising, considering his family's medical history—his father and elder brother both died of coronary disease. The knowledge that Frank was too proud to ask for her help broke her heart and pinpointed the sad state of their relationship. His previous marriage had foundered during his first bypass, and they had got dangerously close to the same edge.

Watching Grace and Murray drifting inexorably towards the rocks had finally woken her up to how much she loved him, needed him, and wanted to be with him. All their other problems, including the fear that Frank's fame would draw down unwanted publicity, were nothing compared to losing him.

She was shocked by his appearance when she got back, partly because she'd somehow managed to ignore the danger signals. He'd been irritable and tired in Oxford when she was too preoccupied with her own grievances to notice how defeated he seemed. She was further bamboozled by how much more himself he'd been in Waterford, buoyed up by the excitement of the TV film perhaps. But even then she, poor goose that she was, didn't observe how he avoided activity. None of his usual vigorous walks with her and Katie trailing miles behind. They'd strolled sedately by the river a couple of times but nothing more. Watching him trying to disguise the effort of moving stuff from the car the night she got home was another matter. He seemed to be thinking and moving through a field of molasses, sluggish of speech and action. The Grim Reaper shifted position.

Cressida walked along the suburban street looking neither to left or right. *I could be waiting for death,* she thought, *waiting for it to stroll around the corner and grab him.* At night, in the darkness of their bedroom, they talked for hours as they faced the best and the worst. The previous day, he'd done one interview with a journalist from the *Daily News,* a man called Sean Brophy, who seemed to know too much about him, and Frank had come home deeply upset. "I'm effing useless at dissembling. I was a complete eejit to allow myself to be talked into it. I'm not doing any more," he promised. "I don't give a fig if it affects the sales or not. Cress? Would you be an angel and ring Rebecca and tell her to cancel everything," he said. "She won't argue with you if you tell her I'm not well."

"I've been trying to get hold of Gil, Frank. I'd like him to come home."

"He's due any day, isn't he? But maybe it wouldn't be a bad idea to get him to come a little earlier?"

We should tell him. We should have told him many things. It was in both their minds. *One day soon,* she resolved for the umpteenth time. *When Frank is out of hospital, I'll take my lovely boy away for a couple of days and tell him everything.*

"If you can get hold of him. He seems to have become very elusive. Did you tell him about Halcyon?"

"No, I couldn't reach him, and I didn't want to leave a message."

Now as she strolled past Gil's old school, in the warm autumnal sunshine, she realised she hadn't actually spoken to Gil for several weeks. He left snappy little messages on her mobile or on the answering machine at home, at odd hours, which he explained was due to the fact that he was now crewing and had little time to himself. She presumed he'd met a girl. She clung to that thought. He'd stopped sending Katie May postcards. Definitely a girl.

She was almost in sight of the school when she heard someone call, "Mrs. Sweeney." Her heart lurched, but she walked on resolutely, turning neither to the left or right. But there it was again. "Oh, Mrs. Sweeney." This time the voice was low, insinuating, as if spoken down a long tube, giving a sense of distance. Cressida froze. Nobody used surnames anymore, did they? She must have imagined it. Then she heard it again. "Oh, Mrs. Sweeney."

After a decent pause, Cressida turned casually and looked up and down the street. Bumper-to-bumper parked cars, one, a mud-spattered black Mercedes, had a sinister-looking bloke with dark glasses, sitting motionless behind the wheel, for all the world like a Mafia boss waiting to pounce. And while Cressida chided herself for imagining things, she was relieved when several pedestrians and a couple of very ordinary young men wheeled their bikes past her, obviously headed for the school. She glanced at the group of women chatting outside the school gate. One of them, catching her eye, nodded vaguely in her direction. Cressie smiled back but made no attempt to join them but instead pulled her mobile phone from her bag and pretended to make a call while the crowd at the gate gradually swelled. Nine women, four men so far. Had the voice been male or female? Hard to tell since it was little more than a whisper. Maybe it was inside her own head?

She was blasted into reality by a loud squawk. "Oh rats, don't tell me the bloody bus is late?" A woman, who had just run her car half onto the pavement, barely avoiding Cressie, leaned out of the window.

"It should be along in about ten minutes," Cressida replied mildly.

"Ten minutes? Are you sure?" The newcomer opened the car door and struggled out. "I'm going to be late. Damn." She tugged nervously at her watch. "I have a dental appointment." She was plump, good-looking, and carelessly but fashionably dressed in black. Like many of the parents, she looked a bit long in the tooth to be the mother of a primary schoolchild. Cressida looked at her more closely. Dishevelled with purpose. The light wool suit was a bad fit but still managed to give off a hint of expense and would have suggested "cool" were it not for the fact that it looked as though it had recently been recycled from a full laundry basket. Her shoulder-length dark hair was well cut and shone. She wore full makeup and an expensive looking silver neckband.

"The headmistress came out a while ago and said the bus was held up in traffic. The driver phoned in," Cressie murmured. She'd never seen the woman before and wondered who she was.

"You're Katie May's mum, aren't you?" There was something vaguely familiar about her face, but Cressida couldn't place her. "Lulu talks about her all the time." She smiled.

"Lulu Stephenson?" Cressida looked at Mrs. Stephenson with interest. Katie May was smitten with her daughter Louise—known as Lulu—whom Cressida had not yet met.

Her companion started rubbing her jaw. "This tooth is driving me insane," she said. "If I miss this appointment, it'll take weeks . . ."

Cressida knew what was coming.

"Would you mind?"

"I could take Lulu home to play with Katie May," she offered grudgingly.

Mrs. Stephenson practically fell on her neck. "Oh, you wouldn't, would you? You sure?" She smiled broadly. "That's really kind. I'll do the same for you sometime, promise. I'm Fiona, by the way," she said and held out her hand. "You're Cressida Recaldo, aren't you? I love your name," she gushed.

Icy fingers clutched Cressie's heart. *How the hell does she know my first name?*

"I prefer Cressie," she said coldly. "Where do you live?" she asked quickly enough to catch the other woman on the hop.

"Blackrock. I'm still waiting to complete on a house." She named a street close to the school. "It's taking an absolute age. Meanwhile I've rented a grotty little flat that costs the earth." She touched her cheek again. "It shouldn't take long, an hour or so. I'll ring you as soon as I'm finished." Another big smile. "I'll just jot down your number."

"Blackrock's very convenient," Cressie said blandly. "I can easily drop Lulu off. Matter of fact, I have to collect something from Merrion Road around six. So if you'll just give me your address?" Game set and match. She watched Mrs. Stephenson leap into her car and drive off. She'd stopped rubbing her jaw. Cressie smiled ruefully. I'm too bloody suspicious, she thought. She relaxed; nevertheless, long practice and her innate caution made her note the make and colour of Fiona Stephenson's car. As well as the registration.

thirty-two

E-mail from Fiona Moore
To: Sean Brophy

Sean, The old toothache act worked wonders. But she was too canny to give me the phone number. Lucky I spotted Frank that day, or what? I've given O'Dowd the bird. If I hear another word about the wrong done to him by all and sundry, I'll scream. The canonization of the saintly Vangie continues. Yuk.
Fi
PS I've come up with another subject—a real peach and a load of sex.
Luv, Fi

KATIE MAY APPEARED to be both overwhelmed and dazzled by Lulu Stephenson's robust personality, though Cressie was less enamoured. Frank dealt with the rise in decibels by shutting himself in the dining room, which had been converted to a study in Cressie's absence. Rafferty alone was

full of enthusiasm, and the two little girls played with him
for most of the afternoon.

Cressie delivered Lulu home well before the arranged
time. Amazingly self-possessed, the little girl sat in the front
seat beside her and kept her entertained all the way. She was
nothing if not informative, and without any prompting from
Cressie, gave out a good portion of her family history. She
was born in San Francisco but lived in London and Cape
Town and other places she couldn't remember the names of.
She had a big brother who was at Cambridge. Katie May
was her best friend ever, in the whole world. She loved
Rafferty, and when they moved, which would be very soon,
she was going to get a puppy just like him. She rambled on
and on, long after Cressie had tuned out her squeaky little
voice. Or almost, since it was quite piercing. Her mommy
had a new friend, a nice man who might one day become her
new daddy. She'd had quite a few in different places, but
Sean was the nicest. Cressie was dying to ask the child what
her mother worked at that took her to so many far-off places,
but knowing how outraged she would be if Katie May was
pumped for information, she put temptation behind her.

"Can I play with Katie May tomorrow?" Lulu asked. "I
love going to your house. Rafferty's only gorgeous." And
she was off again, but Cressie was distracted, looking for the
apartment building. "It's over there," Lulu shouted. "Look,
there's Mommy." She pointed to her mother at a second-
floor window.

As Cressida looked up and waved, the woman stood up.
She bent over behind a curtain for a moment than straightened and waved back. Something about the sequence of her
movements made Cressie wonder if she'd been working at a
computer, shielded behind the half-drawn curtain.

"My mommy's writing a book," Lulu said proudly as
they walked, hand in hand, to the porch. "She writes for a
newspaper as well."

Cressie froze.

"Come on, Mrs. Recaldo, there she is."

Mrs. Stephenson was standing at the door holding her
hand to her cheek. Her speech was muffled as she thanked

Cressie and took delivery of her irrepressible child. She didn't ask Cressie in or offer her a cup of tea—not that Cressie would have accepted. But as she walked stiffly away from the apartment building, her relief at not being asked in did not blind her to how offhand Lulu's mother was compared to her hail-fellow-well-met friendliness outside the school. Somehow or other she didn't think it had anything to do with a toothache.

When she got home, she didn't mention the incident to Frank, who was cooking pasta. Katie May was sitting at the kitchen table, ostentatiously doing her homework. Later, while Cressie cleared away, Frank put his daughter to bed and read her a story.

When he came downstairs, he had Rafferty in his arms. He dumped him unceremoniously into his basket. "The kennel woman told me he was trained," he said. "Disgusting little brute's just peed all over the bathroom."

"Maybe Lulu will take him off our hands," Cressie said absently.

thirty-three

ON TUESDAY MORNING the Recaldos overslept. Plans to go house-hunting in Wexford while Katie May was in school were scrapped over a rushed breakfast. Which was something of a relief to Frank, who hadn't slept well. The previous day Phil McBride had told him about Gil's phone call and he'd lain awake half the night trying—and failing—to find a way to break the news to Cressida. After all their resolutions, he had failed at the first jump and as a result he felt stressed out and was desperate to get out of the house for a

breather. "I'll drop Katie May off, Cress. You stay and fin-
ish your breakfast," he said. Father and daughter were just
going out the door when the phone rang. Frank listened in
silence. "Cress?" he called. "That was Phil. He wants to talk
over something."

"But didn't you see him yesterday?"

"Yeah, that's what he wants to talk about," Frank said
truthfully.

Cressie came out of the kitchen drying her hands. "What
a nuisance. D'you have to?"

"Ye-es, I must." He thought for a moment. "Look, why
don't you go to Wexford on your own? If it's any good we
can all go down at the weekend. I'll pick up Katie May so
you won't have to rush back."

"Oh? That'd be good. Are you sure? It'll certainly be
much less of a rush if I don't have to be back for the school.
You won't forget, will you?"

"Oh, Cress, what do you take me for?" He grinned.
"Don't forget your mobile." He patted his pocket. "I've got
mine. Keep in touch." He kissed her tenderly on the lips.
"We'll have supper ready when you get back."

"Any idea how long you'll be with Phil?"

"He said a couple of hours or so."

Cressie laughed. "That'll be the whole day, then. I'll see
what I can find in Wexford."

"Daa-ddy! I'm going to be late," yelled Katie May.

"Coming. I'm coming, coming, coming," Frank shouted,
though he seemed curiously reluctant to leave. "Bye, darlin'." He kissed Cressie again. "I love you," he said quietly
as she hugged him close.

Cressida went back to the kitchen and poured herself another cup of coffee. She calculated that the rush-hour traffic
wouldn't clear for another half hour or so. She sat down at
the table and opened the morning's paper. It was book day.
She glanced idly through the arts section to see if they'd run
Sean Brophy's interview. They had. *Man of Mystery*. The
photograph was poor. Frank had cleverly sat with his back
to the light so that his face was in shadow. He also wore a
derby she'd never seen before, which made him look shifty

and absurd—like an out-of-work bookie. But definitely unrecognisable. Relieved, she began to read the interview.

The first couple of paragraphs were mainly about the
quality of his writing and the forthcoming TV series. After
that came the personal stuff. She read on with some anxiety.
Frank's whole working history was laid out in some detail,
though his real name wasn't mentioned. But anyone who
knew Inspector Frank Recaldo well would surely recognise
him in Frank Ventry even though Brophy had been skilful in
fudging the edges and there was no mention of his sojourn
in Passage South. His early retirement was put down to ill
health. The travel series was mentioned in passing though
not by the name. It might have been much worse, but she
knew Frank would dissect it, hate it.

She neatly reassembled the broadsheet, slipped the review section inside the main news, and folded the newspaper in two. As she placed it on the table, something she'd
missed the first time caught her eye. The narrow banner on
the front page had a running headline: "Review: Starting
today: True Crime: Unsolved Murder Mysteries by Fiona
Moore."

Cressie opened up the paper for the second time. The top
edges were damp and the first two pages were stuck together, which was probably why she hadn't noticed the article before. She eased them apart and laid the paper flat on
the table. The title ran over both pages: "The Dead Woman
Left Standing in Her Own Garden—The Unsolved Murder
of the Decade."

Underneath the byline was an inch-square photograph of
Fiona Moore. Cressida stared at it for a second or two before
she realised she was looking at Lulu Stephenson's mother.
The woman who'd addressed her as Cressida Recaldo. She
drew in a sharp breath and collapsed over the table. At first
she couldn't focus on the dancing print but she slowly forced
herself to read it several times through, from the twee opening: "This is the story of an abandoned woman, her gay lover,
her murderer, their mentally handicapped child, the handsome policeman, the deaf boy, and the unfrocked priest."

There followed a description of Evangeline Walter's

murder as told to the author by her closest friend and partner, "who every day lives with the pain of his beloved's death." Though the names had been changed, including Cressie's own, it was perfectly possible to recognise Smiler O'Dowd as the narrator. The *gay* narrator. His history was briefly outlined but with deadly accuracy. Cressie, who had never liked Smiler, nevertheless found herself hoping that the poor man had outed himself before Ms. Moore had so comprehensively done the job for him. Had she been less shocked on her own account, she might have wondered how the journalist had wormed her way into his confidence then mercilessly exploited his vulnerability. But that appeared to be her stock in trade. The details of the murder were alarmingly accurate, as were the conclusions. The article managed to be both salacious and holier-than-thou. Ms. Moore started with the difficulties of working single mothers, through the abandoned handicapped child, then neatly paired the rest of the characters. There was a snide innuendo of how John Spain drove his wife to suicide then turned his attention to little boys, specifically the *alleged* murderer's son—she was careful about the finer points of law—while his wife was banging the local policeman. Cressida read on, appalled, as her carefully constructed world caved in on her.

Exposed and defeated, Cressida sat staring into space. Images that she thought she'd buried crowded in on her. One above all: Gil, lying still and injured at the cove that terrible night. She'd gotten back to find Spain asleep, face down at the kitchen table, and crept unseen into the bedroom. Gil was gone. She'd screamed and run down to the estuary, where she stumbled across him, huddled awkwardly against a rock, soaking wet. As she bent to pick him up, she heard Spain cry out, "Oh dear God, he must have followed me." His despair matched hers. She should have walked into the water with her child in her arms, which was her instinct. Walk while Gil was still unconscious, walk until the waters closed peacefully over them. But Spain dragged her away. Once too often she allowed her actions to be dictated by well-meaning blunderers.

The newspaper article had shattered all her hopes for a

happy future with Frank. The same dead feeling of in-
evitability that had kept her at Coribeen all those years
seeped back. Now as then, her soul cried out for someone to
help her through the darkness, but even her beloved Frank
couldn't save her this time. Fiona Moore had damned them
all.

Cressida Recaldo closed the newspaper and nervously
folded it in two, uncreasing it with trembling hands, then refolding and refolding it, over and over. After a long time she
went upstairs like a sleepwalker, collected a warm jacket,
and left the house. She didn't carry a bag and left her mobile
phone lying on the kitchen table.

_____regression 13

thirty-four

Dublin Daily News

New unsolved murder series starts today by award-winning journalist Fiona Moore. Review section pages 2–4.

I LEFT BEFORE seven the next morning and picked up a lift to Cork about a mile out of Duncreagh. I was dropped off at Glanmirc Station and had breakfast while I waited for the train. I spoke to no one. As I went to buy my ticket, I was stopped in my tracks by a read-all-about-it billboard. "Award-Winning Fiona Moore's New Series Starts Today: Unsolved Murders—True Crime." Fiona Moore. I had a premonition about it before I picked up the *Daily News* and read: The handsome policeman, the deaf boy, and the un-frocked priest.

I got fully acquainted with the deadly Miss Fiona Moore on the train. I read her nasty, snide article three times, and each time I felt more and more exposed. Scum. One thing for sure, I didn't want to discuss it or see my parents for a

very, very long time. I pictured their reaction and felt sick.
After that I shut down and stared out the window. I stopped
feeling very much and stopped thinking completely. I felt
my life was over and that there was no way back for me.

I walked slowly along the south bank of the Liffey all the
way from Heuston Station. The day was fine, I think. At
least it wasn't raining. I turned into Temple Bar and cut
across College Green, through Trinity College to the Nassau
Street gate and from there up Kildare Street. I counted off
the streets from a list in my head, like a zombie.

I'd never been in Boswell's Hotel before and arrived a little before the appointed time. It was opposite the Dáil—the
government buildings on Kildare Street. I remembered that
it was well-known as a haunt of politicians and journalists,
when I saw two or three recognisable faces from the telly
while I hovered in the foyer, trying to pluck up courage to
approach the bossy-looking woman at the desk, who in-
structed me to leave my backpack with the doorman. She'd
obviously been forewarned of my arrival, because when I
said I'd an appointment with Inspector McBride, I was
shown into a small room off the lobby. A couple of minutes
later, a waiter came in with a pint of Guinness and a plate of
sandwiches. "D'inspector said you'd probably be hungry."
He grinned.

I was deadly calm by the time Bridie showed up, a quarter of an hour late. Looking at him, the last thing you'd think
of would be senior police officer. Not the most senior at the
Phoenix Park, but pretty nearly. When Phil was promoted to
chief inspector, Frank reckoned he hit his glass ceiling, and
being gay, he'd never make the really top job. He was the
very opposite of camp. He looked more like a successful
businessman than anything else, but with a bit of an edge.
He had a really strong Dublin accent, shaved head, and an
ever-expanding paunch. But he was a sharp dresser: mid-
grey Italian suit, dark shirt buttoned to the neck, no tie. And
to further confuse you, he wore a narrow gold band on the
third finger of his left hand. He and Mark, who was a senior
nurse in St. Vincent's Hospital, had been together as long as

I could remember. As Shay would have put it, Phil McBride was sound.

"Howya, Magillacuddy?" Bridie had a nickname for everyone. Frank was either Amigo or Troilus; for obvious reasons, Katie May was Cutems; and Mark was Suze, don't ask me why.

"Not hungry then?"

"No. Thanks." I pushed the Guinness across the table. "I don't feel much like food."

He sat down. "Understandable, old son, understandable," he said as the door opened and Frank walked in.

I got to my feet furiously. "No," I shouted. "No."

"Calm yourself," Phil said sternly. "This is too important for tantrums." I threw myself back on the sofa and squeezed my eyes shut to stop the tears that seemed ever ready in the last week. I was humiliated at being treated like a child and totally confused, because I didn't know how I felt about Frank anymore.

When I looked up he was still standing just inside the door. His face was white as a sheet. Phil got up, took him by the arm, and led him to a seat opposite me. In spite of my anger, I was struck by how gentle and affectionate he was and how frail my dad looked. I thought he looked pretty seedy at Grandfather's funeral, but now I realised he was ill. "I'd like to stay, Gil, please," he said quietly. "I think this concerns all three of us. But if you insist, then of course I'll leave." Frank never forgot his manners or how to give you space, though God knows I've really put him through it in the past few years. The only time I ever saw him lose it was at that dingy old wake. I wished I'd talked to him that day. He tried, but I pushed him off. I couldn't help myself.

"Stay, if you like," I said ungraciously. I couldn't look at him. "You seen today's paper? Seen what the bitch said about Tar?"

"Yes," he said. His face turned green, and I knew he was thinking of Cressie and her reaction, but he didn't mention her.

"You should have told me all this stuff years ago," I burst out. "You shouldn't have left me to work it out myself."

"We thought—we hoped you'd ask when you were ready," Frank said solemnly. "Me and your mother."

Solidarity or what? "Hoped I wouldn't, more like," I growled. "Hoped I'd forgotten."

"Stop whining, Gil." Phil took command. "You asked for this interview, remember." His voice softened. "I realise how difficult all this is for you. How threatened you must feel, so, can you tell us what you think you found out?" he said. "Take as much time as you like. What made you go to Trianach?"

"I've been thinking about it for a couple of years. Longer even." I glared at Frank. "Christ, I didn't even know who my father was until Grandfather talked about him one day. I didn't even know my own bloody name, for God's sake."

"I am your father, Gil. You are my son; Katie May's your sister. I've never thought of you otherwise." Frank looked so sad.

I fought back more tears. "I know, Dad, but there's also Gil Sweeney, the murderer's son, isn't there? Halcyon Walter's brother?"

"Oh God almighty." Frank put his head in his hands.

"Half brother—if that," Phil cut in. "Let's cut the dramatics."

I swivelled around. "You could have done a DNA test," I snarled. Bloody stupid really, since neither of them were denying it.

"To what purpose?" Chief Inspector McBride asked mildly.

"So I'd bloody well know whether I was half-witted as well as . . . as . . ." This time I couldn't control the tears.

I heard Frank say, "Jesus Christ, Phil, what are we going to do?"

And then, as usual, when I'm stressed out, I blanked out sound.

Frank knew immediately. He came over to me, took my face in his long, slender hands, and looked straight into my eyes. "Start at the beginning, Gil." He formed the words carefully. "When did you get back from France?"

"I only stayed there a week or so after the funeral," I

mumbled, then I pulled myself together and started. At first I spoke into silence, but slowly I began to hear my own voice and Phil's when he had a question or let out a string of expletives. Frank didn't say a word until I finished describing what happened in the garden; then he simply said, "You thought your mother murdered her? It's not true." Frank shut his eyes and tried to control his breathing. "You've got to believe me, Gil. Cressie did not kill that terrible woman."

"But she thumped her, knocked her down." Neither of them looked surprised. *They knew?*

"And that's all she did." Phil spoke slowly and clearly as if he wasn't sure I could hear him properly. "Your mother didn't kill Evangeline Walter; the wound to her head was superficial. We thought it might be important, but the pathologist put us right. There was absolutely no doubt a severe blow to the stomach killed her. Look at me Gil. The autopsy was conclusive. The evidence against V. J. Sweeney was incontrovertible." He spoke the name as if it meant nothing to him and should mean nothing to me. But it did.

"My father?"

"Yes." He looked away.

"So either way, according to you, I'm a murderer's son." He didn't get it.

"I'm sorry. But better him than your mother," Phil said roughly, in police mode. "That bastard was never much of a father to you, Gil." He somehow managed to lower the emotional level. Thank goodness he didn't try to make me feel better, because had either of them touched me or commiserated, I don't know how I'd have coped.

"I want you to tell me about the investigation," I said stiffly. "That's why I'm here."

They exchanged glances. Frank sat on the opposite side of the room, and Bridie paced up and down. He did the talking. He told me as if he was reporting the investigation to a colleague or even a superior. He was completely unemotional and factual, and he got it wrong. At least that was what I was struggling with. Because as far as I could remember, all three of them—my mother, father, and Tar— had all done their bit.

"When did you realise that Mrs. Walter was Halcyon's mother?" Bridie broke in on my thoughts. I don't know how he knew how critical that piece of information was for me, but I suppose that sort of intuition makes him a good copper. It took me a while, but somehow or other I told them about seeing her at the garage and carried on to what had happened when we got home. I described my father throwing the glass at my mother and knocking me over.

"Now can you explain to us what happened when your mother took you away from the house?"

I told my long, rambling, incoherent story. Frank looked absolutely stunned. It was Phil who asked me about seeing my father in the garden. "Go over that bit again," he said. So I did, starting from the shoe coming down on my foot. This time I remembered the colour of the muddy cords was not brown but buff. They exchanged meaningful looks. "Why is it so important?" I asked, and they told me how they'd found the evidence against my father in the boot of his car. *Including* the tape recorder. Though they didn't know who put it there and I didn't enlighten them.

"His clothes?" I asked.

"Yes. Her blood was all over them," he replied, and I remembered that my father had a lot of clothes, sometimes duplicates, and that Tar was in and out of the house.

"What else?"

"Her laptop, bag, that sort of thing."

"And a big box?"

Frank's jaw dropped. "Yes," he said. "A painted Italian chest from her house. How do you know that?"

"I saw him put it in."

I thought Frank was going to leap across the room and shake the information out of me, but Bridie put up his hand. "What happened *after* you left the garden?" he asked. "Can you remember?"

I closed my eyes. "Tar's cottage. Cressie and me lying on his bed. She fell asleep. In the morning, he carried me to the car."

"But before that, you went back to the garden, didn't you?" he said softly. "Did you follow Tar?"

Well, I'd got myself into that one, all right, but I was afraid of what he'd drag out of me. I felt I was seeing him for the first time—the tough copper—and I was afraid. He was much more clever than I thought, and a hell of a lot smarter than me, so I felt I had no choice but to tell it like it was—I knew that he'd keep at me until he got the full story. The only thing I kept back was all mention of my mother. I simply implied she was sleeping when I left and when I got back.

"What did he do with the bundle he took from the house?"

I shook my head. "I don't know. I didn't see."

And like before, he moved on as if he'd lost interest. No chance. "What happened in the morning?"

"He carried me out to the car. It was in a field, I think. We drove a long way." It was only then something else came back. "A hospital. We were in hospital. Talking to a woman. She was sick, lying in bed."

"Marilyn Donovan," Frank said.

"That was Marilyn? Oh." Another with her own agenda, she hadn't said a word about us coming to the hospital.

"She had a miscarriage two days before the murder," Bridie said. "Your mother drove her to the Bon Succours in Cork." He was silent for a while after that, which made me even more tense. "In all, you were in the garden twice?" A faint smile. "I'm a bit confused. Let's go through it sequentially, will we?"

"I'm the one supposed to be asking the questions," I said. "Why are you interrogating me?"

He wasn't in the least put out. "You think this is interrogation, old son?" He laughed mirthlessly. "Look, Gil, I want to help you understand, but it's your interpretation that's to cock. I can't clear it up until I hear what you think. OK?"

I nodded, but I really hadn't a clue what he meant. At the same time, I wanted to stop playing games, to clear it up in my mind. I think I wanted him to make the decisions.

"So. Go back to the cottage after you got back the first time. You fell asleep?"

"No," I said, feeling my way back into the dark bedroom.

"Cressie fell asleep. John Spain was next door, drinking whisky, at the table."

"How do you know?" Phil asked.

"I could smell it." You could hear a pin drop. "I got out of bed, but I didn't go into the living room. I peeped around the door and watched him. He was crying. His shoulders were shaking. After a while, he got up and went out." I looked at Frank. "I crept out after him. I tried to call him, but I couldn't get the words out, so I followed him down to the cove. He took the boat out. I climbed up on the spit to wait for him."

Phil looked at Frank. "What spit?"

"It's a rocky outcrop, quite high, edging the cove where he kept his boat."

"They call it Spain's Cove now," I said inconsequentially.

"Go on," Bridie ordered brusquely, but the spell had been broken. So he made me start all over again.

"My arm was hurting, and I kept slipping. By the time I got to the top, Tar had disappeared. I was just going to run back to the cottage when the launch came shooting out of the night and across the river."

"Launch? What launch?"

"My father's launch."

"Are you quite sure? You heard it?"

"Of course not; I saw it. He was at the wheel. There was a full moon. It shone on his hair." I touched my own. "Like mine, same colour. He wasn't wearing a cap. Dark sweater, no coat. It was cold." I was talking to myself.

"Then what?"

"I sat down again and waited for Tar."

"You weren't afraid of him after what you'd seen earlier?" Bridie asked gently.

I was surprised myself. But maybe that was looking at it from an adult's point of view. As me, aged eight, I had no fear of him whatsoever. I just wanted him to come back and look after me. "None, except the fear that he wouldn't come back for us."

"How long did you wait?"

And back over it I went, adding the detail. There no

longer seemed any point in leaving things out. Except for that one thing. I didn't tell them I thought I saw Cressie.

"And Spain was there next morning?" Phil said when I finished.

"Yes. But I don't know if it was morning; it was still dark. He carried me out to the car."

"I'm sorry you had to do all this alone, Gil." Frank broke a long silence.

"Yeah, you really blew it, didn't you? Why didn't you tell me?"

"Oh for crying out loud, Magillacuddy, get real. How the fuck were they supposed to tell an eight-year-old, or a ten-year-old, or a twelve-year-old all that stuff? How? You want to tell me that? Look at me, son. You think they knew how much you saw? How much you were taking in?"

"I should have been told about Halcyon, about my father," I said stubbornly.

"I'm sorry," Frank said. "Oh, Gil, I'm so sorry. Cressie and I agonised over it all the time, but when it came to the point, we were afraid of what it might do to you. We screwed up."

"Oh stop it!" Bridie exploded. "Weren't you only trying to protect the child? You did your best, Frank."

"It wasn't good enough though, was it?" I said.

Phil gave me such a dirty look I was glad I wasn't a criminal. "Maybe you could have done it better? Put yourself in their place, lad. Ask yourself how you would tell Katie May now, aged ten? Where would you begin?" That got to me more than all the rest, because I suddenly saw Halcyon send my baby sister flying through the air, damn near killing her.

"I don't normally do this, Gil, but I want you to hear the story from my point of view." Bridie talked for nearly half an hour, starting from the moment he arrived with his superior from Cork to take charge of the murder investigation. He went through the whole process, ending with the burning of Tar's boat. And when he'd finished, he told me that Frank, Spain, and my mother had all been suspects, at one stage or another. Spain and Cressie for the murder, and Frank for fudging the evidence.

I pricked up my ears at that.

"He nearly scuppered it, you know, with his bloody meddling and very nearly ended in jail himself, trying to save your mother. Thought I was a feckin' eejit."

So they thought Cressie did it as well. But not now? Why were they so sure?

He said it was only when they got their wires uncrossed and worked together that the real evidence was found. That's when they believed Spain's story of seeing Sweeney in the garden later that night. "The story you've just corroborated, Magillacuddy. You're a bloody great witness, d'you know that? We could have done with you at the—" He put his hand to his mouth. "Aw, Jaysus, what am I saying?"

"I don't think I'd have been much good, would I? At the time? Seeing I couldn't really talk all that well? Or hear." I put my hand on Frank's arm. "Anyway, I was terrified of my father. He nearly killed me and Cressie the same night." I swallowed hard. "Yet my mother lived with him, stayed with him. For what?" Even to my own ears I sounded hysterical. "For the sake of a fucking house?"

That silenced them.

"I have a question." I couldn't look at either of them. "Was Tar trying to save him when they drowned?"

Bridie turned to Frank. "Over to you, Amigo. What's your take on that?"

Frank hesitated. I had a horrible feeling he was going to get all pious, but I should have known better. "Spain went to pieces after the murder. He practically lived in his boat. We realised too late that he must have been lying in wait for Sweeney."

"We found out that Sweeney sold his shares in the Atlantis Hotel in Passage South—forty K's worth in hard cash. Evangeline was after them, but he sold them to someone else. It was my opinion Sweeney had already got away by car," Bridie put in. "But Frank always thought if he was going to make a run for it, he'd use the yacht, and Spain must have been thinking along the same lines. The yacht slipped anchor the Saturday morning around six. We missed it, but Spain was right there. He took the motor launch and gave chase. They were caught in a storm."

"Cressie thinks he may have nudged the yacht on to the rocks," Frank said.

The man they were discussing was my father. I kept telling myself that, and it hurt like hell that they talked as if he was a wild animal. "Why does she think so?" I asked, though I knew what he was going to say.

"He'd have done anything to protect you. I believe he figured that if a trial could be avoided, then the scandal would die."

"In a manner of speaking."

It hadn't worked for him, had it? Marilyn had told me how "everyone knew John Spain wasn't a paedophile," but the fact that she felt she had to say it was damning in itself. Ten years after his death, the same old lies were being denied, and that didn't seem to me to be much different than making an outright accusation. Either way, the dirt stuck. For a split second I was glad that the bitch that started it all had been killed. But there was still one more: Moore.

"Why did Mrs. Walter make up those terrible lies about Tar?"

"Well now, that's the feckin' million dollar question," Bridie said, but at last he got to the reason for the murder. He confirmed what Tar had said in his letter.

"She was trying to get at Sweeney, destroy him and everything he had, including his family." Frank seemed to be thinking it out as he spoke. "Sweeney used those stories about Spain to threaten Cressie. He said he'd inform the social services if she didn't give up the house. I'm not sure that was what Evangeline Walter intended him to do, but that was the effect. She and Sweeney weren't having an affair as everyone, including Cressie, thought. Not an ongoing one. They had been lovers, but he abandoned her when Halcyon was a baby. Murray admitted to your mother last week that Sweeney was responsible for her condition. Evangeline certainly believed so. She stalked him for years, looking for revenge. For herself? For the brain-damaged child? Cressie and I've thought about it a long time," Frank said, "but we still can't figure it all out. She publicly humiliated him. She bought the yacht—"

"The name was changed to *Halcyon*." I said. I drew in a deep breath and quietly placed the mobile phone on top of the plate of sandwiches. Phil leapt on it.

"Where did you get that?" Frank whispered.

"Tar left it for me to find. In a place only I knew about. He must have known I'd go back. It's hers, isn't it?"

"Probably. Hers certainly went missing."

Frank came across the room, put his arms around me, and held me tight, like he used to when I was a child. We both cried. He asked if I'd go home with him.

"No," I said. "I couldn't face it. I'll go away for a while."

"Where? What about university?"

"What about it? You think I could hack university after all this? You've had ten years to bury it; I'm just beginning. So I'm heading out. Back to France for a while, then I'll probably go to Australia or somewhere."

"You'll need money. I'll put some in your account. . . ."

I stood up and headed for the door. "No, I'm OK. If I need it, I'll ask. Thanks. I'll ring in a day or so and let you know my plans. OK?"

Frank came after me. "Cressie will be very upset. Won't you come and see her before you go?"

I shook my head. "I'm sorry. Tell her I'll be in touch when I get my head together." To his credit, Frank didn't try to change my mind. And he didn't play the heart card, either. He just stood looking at me, stroking the beginnings of a beard.

"You can come and stay with us for a few days while you get sorted," Bridie suggested.

"No thanks," I said. I was almost at the door when I turned back to face them. "You got a few things wrong," I said and held out the car keys with the Lexus symbol prominent. "I found these with the phone. See if you can figure out what Tar was trying to tell me."

I turned and crashed into a waiter. "Turn on the television, sir," he shouted. "New York's just been bombed."

_____regression 14

thirty-five

Duncreagh Listening Post

Trianach businessman Jer O'Dowd, after five attempts, finally gets permission to develop new marina and clubhouse at Coribeen.

I SLIPPED OUT unnoticed. I didn't bother with my backpack. The foyer was full of people gawping at a television screen mounted above the reception desk. In the couple of minutes it took me to push my way through, I saw the aircraft fly into the World Trade Center twice. It seemed unreal. I didn't linger.

Out on the street, people were hurrying towards public buildings looking for TV sets. Several times I heard voices cry out, "Did you hear? Did you see?" I walked swiftly down Kildare Street and along Nassau Street, where I found a hairdresser and watched the newsreel while I had my hair cut close to my skull.

After that, I rang the hotel I'd worked in before I went south, and they said they could give me a room for a couple of nights at half the going rate. I bargained a bit more, and Fred, the guy at the desk, eventually said, "Ah, you're all right for a couple of nights. You've heard the news? I bet we're in for a mountain of cancellations. You mightn't get sheets but." Which was fine by me. I headed for O'Connell Street, which was crowded. Either the word hadn't spread or people had other things on their minds. As I had. I went straight to the newspaper office, where there was total chaos. Phones were ringing, staff were flying about, two of the girls behind the reception desk had headsets clamped to their ears. If I'd planned it myself, I couldn't have done better. I took my hearing aid out of my pocket and stuck it in my ear. There was no need to switch it on.

The front of the huge counter had a series of posters, some with pictures of the star reporters, others announcing forthcoming features. Bang in the middle was "The Dead Woman Left Standing in Her Own Garden—The Unsolved Murder of the Decade. Read award-winning Fiona Moore's great new series: *Getting Away with Murder: The Unsolved Crimes of the Century.* Exclusive to the *Daily News.* Starts Tuesday."

I took an envelope from my jacket pocket and waved it in front of a receptionist's nose. I'd printed Fiona Moore prominently across it, in big letters. "Urgent," I mouthed and twisted my head, bringing my aid into full view. She smiled and scribbled "Third floor, Room Four" on a Post-it label, attached it to the envelope, then picked up another phone and shouted into the receiver.

I took the stairs two at a time. The third-floor corridor was deserted, but every room I passed had men and women standing open-mouthed in front of televisions. In rapid sequence along the corridor I saw one of the Twin Towers collapse, read the flash at the bottom of the screen: "Pentagon hit. Thousands feared dead," then saw it all over again. Neither image impinged on me. I pressed on.

The door of room four was wide open. Just as I reached it, a red-haired man came charging towards me and slid to a halt at the open door. "Fiona," he shouted. A woman peered out. "Come in, Sean," she said. "It's totally unbelievable."

She was older than I expected, big and busty with huge brown eyes and a lot of makeup, dressed in black from top to toe. Her hair was dark, shoulder length. Neither of them paid me any attention. I held back until they went inside, leaving the door wide open, then I sauntered past. The man had his arm around her, nuzzling her ear as they watched a TV mounted on the wall above her desk.

I went back down, this time by the lift. The ground floor was even more crowded, but stunned. I removed my hearing aid as I left the building and went into a Starbucks next door and nursed a double espresso for an hour or so until Fiona Moore came racing past. I followed her to the Tara Street DART* station and onto a southbound train. She didn't pay me any attention. She put on earphones as soon as she sat down. I sat halfway down the carriage, pretending to look out the window. She got out at Blackrock and went to an apartment block on a quiet road about a quarter of a mile from the station. About five or six minutes after she went into the block, she came out and got into a green Saab parked outside. It was four o'clock. I found a convenient low garden wall a little way down the road and sat down and waited. At five-fifteen, she came back with a little blonde girl, about the same age as my little sister, and an older woman. The kid never stopped talking as they went inside.

On the supposition that journalists work in the evening, I waited for another hour and a half. It was growing cold and started to drizzle. I pulled up the hood of my jacket and strolled slowly up and down the road. I felt a bit conspicuous until people started coming home from work and I just melted into the background. By seven the light was beginning to go, when a young guy, about my age, came out of the apartment and drove away in the Saab. That was my main worry out of the way. I stepped back into the dubious shelter of a nearby hedge and hung on. There were cars parked on either side of the street by now. A big black Mercedes with dark windows and the name of a Cork dealer on the

*DART: Dublin Area Rapid Transport

rear window had been there on and off since I arrived. I noticed the windscreen wipers switched on once or twice so I
knew there was someone sitting in it. And I had a good idea
who. I was almost certain it was the same car Marilyn had
pointed out to me the day she gave me breakfast. Having
read Fiona Moore's article, I wouldn't have been surprised
to get to see the legendary O'Dowd hop out of it. But maybe
I was mistaken because on reflection I thought it more likely
that the poor guy would have disappeared into the wood-
work to lick his wounds. In his position, I would. There was
also a VW Beetle the same colour as my mother's halfway
down the road, but I couldn't make out the number plates
without showing myself. I could see that it was empty. I almost weakened at the thought of Cressie, alone and worrying about me, about all of us. But anger and resentment
swiftly overcame sentimentality.

At last, at half past eight when the rain was lashing down
and I was soaked, she came out. I didn't mind; the weather
was perfect for my purpose—people slipped on wet pave-
ments all the time. Railway platforms were even better—
and that is what I had in mind—a swift shove onto the
tracks and she'd be pulverised. I wondered vaguely how
many people the DART killed every year? She stood in the
doorway looking up then went back inside for a few minutes
and came back with a big black umbrella. She was wearing
flat shoes and was a lot shorter than I thought. I held back
until she'd gone about fifty yards or so down the road in the
direction of the railway station, then started after her. The
Mercedes went past in the opposite direction sending up a
huge filthy spray. The pedestrian light at the main road was
against her. I held back waiting for it to change, but Fiona
didn't, she just stepped fearlessly out on the road and wove
in and out of the traffic. I followed. We passed the supermarket at the corner and down the quiet local-traffic-only
road into Blackrock village. She held the black umbrella low
over her head, against the wind. I was bent over holding on
to my hood, about twenty paces behind her but beginning to
catch up. As we turned the next corner, the station was
ahead, across a deserted car park. I was close to her now; if

I put out my hand I could have touched the umbrella. Something made me half turn my head. The black Mercedes was bearing down on us. Fast, too fast. Out of control. The driver's face was huge, huge, grinning at me. I gave an involuntary scream, then I was slammed against the wall.

thirty-six

"PHIL?"

"Frank. What's up?"

"Cressie hasn't come home."

"But it's only six o'clock—she's probably glued to some television set like the rest of the world. The news is only desperate isn't it?"

"Phil, she didn't take the car."

"What? I thought she was going to look at houses in Wexford? Maybe she went by train? Did I tell you I think you're both mad? What do you want to bury yourselves in Wexford for . . ."

"Phil, listen to me. The car's outside. Cressie left her bag on the table. The keys were in it. Her mobile as well. She's gone."

"That's why you couldn't get hold of her. Oh my God, Frank, the paper. She must have read that feckin' article. I forgot all about it with the Trade Center thing. Fifty thousand dead, they're saying. Cressie is probably . . ."

"You already said that. I should have come home. I didn't even see the bloody article until after Gil . . . God why didn't I . . . ?"

"I guess you were distracted by the profile," Phil said. "Any sign of Gil?"

"No, no."

"Well then, that's probably it. I bet he came straight home to see her. They'll be together somewhere."

"No. They won't. She's been gone eight hours. My next door neighbour saw her leave the house this morning. On foot. I told you, her bag's in the kitchen."

"Calm down, Frank, I'm on my way. What was she wearing?"

thirty-seven

Dublin Daily News, Thursday, September 13

Dublin Gardai are appealing for witnesses to a
fatal incident on the approach road to Blackrock
station on the evening of 11 September around
nine o'clock, in which a woman was killed and a
young man seriously injured as they crossed the
road. A large black car was seen leaving the vicin-
ity shortly afterward, make and registration unknown. Anyone who saw the incident or has any
information about the car or driver should contact
the duty officer at Blackrock or at Pearse Street
Garda Station.

Moore, Fiona 11 September
Victim of a hit-and-run incident at Blackrock,
Dublin. Fiona (48), beloved mother of Sebastian
and Marie Louise (Lulu), and dear daughter of
Brian and Annie Moore of Daingean, Co. Cork.
Funeral details to be announced.

FIVE DAYS AFTER Gil was admitted to hospital, he was moved from the intensive care unit into a single room, though he was still hooked up to a phalanx of monitors at the head of the bed. His head was swathed in bandages and his right arm and leg were in splints. His face was deathly pale and his breathing barely perceptible; he appeared to be asleep. Mark, appalled, stood inside the door uncertainly before approaching the bed.

"Gil?"

"Mark?" Gil opened his eyes groggily. "What are you doing here?" His speech was slurred.

"I might ask you the same. I brought a few grapes."

"Not sure I can eat. My jaw hurts like hell."

"Poor Gil." Mark sat close to the bed and took Gil's hand. "We'll look after you, kid," he said.

"Hmmm."

"What happened? Did you see what hit you?"

"Not a thing."

"So Bridie says. He also said you're taking another year off, is that right?"

"Not sure what I'll do."

"If you're free, what about coming to work for me?"

Gil managed a laugh. "Doing what? I've a broken leg, arm, and my head feels like a balloon."

"I have a plan. Come on, it'll be great *craic*."

"Is that right? I hope you can wait. What had you in mind?"

"I've given up the nursing. Feel like a bit of a change. I'm opening a restaurant so I'll need a good waiter. You're it."

"You're off your head." Gil sounded a bit more lively. "When?"

"Oh, in about six months. You'll be well better then. But I'll need a bit of help in the planning stage as well. We could start on that pronto. It'll be a laugh."

"Where is it going to be?" Gil asked cagily.

"On the waterfront?"

"New York?"

"Don't be an eejit. Ringsend of course. I'm going to call it Wagner. Get it?"

"Not yet, but I'm sure you'll tell me. I was thinking of going to Australia or somewhere."

"So your dad said. I'd be really pleased to have a pal around at the beginning, Gil. I'm begging. On my knees." He laughed.

Gil blinked back the tears. "I'd be no good. I'm only out of school."

"You're the best I'm likely to get for what I'm paying," he said.

"I'll think about it. If you don't mind waiting. Thanks, Mark."

"Seen the folks yet?" Mark asked casually.

"Yeah. Dad's been here a few times. Cressie's in and out the whole time."

Mark choked back a cough. "Oh? Was she here today?" His voice was strained.

"Not yet. She usually comes at night when Katie May's in bed. She's got a new dog."

"Who? Your mother?"

Gil's eyelids drooped again. "No. Twink."

"Cressie in good form then?"

"Yesh. The ushual. She never says much but it's nice . . . bit like it was when I was little. Her sitting at the end of the bed, smiling. Old times. She understands why I went back to . . . to . . ."

"So everything's OK? Gil? You awake?"

"Sleepy. I promised her I'd go home for a while." He opened his eyes and made a feeble attempt at a grin. "Bit ironic, really. Now that Cressie's rid of Grandfather, she's lumbered with me. Doesn't seem fair, does it?"

"No, but I'll help. I'm moving in for a few days when you come out of the hospital. Might as well make myself useful, as long as I'm out of a job."

"Mark?"

"Yeah?"

"Why does Bridie call you Suze?"

"Ah now, that would be telling," Mark said as the door

was tentatively pushed open and a wide-eyed girl edged into the room. Just as Mark had done, she stood with her back to the door, using it for support. Mark stood up and the girl began to sob very quietly, wiping her eyes and nose with the back of her hand. She appeared rooted to the spot. "He's just dropped off to sleep," Mark whispered. "Come and sit down." When she didn't respond, he went over to her, put his arm around her shoulder, and led her to the bedside. "I'm Mark—a friend of the family."

She turned her head to him. "Is he going to die?" she whispered.

"No, he's going to be OK. It'll take a while, but he's strong."

"Does he know about his mother?" she whispered. Mark put his finger to his lips and shook his head.

"Shay? Shay?"

The girl knelt beside the bed and held her face to Gil's. "Ah Sweeney," she said softly, "look at the cut of you; sure you're not fit to be let out on your own."

Dublin Daily News, Saturday, September 15

The body of a woman washed up on Sandymount Strand yesterday morning has been identified as mother of two, Mrs. Cressida Recaldo (43), who was reported missing by her husband, ex-Garda Frank Recaldo, on Wednesday. Mrs. Recaldo's son Gil was seriously injured in the hit-and-run incident, which killed award-winning journalist Fiona Moore late the previous evening. Mr. Recaldo is the popular crime writer, Frank Ventry.